RAY OF LIGHT

Also by Shelley Shepard Gray

Sisters of the Heart series
HIDDEN
WANTED
FORGIVEN
GRACE

Seasons of Sugarcreek series
WINTER'S AWAKENING
SPRING'S RENEWAL
AUTUMN'S PROMISE
CHRISTMAS IN SUGARCREEK

Families of Honor series
THE CAREGIVER
THE PROTECTOR
THE SURVIVOR
A CHRISTMAS FOR KATIE

The Secrets of Crittenden County series
MISSING
THE SEARCH
FOUND

The Days of Redemption Series
DAYBREAK

RAY OF LIGHT

The Days of Redemption Series, Book Two

SHELLEY SHEPARD GRAY

AVON
INSPIRE
An Imprint of HarperCollins*Publishers*

This book is a work of fiction. The characters, incidents, and dialogue are drawn from the author's imagination and are not to be construed as real. Any resemblance to actual events or persons, living or dead, is entirely coincidental.

HarperCollins books may be purchased for educational, business, or sales promotional use. For information please write: Special Markets Department, HarperCollins Publishers, 10 East 53rd Street, New York, NY 10022.

FIRST EDITION

Designed by Yvonne Chan

Library of Congress Cataloging-in-Publication Data has been applied for.

ISBN 978-0-06-220442-4

13 14 15 16 17 OV/RRD 10 9 8 7 6 5 4 3 2 1

To Tom. Because of you, I can be me.

Till at last the day begins
In the east a-breaking,
In the hedges and the whins
Sleeping birds a-waking
~from "Night and Day" by Robert Louis Stevenson

Light shines on the godly, and joy on those whose hearts are right.

~Psalm 97:11(KJV)

RAY OF LIGHT

chapter one

It hadn't been easy, but Lovina Keim had gotten her way. She was going to be the one to read her grandson's very first letter from Florida aloud.

Holding the envelope carefully on her lap, she adjusted her glasses and waited for her twin granddaughters, husband, and daughter-in-law to get settled. Actually, she was drawing out the moment. It was nice to feel like the focal point of the family once again. Too often she felt like as much of an add-on as her *dawdi haus*.

But, as usual, her granddaughter Viola was anything but patient. "Mommi, open the envelope. We're all here and sitting quietly." Under her breath, she added, "As you insisted."

Lovina heard that, of course. But she pretended not to.

Instead, she shook the envelope importantly. "Patience, Viola. I'll get to it in my own time. After all, none of us makes you rush to share Edward's letters."

"That's because she doesn't share them," Viola's twin, Elsie, said. "At least none of the good parts."

Crossing her ankles primly, Viola glared at her sister. "Ed's letters are different. He's my fiancé, you know."

"I believe we all know that, dear," Viola's mother, Marie, said behind a smile.

Standing behind her rocking chair, Aaron leaned over and pushed the kerosene lantern on the table closer to Lovina.

"You'd best read Roman's letter from Florida before this whole family dissolves into another heated discussion."

Her husband had a point. Over the last few months, even the most benign topic seemed to ignite tempers. With a sigh, Lovina carefully opened the envelope, smoothed out Roman's note, and began reading. "Dear Family, Greetings from Pinecraft!"

Elsie chuckled. "He sounds like he's an advertisement."

"Indeed," Lovina said with a small smile. Clearing her throat, she continued. "Now that I've been here for three days, I'm beginning to get into a routine. Every morning, I sit with one of the cousins and drink coffee on the patio, looking out at the ocean. I never get tired of watching the waves crash along the shoreline and can only imagine what it must be like to get used to such a sight."

Marie sighed. "Being at the beach sounds *wunderbaar.*"

"You should go soon, Mamm," Viola said. "I mean, you should go when Daed gets better. . . ."

"Perhaps."

Not wanting to think about Peter's problems, Lovina rattled the pages a bit to claim everyone's attention again. "Next door, another woman starts her morning the same way as me. She seems to be about my age. She's Amish, too, and has blond hair and blue eyes. She's quite pretty. I hear she's a mother and a widow, but I don't know if that's true or not. But whatever the reason, I can't help but be curious . . . but so far, I've had no reason to speak to her. But maybe one day soon."

Just as Lovina paused for a breath, the room erupted into excited chatter.

As Elsie and Viola discussed who this mystery woman might be, Lovina found her gaze straying to her husband and then felt her stomach drop. Aaron was looking out into the distance with such a heartbreaking expression, she knew he could only be thinking of one thing: his first wife and child.

Little by little, the other occupants noticed, too.

"Dawdi, what is wrong?" Viola asked.

Lovina was just about to tell her nosy granddaughter that not everything was her concern when Aaron slowly stood up.

"I'm all right, child. Roman's note simply made me think of something that happened long ago."

"What was that?"

Aaron looked Lovina's way, shrugged, then said, "It got me thinking about the time I buried my first wife and son."

As Marie, Viola, and Elsie watched him leave the room in shock, Lovina felt her world tilt. She and Aaron had agreed never to talk of that. Tears started to fall on her cheeks as she thought of his heartbroken expression. Even after all this time, it seemed that Aaron still carried a torch for his first, beautiful, perfect wife.

When they all heard the back door close, Viola gripped Elsie's hand. "Grandpa was married before? And had a child? Mamm, did you know about this?"

Even in the dimly lit room, Lovina saw that Marie was rattled. "*Nee*."

Elsie shook her head in wonder, staring at Lovina with accusation in her eyes. "I assume you knew about this. First we find that Mommi was once an *Englischer*, then that Daed is secretly drinking. Now we find out that Dawdi has been married before. How many secrets does this family have?"

Thinking of her other secrets, the ones she hoped and prayed were buried so deep that they'd never be let out, Lovina shrugged. "Too many to count, it seems." Wearily, she stood up. "I better go see how your grandfather is doing."

No one seemed to notice that Roman's letter floated to the floor, only half read.

Roman Keim wasn't stalking the woman staying in the condominium next door to him at Siesta Key. He just couldn't seem to stop watching her whenever he could.

It seemed she enjoyed the morning sunrises as much as he did. As the sun continued to rise, he sipped his coffee, wiggled his toes in the sand, and watched Amanda Yoder slip through the white wooden gate that separated the condo properties from the public beach, and walk down the path to the water.

Today she wore an apricot-colored dress that set off her blond hair, prim white *kapp*, and lightly tanned skin. As she walked along in her bare feet he was captivated. Her steps looked light and smooth. Happy. He'd heard that she was a widow. He wondered if it was true.

Actually, she looked like her own ray of sunlight, and he felt himself unable to look away when she tossed down a towel, spread it smooth, then sat right down on it, all while holding a cup of coffee in her right hand.

He was trying to think how he'd ever get the courage to talk to her when his cousin Beth stepped through the open sliding door. "May I join you, Roman? Or are you attempting to find a few moments of peace and quiet?" she asked with a wry smile. "I know we can all get to be a bit overwhelming sometimes."

"Not at all," he said, thinking what a nice change of pace his uncle Aden's family was compared to his own family's exhausting problems. "Of course I'd like your company." He leaned over and pulled another chair closer. "Come sit down."

"Danke." She, too, was sipping coffee and, to his delight, had brought out a thermal carafe. After topping off his cup, she sat beside him and followed his gaze. "Ah, I see you've found Amanda Yoder. Again."

He was embarrassed that his interest was so transparent. "I can't help it if she enjoys the sunrises as much as I do."

"You know, I met her yesterday when Lindy and I were out."

Surprised, he glanced her way. "You did?"

"Uh-huh. My Lindy and her daughter seemed to get along."

Roman struggled to not show his interest. "So, *is* she married?"

"No . . . No, she's not. She's widowed. It seems the rumors we heard about her were true."

"That's too bad," he murmured, trying to do the right thing and think of her loss—and not his interest. "She's a young woman."

"Indeed. Only twenty-five." Cradling her cup, Beth leaned back and closed her eyes. "I don't know the whole story, but she did say that her husband's death was a difficult thing. I guess he lingered for months in pain."

Roman inwardly winced. Her story made his family's troubles seem insignificant in comparison. "Did it happen recently?" he asked before he could remind himself that he shouldn't care.

"I don't know that answer, but I'm guessing no. She doesn't seem to be mourning." Looking at him with a new gleam in her eye, she added, "Actually, Amanda seems like one of the most restful women I've ever come across."

Restful. Now, that was an unusual descriptor. But he fancied it. "Hmm."

Before he knew what was happening, Beth stood up and grabbed his empty left hand. "Come on. Let me introduce you."

"Beth, *nee*. I was merely curious."

"If you're only curious about her, then it won't hurt you to say hello."

"But—"

"Roman Keim, didn't I hear you say that you wanted to experience something new this week?"

"*Jah*, but I was thinking about surfing. . . ."

"Meeting a new woman counts, I believe."

Because she had a point, he let himself be dragged across the gated patio, through the gate, and down the steps to the sand.

As she heard the hubbub behind her, Amanda turned and watched them approach, her eyes brightening when she recognized Beth.

Roman's mouth went dry. Amanda was even prettier up close.

With effort, he forced his expression to remain impassive.

It would never do for her to know how captivated he was by her. At least . . . not yet.

chapter two

Even at this distance, Roman realized, Amanda Yoder had a peaceful way about her. As she watched Roman and Beth approach, she didn't look startled or suspicious. Merely curious.

But it was more than that. She was stretched out on her beach towel as if she'd never had a thing to worry about in her life.

It was the exact opposite of the way he functioned. He got up early and usually hit the ground running. He made to-do lists and crossed off each completed task with a dark *X* to signal his satisfaction. He kept to himself and concentrated on working hard.

Amanda, in contrast, looked as if she never hurried through anything. She seemed like she took the time to enjoy each minute of the day, instead of worrying about plans and goals and what was up ahead.

It was completely attractive.

When she looked his way and smiled slightly, he felt his body's temperature rise another degree. Most likely, his cheeks were flushed. With effort, Roman looked toward the sea and tried to calm his wayward thoughts.

Beside him, Beth had no such compunction. She was beaming so brightly that it was a wonder Amanda didn't look away to shield her eyes. "Amanda, hi!" she called out. "*Gut matin!* How are you?" she continued, not letting more than the briefest of seconds pass before she continued. "We saw you sitting here alone, so my cousin Roman and I wanted to say hello."

"I hope we're not disturbing you," he said, then cursed his tongue. It was barely seven in the morning, and she'd been sitting alone, obviously enjoying her own company. Of course they were disturbing her.

"You aren't disturbing me in the slightest. I was simply sitting here, enjoying the morning sun," Amanda replied. After glancing his way for a split second, she focused on Beth. "Regina enjoyed playing with Lindy yesterday."

"We should get them together again soon. It's so wonderful that our four-year-olds have found each other. And they play well together, too."

"I've been thinking the same thing."

Beth looked toward Amanda's condo. "Is Regina still asleep?"

"*Jah*. My Gina likes to sleep in, I'm afraid. She's something of a night owl."

"It would be hard to go to sleep early here," Roman said. "It's a beautiful area. . . . I don't want to miss a minute of daylight."

As if she was amused, she slowly smiled. "It is a beautiful place. I'm Amanda, by the way."

"Roman Keim."

"Pleased to meet you. Do you live in Indiana as well?"

"Ohio. Where are you from?"

Her smile widened. "I live in Pinecraft."

Without being invited, Beth sat down on the sand. "This is your home? I thought you were on vacation, too."

"Oh, I am on vacation, for sure. I live in town. My, uh,

husband's family owns this condominium. They're encouraging me to take a week's rest." She rolled her eyes. "They seem to think I work too much."

Feeling awkward, being the only person standing, Roman sat down as well, stretching his legs as the warm sand shifted around him. "Do you?"

Her eyes widened, then she nodded after a moment's consideration. "I suppose I do. But I don't mind working. To me, it makes the days fly by."

Beth nodded. "My two kids make my days fly by, too. Well, most days."

"Mamm?" Lindy called out from the condo patio. "Mamm, I'm hungry."

Beth scrambled to her feet. "That's my cue to pour cereal," she said with a laugh. "No doubt her *daed* is standing right there, but for some reason Lindy and Cale like me to do the serving."

Amanda chuckled. "That is a mother's duty, for sure."

Backing away as Lindy called out for her again, Beth said, "Amanda, we'll knock on your door later to see if Regina can play."

"See you then," Amanda said with a smile.

With a spray of sand, Beth trotted back to the patio. In a flash, she was out of sight, leaving Roman and Amanda relatively alone.

There in the morning sun, it felt as if they were the only two people on the beach—the only two people smart enough to take time to enjoy the day's glorious start. Reluctantly, Roman realized he should probably get up as well, but he couldn't bring himself to do it. The sand was as soft as powdered sugar, the salty, faintly damp breeze coming off the water felt good on his skin, and he was enjoying the novelty of being one of only two people out on what was usually a very crowded beach.

And then there was his companion.

He thought Amanda was one of the loveliest women he'd ever met. But attracting him more than her pleasing features was the calm way about her.

"So, what is it you do?" he asked. When a line formed between her brows, he clarified. "I mean, what work do you do too much of?"

"Oh! I work at a bakery that my husband's family owns, Pinecraft Pastries. Do you know it?"

"*Nee.*" Though she was talking about the bakery, he couldn't help but fixate on the way she spoke about her husband. This was the second time she'd brought him up. Obviously, his cousin had gotten her information wrong. "Does your husband work there, too?" he asked politely.

Her eyes widened. "*Nee.* Oh, no," she blurted. "I guess I need to stop doing that. I keep saying 'husband,' but he's gone. I mean, he went up to heaven two years ago. I'm a widow."

"I'm sorry for your loss." Why did he have to prod her to divulge that? Here he was, making her uncomfortable. He would've thought he could have shown a little bit more tact.

"*Danke*. I am sorry about Wesley, too." Her chin rose. "But I am thankful for my many blessings. I have a sweet daughter and a good life." Leaning back on her hands, she said, "What about you?"

"Me? I'm not married."

"And your work?"

"I work on my family's farm," he began, then realized that was about all he could say. His family was in turmoil, he'd never had a steady girlfriend to speak of, and at the moment, he couldn't seem to count very many blessings. He couldn't think of another thing he did besides work and try to stand apart from everyone else's drama.

"What kind of farming do you do?"

He shrugged, not really wanting to talk about taking care of livestock or walking behind a plow. It all sounded boring and dirty—the exact opposite of life where they were. Here on the beach, everything felt bright and new and clean.

After another second of looking at him expectantly, her warm expression cooled as she got to her feet. "I see. Well, I should probably go inside now."

"So soon?"

Bending down, she shook out the bright turquoise beach towel, then folded it in her arms. "I don't like my Regina to wake up without me being around."

"Well, it was nice to meet you, Amanda. Maybe we'll see each other around this week."

"I imagine we will," she said. "We are neighbors, after all."

Side by side, they walked back to their units, Amanda carrying her towel and empty mug of coffee, Roman empty-handed.

It was obvious to him that she was in no hurry to get to know him.

He wondered if that was because she was still mourning her husband. Or if she simply wasn't interested in him.

Well, he couldn't blame her. Roman realized that he had terribly little to offer. He was reasonably attractive, but not much more than that. He was reserved by nature, and a lifetime of standing on the sidelines and keeping to himself meant there were few bright spots in his life. In his anxiousness to remain calm and collected, he let much of life pass him by.

Back in Berlin, he'd been proud of that fact. Unlike the rest of his family, he'd had little pain, no secrets, and nothing to be embarrassed about.

But now his lack of excitement made him feel curiously flat. One-dimensional instead of three. As if he'd simply existed instead of lived.

It wasn't a good realization. Not at all.

Amanda didn't find it difficult to say goodbye to Roman Keim. Though he was lightly tanned and fit, had handsome features and attractive brown eyes, she found him to be too reserved.

She could understand a man's need for privacy, but not about such things as his occupation or his family.

Roman had reacted to her questions as if she were attempting to learn all his secrets. She definitely hadn't cared to know his secrets or his problems.

After all, she had plenty of her own to worry about.

In her twenty-five years, she'd had more than her share of hardships. She'd been scarred by her husband's failing fight with cancer, and before that, she'd married against her parents' wishes. They'd wanted her to wait to marry.

She'd insisted on marrying at nineteen.

They'd wanted her to live near them in Pennsylvania. She'd wanted to live with Wesley near his family in Florida.

And after Wesley's death, she'd gone her own way again. Instead of succumbing to her parents' demands and moving back to Intercourse to live with them, Amanda had chosen to live in the little house she and Wesley had bought with every last bit of their savings.

Now she was working hard to make the mortgage payments and take care of Regina. Her life was busy, with few moments for regret. Instead, she was surrounded by her daughter's joy. And, if, in the middle of the night, when the chores were done and Regina was asleep, she felt lonely and depressed? Well, that was her concern. Not anyone else's.

She had nothing in common with a man who had little to say for himself other than he worked on his family's farm.

Opening the refrigerator, she pulled out the quart of strawberries she'd bought at the market, and bit into the plumpest, juiciest one she could find.

The sweet taste exploded in her mouth, and she savored the flavors.

And couldn't help but contrast that zing with Roman's curiously bland manner. She wondered why he'd even agreed to walk over with his cousin to say hello.

After shaking out her towel again and hanging it on a rail on the back porch, she poured herself another cup of coffee and sat down at the kitchen table, irritated now.

She'd lied to Roman on the beach. The truth was that Regina wouldn't be up for another hour at the earliest. She just hadn't been eager to sit next to him for another moment, waiting for him to tell her something about himself.

Especially since she'd told him about Wesley being gone.

So, essentially, Roman had ruined her morning routine, her very favorite part of the day while on vacation. It was really too bad that he was staying right next door.

She couldn't very well go back outside without looking rude.

Looking around, she thought about making some jam with those strawberries. They had a refrigerator full of fruit. But that meant hours of working in the kitchen.

And that sounded like too much effort.

Amanda supposed she could read her book. Or practice on those Sudoku puzzles everyone else seemed to do with ease.

But those things didn't really appeal to her, either.

The phone rang and startled her out of her stupor. She eagerly ran to pick it up before it woke Regina.

"Hello?"

"Amanda, it's Marlene, dear. I was thinking of hopping on the bus and visiting Siesta Key today. Would you like me to bring you anything? Or have lunch together?"

Her mother-in-law was a *wonderful-gut* woman. But she was a talker. And a worrywart. And a bit controlling. Having her around today would not be relaxing.

Actually, Amanda had a feeling Marlene was worried about Regina. Marlene often watched Regina when Amanda worked at the bakery. She made no secret about how much she worried about Amanda's withdrawn little girl.

It did no good to tell Marlene that Regina was still recovering from Wesley's death. And that it didn't always make Regina feel better to be surrounded by constant talk and memories of a father she only remembered living in a hospital bed.

When she'd finally accepted her in-laws' invitation to use the condominium, Amanda had promised herself that she'd try to make this a carefree week. A happy one. She was looking forward to a few days of doing what she wanted, when she wanted to do it.

If Marlene stopped by, she would certainly comment on the unswept floors and unmade beds. The crayons strewn across the table and the sand toys in buckets by the back porch.

Worse, she would likely settle in and tell Regina a dozen stories about when her father went to the beach as a child . . .

and how sad he'd been when he'd gotten too sick to see the ocean.

That wouldn't do. That didn't sound like the kind of vacation Amanda had in mind.

"*Danke*, Marlene, but I don't need a thing."

"You don't? Oh." She took a breath. "Well, how about I simply stop by for a chat? I'm worried that you're sitting by yourself day after day."

In the privacy of the kitchen, Amanda let herself smile. After all, she'd only been gone for two days. "I haven't been sitting alone."

"No?"

"Not at all. I've made friends with the family next door. Regina has, too. The Keims have a little girl named Lindy, and she's almost exactly Gina's age. They have become fast friends. We've got plans to get together with them later."

"Oh."

Amanda winced. That one sound held multiple meanings, for sure. Wesley's mother loved her very much. But she also envisioned Amanda memorializing Wesley for the rest of her days.

"Thank you for checking on me, Marlene. I'm glad you called."

"Me, too. Is Regina right there with you? Could you put her on? I'd like to say hello."

"Gosh, I'm afraid she's still asleep."

"Still? It's almost eight."

"I know." Purposely, Amanda left the conversation at that. No way did she want to try to explain their late nights to her mother-in-law.

"Oh," she said again. "Well, then . . . I suppose I'll call you later."

"I'll be talkin' with you then. Goodbye, Marlene."

After hanging up, Amanda stared at the empty spot on the beach where she'd been sitting. She wished she were still sitting outside. Then she wouldn't have heard the phone ring or picked it up.

She could've still been sitting quietly, giving thanks for the day and enjoying the antics of the seagulls as they flew in circles over the water.

Now? She was feeling guilty about rejecting her mother-in-law's invitation and about letting Regina stay up late and sleep in.

And she couldn't stop thinking about Roman Keim. The first man to tangle up her thoughts in years. For the first time in a long time, she felt a fresh slice of pain. Almost as if she was suddenly living again.

It was as if one of those rays of light from the rising sun had struck her skin and were blazing inside her.

Waking her up.

chapter three

"Momma?" Regina called out from her room. "Momma? You here?"

"I'm right here, dear," Amanda said with a wry smile as she walked to the hallway. "Where else would I be?"

"I don't know," her daughter said around a yawn as her bare feet padded along the white tile floor. Every few feet, she stopped and gathered up her stuffed dog in her arms. When she did that, her toes curled away from the cool surface, as if the cold tile was a little too chilly on her skin.

As she came closer, Amanda noticed Gina's white nightgown was wrinkled, and it fluttered around her ankles. It was the perfect complement to the long brown hair falling in thick waves to her shoulder blades.

As she stopped and yawned yet again, Amanda felt her heart fill with love for her little girl.

Regina always looked like an angel to her, but of course, she wasn't the quiet, peaceful sort.

Not at all!

Instead, Regina had a way about her that brought a smile to your face. Since Wesley's death, she was just a little hesitant, a little apprehensive about new things. But once she felt secure, her smile could warm anyone's heart.

Amanda didn't know how she'd been so blessed to have such a sweet little girl. "Are you hungry, sweet pea?"

"Uh-huh."

"What will it be this morning? Scrambled eggs and bacon?"

"Do we have Pop-Tarts?" Regina's eyes sparkled with mischief.

They'd played this game before. "Pop-Tarts? Here?" she asked in mock surprise.

"We might have them."

"Truly?"

Regina giggled. "*Jah*, Momma."

"Well, if you say so, I suppose I'd best go check." She made a great show of opening several cabinets and looking around in wonder, but of course, it was all in jest. In truth, strawberry Pop-Tarts were their little secret. On vacation, the two of them ate foods that were decidedly different from their usual healthy diet.

Instead of bowls of nutritious oatmeal or eggs and toast, they enjoyed box cereal with tigers and other cartoon characters on the cartons . . . and indulged in their shared love of the boxed pastries. Regina loved the strawberry ones. And Amanda? She didn't even pretend to be healthy—her favorite were the brown sugar cinnamon ones.

Regina got on her tiptoes, trying her best to peek on the counter. "Mamm, do we have any today?"

Her daughter's voice was so hopeful, Amanda couldn't continue the ruse any longer. "Of course we do, dear."

"*Aeb-beah*?"

"*Jah*. You may have strawberry and I'll have cinnamon sugar. But you must drink your milk, too."

"I will." As Amanda was pouring milk into a sippy cup, Regina asked, "What about you?"

"What about me what?" This time, she really was confused.

"Are you going to drink healthy *millich*, too?"

"*Nee.*" She held up her mug. "I'm going to stick to my *kaffi*."

"But Mommi says you don't take care of yourself."

Surprised, Amanda set the carton of milk down. "When did your grandmother say that?"

Eyes wide and innocent, Regina said, "Mommi says you don't take care of yourself like you should. 'Cause you're still missing Daed."

"I'm taking care of myself." Seeing the stress in her daughter's eyes, Amanda felt a flash of annoyance. She didn't appreciate Marlene causing Regina unnecessary worry. Regina had already had more than enough pain and worry in her short life. "Don't worry about me, child. I am fine."

"But—"

"I am perfectly fine, Regina. Please, don't worry that I'm not," she said with a bit more emphasis than she'd intended.

Just as Regina started to get that pout in her lip that signified she was going to argue, Amanda set the red plastic cup on the table and placed one strawberry Pop-Tart on a napkin beside it. "Now, what would you like to do today?"

"Go to the beach."

That was the top of Regina's list always. She loved the beach and hunting for crabs and building sand castles, and swimming, too. Never did she complain about sunscreen or getting salt or sand in her eyes. If she was outside at the beach, she was a happy girl.

"I think we can go to the beach," Amanda said with a smile. "And maybe we can go for a walk and look for shells?"

Regina nodded, as if they were discussing extremely important matters. "And maybe get some ice cream, too?"

"Perhaps. Also, Lindy might have time to play. Would you like that, too?"

"Uh-huh."

"Eat up, then." Amanda smiled, but felt her insides churning with doubts all over again. As much as she loved spending time at the beach with her daughter, something about those few moments with Roman Keim had reminded her of what it was like to have a man by her side. To be more than just a *mamm*.

Yes, she was calm and relatively content. But she was beginning to feel as if she were only half alive. Suddenly, a lazy day at the beach didn't sound as if it were the best day ever.

No, it sounded like another day to pass while she waited for something better to happen.

Was that true? Had she begun to confuse contentment with happiness . . . simply because both were far better than grieving for things that couldn't be?

"Have you heard from Roman again, Marie? Has he called, by chance?" Lovina asked from across the room where she'd been hard at work at the treadle sewing machine for two hours.

They'd been working in almost complete silence, each lost in thought. At least, that was what Marie suspected. For herself, she kept thinking about Peter . . . and wondering how he was going to react to the latest bombshell about his parents.

Marie kept waiting for Lovina to bring up the matter again. But, like always, it seemed she was content to push their problems to one side . . . almost as if they weren't happening.

"Have you heard anything?" Lovina asked again, her voice now tinged with impatience.

"Not a thing." Looking up from the pattern she was tracing for Lorene's wedding dress, she said hesitantly, "Perhaps Roman is trying to forget about us this week. If he stayed in constant touch, he'd hardly be taking a vacation from the goings-on around here." She paused, half expecting Lovina to say something caustic.

But instead, her mother-in-law chuckled. "I suppose you're right. We've had enough drama in this home for a lifetime. If I were a young man, I'd try to stay as far away as I could. At least things seem to be calming down here, I think."

"Are they?" Marie asked. "Lovina, when are you planning to explain this news about Aaron's first wife and son?"

Lovina clenched her hands on her lap. "I wasn't planning to discuss it."

"But we deserve to know more. I mean, if he lost his wife and child . . ."

"It's not my place to discuss my husband's past."

"Since he doesn't seem ready, I wish you would."

The tension in the air thickened. Marie stared at her mother-in-law, tired of playing games.

"We need to have everything out in the open," she whispered. "Only then can we begin to heal."

"Perhaps," Lovina said, but she didn't sound too convinced.

For a moment, Marie was sure Lovina was going to talk. Was finally going to share her feelings and talk about their past. Chest tight with unspent emotion, Marie waited.

And waited.

Then watched as her mother-in-law shook out her fabric and cleared her throat. "Well, now. At least Viola is happy. That is a blessing, for sure."

So that was going to be the way of it.

With a sigh, Marie relaxed her posture and played along. "It is a blessing, to be sure. I fear the postman is going to start coming to our house with body armor on. Viola practically tackles him when he delivers the mail."

"She's in *lieb*. She can't be faulted for wanting to hear from Edward."

There was such fondness and whimsy in her mother-in-law's voice that Marie looked her way in surprise. "So, you don't think I should be worrying about Viola marrying a missionary? Moving to Belize is a big step."

"It is, but I've never known your daughter to do anything she doesn't want to do. Or to take advice." Carefully clipping some stray threads, Lovina held up the portion of the pink dress she'd just pieced together. "Elsie now has half a dress for Lorene's wedding."

Marie noticed how perfectly the sleeves were attached and again marveled at what a competent, skilled seamstress Lovina was. "Viola's dress is already done, right?"

"It is. As is mine. I only have Elsie's to finish, and yours."

Thinking about her sister-in-law Lorene, her husband's youngest sister, Marie said, "Lorene is as giddy as a schoolgirl, don't you think? I've never known her to be so full of life. It's fun to see."

"It is *gut* to see. It is time she had some giddiness, I think." Smoothing out the pink fabric in front of her, Lovina added, "I truly thought John Miller wasn't the right man for her all those years ago. I thought interfering in her life was the right thing to do."

"Maybe it was? Not everyone is ready for marriage at twenty."

"I should have let her make that choice." Lifting her chin, she gazed at Marie. "I regret my actions."

"It wasn't just your choice, Lovina. Aaron agreed, and both John and Lorene went along with your decision." Smiling slightly, she said, "But could you ever imagine Viola giving in so easily?"

Her mother-in-law chuckled. "I can't even imagine Viola eating carrots! She never was one to do something she didn't want to."

Marie smiled. "I had forgotten about that. When they were little, that was one of the ways Peter and I could tell them apart! Elsie always loved all vegetables. Viola? Not so much."

"Those were the days, weren't they? It was such a busy house, with those twin girls constantly causing mischief."

Marie felt the same spark of nostalgia. "I thought I'd never get a moment's rest when the girls were two and Roman was three. Oh, the three of them together were a handful."

"Remember when Roman announced he wanted to live in the barn, because there were no little girls there? Aaron and I couldn't stop laughing." There was more than a touch of fondness in Lovina's tone . . . and a bit wistfulness, too.

Which made Marie realize she was feeling the absence of another member of their family.

Marie hesitated, then decided to let the cat out of the bag. "I hope Peter will be able to attend Lorene's wedding. They're so close, it would be a shame if he missed it."

"So . . . I don't guess you've heard from him?"

"Only one phone call so far." Her husband had warned her that his time in the alcohol rehabilitation center would be restrictive. But somehow, she'd thought they'd talk more often. She missed him so much. Before he'd left, they'd never been apart more than two nights, when he'd sometimes go with his father to a horse auction. They'd been together so long, she felt his absence acutely, as if she were missing one of her limbs. "I sure hope he calls soon. I wonder why he isn't writing?"

"Are you worried about him, Marie?"

Once again, Lovina's voice was so kind, it almost caught her off guard. Lovina had never been one for sympathy, or understanding people's weaknesses. But ever since it came out that Lovina had grown up English, and that she'd kept it a secret all these years, there was a bit of humility in her that Marie didn't know what to do with.

Little by little, Marie had lowered the defensive wall she'd erected for self-preservation. It was time to speak the truth—even if it made her vulnerable. "Of course I'm worried. I mean, I don't want to think the worst, but hardly hearing from him for two weeks . . . my imagination takes control and I start worrying that he's sick. Or that his drinking problem has gotten worse."

"I doubt he's worse. He can't be getting into any alcohol there. And if he was sick, you would have heard from the center."

"I suppose. I'm just worried."

"Why? He is finally getting help. You should be relieved."

"I'm worried that the center won't be able to help him," she admitted, hating to even say the words out loud. "Or I fear that Peter will lie about his progress, that maybe everyone will think he's cured but he won't be. Or that it will take even longer than we thought." She worried about his faith, too. Was he clinging to it, like she was? Or was the program encouraging him to compromise—or to even set aside his beliefs in order to heal?

"I'm sorry," Marie said. "I sound hateful and selfish, don't

I? I do believe in him. And I do love him. It's just, well, at night, I find myself wishing for the way things used to be."

"When he was keeping things from you?"

That was an apt question. Wryly, she said, "I want things to be like I *thought* they were, like I wanted them to be. I'm sorry, Lovina. I hate to burden you with this."

Interrupting her thoughts, her mother-in-law spoke again. "You're not burdening me, Marie. Your worries are justified." Hesitantly, she added, "I have also thought the same things a time or two."

So thankful that Lovina wasn't berating her for not being more positive, she said, "I suppose you don't know what to think of any of us."

Lovina laughed. "If you're thinking that, you would be wrong. I think you've been doing the best you can during a challenging time. Your sister-in-law is practically eloping, she's in a such a rush to get married. Your daughter is engaged and will likely move out of the country, and your husband is in a drug treatment facility. Then, Aaron lets it slip that he was married before. It's a lot to have on one's plate, I think."

The summation of their family's troubles almost made Marie smile. Almost. "And you didn't even mention Elsie." Viola's twin was the sweetest, most even-tempered daughter you could ask for, in great contrast to her twin. But she'd been diagnosed with a degenerative eye disease when she was but a child. Little by little, her dear daughter was going blind.

"That's because I'm not worried about her, Marie, and you shouldn't, either. I feel certain that Elsie will be all right, with the Lord's help. And we'll all be there for her, even if the worst happens and she does go blind."

"I'll always be there for her. As long as I'm able, that is. Thankfully, Viola and Roman have promised to always look after Elsie, too. . . ."

"What are you talking about? What are you two saying about me?" Elsie said sharply from the doorway.

"Nothing, dear," Marie replied quickly, but the look of hurt in her daughter's eyes revealed her fib wasn't appreciated.

"No, I know what I heard." Looking from Lovina to Marie, Elsie scowled. "Mamm, you two were talking about taking care of me as if I were a burden. Weren't you?"

"I was only saying that I want to make sure you always have our help. And you will, *maydel*," Marie said weakly.

"I won't always need your help, Mother. I am not a child."

Looking at Lovina in a silent request for help, Marie bit her lip. "Of course not," she said in a rush.

But Elsie wasn't buying that. "Mamm, I am not helpless."

"I never said you were." Because she didn't know what else to do, Marie found herself snapping at her dear daughter. "Don't put words in my mouth, Elsie."

"I'm not. But you need to stop treating me as if my destiny is living at home and being tended to. I will be just fine."

But how could she be, if she couldn't see? Marie felt her reply stick in her throat.

"We were only discussing your disease, Elsie," Lovina interjected smoothly. "And you are fooling yourself if you don't think your health concerns us all."

"But I am not blind. Yet," she blurted, then turned around and walked away. Two minutes later, they heard her close her bedroom door with a decidedly firm click.

Marie shook her head. "Well, I didn't handle that too well."

After a moment, Lovina spoke. "Roman has every right to

enjoy a few days away from here. If I were him, I'd consider staying in Florida even longer. This family of ours has more problems than a squirrel has nuts."

Marie thought that was putting it mildly. Feeling tense, she began carefully cutting fabric. Only when the slow whir of the sewing machine started did she feel able to exhale.

When would things ever settle down?

chapter four

One of Roman's favorite things to do in Pinecraft was to watch the older men play shuffleboard. The numerous courts that were scattered around the boardwalks always gave a man someone to compete against, and the congenial conversation that took place around the playing was as entertaining as the game itself.

Usually, men his age played volleyball or basketball, but Roman was partial to the shuffleboard courts. Maybe it was because of his close relationship with his father and grandfather, but whatever the reason, he found he enjoyed watching the older men strategize and joke with each other. And, of course, Roman was always happy to give the men a run for their money when he could.

Walking with his cousins Evan and Jonah, and Beth's husband, Paul, Roman felt almost like his old self . . . or maybe even a better version of his old self.

The guys were an easygoing lot, and the jokes they passed back and forth made his mood lighten even more.

Especially since at the moment they were teasing Evan, who couldn't seem to make a choice between the three girls he was halfheartedly dating at the same time. Three!

"It takes a special man to manage three women, Evan," Paul commented. "I can hardly handle your sister."

Jonah snorted. "That's because she's got two *kinner* underfoot."

"That's not it," Evan countered. "It's because Beth was always difficult. Even when she was four, she was demanding."

Jonah chuckled. "Evan, you're only saying that because she constantly tattled on you."

Evan sighed, like he was the most put-upon man in Florida. "That is true. No matter what, Beth always told on us. Even when we practically begged her not to, she went running off to Mamm and Daed and told them everything."

"You mean *threatened* to tell them everything," Jonah murmured. "I happen to know of a couple of things that never reached our parents' ears."

"Oh, yeah?" A spark of interest lit Evan's expression. "Like what?"

Jonah grinned Roman's way. "I'm not telling. We don't know if we can trust Roman yet."

"Believe me, I've got my own secrets to keep," he said. Though he kind of didn't.

But maybe that was his secret? That he'd lived his life so carefully that he had nothing special to keep close to his heart? Twenty-three years of being dutiful and reserved hadn't brought him much excitement.

Now that he thought about it, it hadn't brought him a great deal of happiness, either.

"Anyway, Paul, we were mighty glad when you married Beth. You got her out of our hair," Jonah said. "The *haus* became much more peaceful when she left."

Paul grinned. "I'm right fond of Beth, even though she is a stickler for order. But as far as our falling in love? Why, I couldn't help myself. From the moment I first saw her, she claimed my heart." He paused. "But even though I'm happily married, I can't help but be interested in Evan's, uh . . . love triangle. It's fun to watch someone else's exciting love life."

"I don't think it's a triangle if there's four involved," Roman pointed out. "Three women, one man."

Jonah grinned. "It's more of a love rectangle. Evan, you're impressive, for sure."

Evan's cheeks were now bright red. "Stop; it's not like that. Well, not that bad! I simply can't choose. And Carrie, Trisha, and Sally all know about each other."

Jonah pretended to choke. "Kind of."

"You're one to talk, *bruder*," Evan retorted, his face still flaming. "You're hardly seeing any girls."

"That's only because you're dating them all. Save some women for the rest of us."

That comment, of course, brought forth a whole new round of ribbing and laughter.

Roman joined in a bit, but mainly stayed an observer. At home with his twin sisters, he was often the odd man out. Though he had many friends, it was rare that a group of them would have so much time to simply hang out. At home, chores and duty were his first priorities.

And, of course, he'd chosen to order his life that way.

Now, for the second time that day, he was regretting that. He would have liked to have fostered this kind of relationship with some of the other men in his church community.

Roman was surprised by these thoughts. Maybe it was being away from all that was familiar and his strict routine that made his heart long for more.

Here, in Pinecraft, the sun was shining on his shoulders

as they walked along the boardwalk. At home? All he'd felt lately was a miserable, cold wind.

Here, the scent of sand and ocean permeated the air instead of dirt and horse and manure. Here, people were smiling and joking with each other—not complaining about the snow or the crops or the latest family drama.

Here, he felt as if anything was possible. Surrounded by short sleeves and vibrantly colored dresses and blue skies, everything seemed better.

Even the heat coming off the hot cement felt rejuvenating, like he was suddenly alive after sleeping too long in a dark room.

He envied everyone who was fortunate enough to live in such a place for months at a time.

When a group of men their fathers' ages invited them to play shuffleboard, he jumped right in, but wasn't too disappointed when he was eliminated after the first round. He enjoyed people-watching as much as anything.

Though most of the people were either Mennonite or Amish, being in Pinecraft had afforded Roman an unusual opportunity to be around men and women from all parts of the country. Many Amish came here for vacation, a way to be away from home but still among their people. The relaxed atmosphere gave him the chance to notice the differences in everything from women's *kapps* to men's hats and dialects.

Evan, Jonah, and Paul seemed to understand his preference to simply observe. When Roman took a seat on a bench and stretched out his legs, none of them seemed to care that he was sitting alone and watching the game.

And then he saw her.

Amanda was walking toward him on the sidewalk, her hand clasped around a little girl's. Amanda was wearing the same apricot-colored dress that she'd had on that morning. Her daughter's dress was a more vibrant shade of orange, and the combination of their bright dresses made Roman smile.

As did their expressions. Both were chuckling as they sidestepped the men who were gathered around the shuffleboard courts and the older ladies who'd stopped for a quick chat.

When they moved off the sidewalk to pet someone's puppy, Roman found himself moving to one side of the bench and craning his neck to see them better.

His focus was probably obvious. Maybe bordering on rude.

But for the life of him, Roman couldn't find the will to look away. Not even when Amanda glanced in his direction, caught sight of him, and then looked a little apprehensive. Obviously she was finding his unwavering attention more than a little off-putting.

The smart thing to do would be to look away. To turn back to the men he was with. To let her have her space.

But instead, he approached her, just as if his feet had a mind of their own.

"Hi, Amanda," he said. "I thought that was you." As if he could have been mistaken.

Politely, Amanda stopped, but she didn't look all that happy about it. "*Gut matin*. Again." She reached for her daughter's hand again—an unmistakable sign of protectiveness.

He ignored it. "I'm Roman," he said to her daughter. "I met your *mamm* this morning on the beach. She said you've been playing with my niece, Lindy."

There, he was no longer a stranger, and had effectively eliminated any opportunity Amanda might have taken to keep them apart.

Looking at him with wide blue eyes, her daughter stared at him warily.

"This is Regina," Amanda said. "She's a little shy."

Roman inwardly chastised himself. He shouldn't have been so gregarious. "It's nice to meet you, Regina," he said softly.

After a few seconds of studying him, she held up the hand Amanda wasn't holding and displayed a bright blue bandage on one of her fingers. "I have a Band-Aid."

He bent down so he could examine it more closely. "Indeed you do. What happened?"

Her lips pursed. "I was stung by a bee."

"Oh my goodness, that hurts."

Patting Regina's back, Amanda said, "She was a brave girl."

After studying Roman again, Regina blurted, "I cried, but I'm okay now." Then she waved her finger as if to illustrate its good condition. "Mamm put some ice on my finger and wrapped it up."

He noticed that pink unicorns decorated the bandage. "I like those horses."

"They're unicorns, not horses. Unicorns have horns. And they're pink," she said solemnly. "They're not real, but I still like them."

"Me, too." He smiled. He liked how protective Amanda was of her daughter, and how Regina continued to carefully study him even as she schooled him on the differences between horses and unicorns.

Straightening, he faced Amanda. "You know, I was just thinking that some ice cream sounded like a good idea. Would you two like to join me?"

Regina's eyes widened. "Can we, Mamm?" she asked in a loud whisper.

Amanda gave him a chiding look that said exactly what she thought about him offering such an invitation in front of her daughter. "We may," she finally said.

Roman grinned. "Great, let me just tell these guys that I'm off. Don't go."

"We won't," Regina said.

As he walked toward his cousins, Roman noticed that his visit with Amanda and her daughter hadn't gone unnoticed. Evan and Jonah were looking at him with knowing grins.

"What's going on?" Paul asked.

"I'm going to take Amanda and her daughter out to ice cream."

All three men looked in their direction. Jonah squinted. "Ain't she our neighbor over at the condo?"

"Yep." Roman grinned.

Evan took a step forward. "What's going on? Do you like her?"

"I don't know. I mean, I just met her."

Evan brazenly looked at her again. "She's pretty."

"Don't look at her anymore. You already have three women," Roman quipped. Then couldn't believe he said such a thing.

Evan held up his hands. "Don't worry, cousin. She's all yours . . . if she'll have you."

Now he felt awkward. "I don't *have* her. Like I said, we just met. We're merely friends." And they weren't even that. Not really.

"Of course," Evan said, smirking.

Jonah and Paul exchanged knowing looks. "I think it's a fine day to go get ice cream. Enjoy yourselves. We'll see you later," Paul said. "You'll take the bus back to Siesta Key?"

"Yep, no problem." The bus ran between the two places regularly.

Roman turned back to Amanda and Regina, half expecting to find that they'd disappeared into the crowd. But there they were, waiting for him to return to their side.

He didn't want to contemplate why that made him feel so good. But it did.

chapter five

"I'm sorry about that," Roman said as he strode back to Amanda and Regina. "I didn't want the guys to think I abandoned them."

Amanda coolly looked at the men who were standing like a klatch of housewives, watching their departure with unabashedly amused expressions. "Is everything all right?" she asked. "They looked a little worried."

No, they'd looked amused, Roman mentally corrected. "Everything couldn't be better. They were just giving me grief," he said lightly. "You know how that is."

The look she gave him showed that she knew anything but how that was. "Are they all members of your family?"

"Yeah." Remembering how she'd seemed to like for him to talk a lot, he forced himself to keep talking. "Actually, they're my cousins. They live in Indiana. I'm vacationing with their family. Oh, and one of the men is Beth's husband. Beth's my cousin, too."

She peered at them again, then nodded. "Ah, now I remember Beth talking about them all."

"They're great, the whole family is. I am really having a good time with them. They make me laugh."

Amanda looked at him again, her blue eyes studying him seriously. But this time, he noticed that she was looking at him a little differently, as if she'd suddenly found something new about him that took her by surprise.

He was finding that this new, chatty, gregarious side of him was taking him by surprise, too. Usually, his sisters would have to prod and badger him to chat longer than five minutes.

Now, however, he couldn't seem to stop the words from coming. He seemed to be keeping her interest, though, so that was something, he supposed.

Leaning over to catch Regina's eye, who was walking on the other side of her mother, he said, "So, I can't believe you two are lucky enough to live here in Florida. You're certainly blessed to get to spend all your days in this sunshine."

Regina smiled up at him, looking happy to be included in the conversation. But she didn't say a word.

He tried again. "I love going to the beach. Do you?" When she nodded, he felt like he'd won a prize. "What do you like to do best at the beach?"

After a second's silence, Amanda started to speak. "She likes—"

"Sand castles," Regina whispered.

"I like making those, too," he said gently. "And digging for shells."

Her eyes widened. And then, she did the most amazing thing. She circled around her mother so she was now walking between the two of them. After clasping Amanda's hand, Regina said, "I like digging for crabs."

Roman glanced at Amanda. She looked stunned. It was obvious that this wasn't Regina's usual habit.

Roman was thrilled by the little girl's acceptance but didn't want to make a big deal about it. So he continued to chat. "You like digging for crabs, do ya? Aren't you scared that one is going to snap at your fingers?"

"One did! I got a Band-Aid then, too. But it wasn't a unicorn one. It was plain old brown."

He was charmed. "I like the unicorns better."

"Me, too."

While Roman laughed, Amanda felt herself smiling, almost against her will. It was rare that people thought to include her little girl in their conversation. It was rarer still for Regina to respond like she was with Roman.

Ever since Wesley got sick, Regina had become withdrawn. More of a worrier and far less outgoing.

But now Amanda was seeing glimpses of her daughter that she'd feared would be gone forever. It was amazing, really, and made her feel flustered.

Roman, on the other hand, looked anything but flustered. Actually, he looked as if he was determined to make sure Regina didn't feel left out in the slightest.

As she watched Regina blossom under Roman's gentle, teasing banter, Amanda felt herself warming toward him. Slowly, her first impression of him was transforming. Truth be told, she was appreciating Roman's efforts to be more open about his life, too.

Instinctively, she knew he was working hard to make himself agreeable to her. He wanted her to like him. That was flattering, indeed. When was the last time someone had made her feel like an attractive woman, not only Wesley's widow?

Gosh, when was the last time she'd even felt attractive? She could barely remember such feelings.

When Wesley was battling cancer, she'd forgotten to eat, neglected to take care of herself. After he passed away, she'd had a series of illnesses—the result of being so rundown and unhealthy.

Then, of course, it had been a struggle to get through every day. She'd worn somber dresses and only focused on Regina. Only over the last eight months had her attitude shifted. She'd started to notice the blue skies again, and the kindness of other people. She'd started to find peace within herself and enjoyment from small things.

And now it looked like she'd almost come full circle. She'd attracted a handsome man's regard . . . and she didn't hate it.

These realizations made her want to try harder, too. "So, Roman, where is your favorite place to go get ice cream?"

"I don't have a place in mind." With a wink in Regina's direction, he said, "I simply thought it sounded like a good idea."

"I love ice cream," Regina quipped.

Raising his head, he met Amanda's gaze. "Is there somewhere you two like to go? Wherever you have in mind is fine with me."

"I don't have a favorite spot."

"I do! I like the Swirl," Regina exclaimed. "They have orange swirls."

"That sounds great." He looked around. "And where is that shop?"

"Here!" Regina said, pointing to the charming white-washed building one block away that had silly swirling ice cream pictures on the windows. It also boasted a line of at least twenty people.

"And just in time, too. I was tired of walking," Roman said with a smile. As they got in the back of the line, he looked down at Regina. "What do you think I should get?"

"Orange swirls, just like me."

"What do you usually get, Amanda?"

His voice, warm and kind, melted her more than the sun ever had. "Oh, any kind," she said, because, suddenly, for the life of her, she couldn't remember what she usually ate. Was it vanilla?

"Mamm likes vanilla swirls with rainbow sprinkles," Regina supplied.

Roman looked intrigued. "Rainbow sprinkles, hmm?"

"Ah, only on special occasions."

They continued to stand in line, slowly edging forward as person after person walked away with napkin-wrapped cones.

Amanda had stood in this line dozens of times, but it had been quite some time since she'd felt so happy or relaxed.

What was it about him that intrigued her so much?

Was it the way he was revealing himself to them bit by bit, as if he were peeling back layers of an onion?

Was it his handsome good looks, the way his dark hair, brown eyes, and muscular build looked like it could handle anything? His physique was so different from Wesley's. Wes had been slimmer, shorter. And at the end, of course, far weaker. She'd had to be strong for him.

Roman, on the other hand, looked like he could shoulder any burden easily.

All she knew was that she was terribly eager to learn more about him.

"Tell me about your family," she blurted when he and Regina had a break in their conversation. "I mean, do you have any sisters or brothers?"

"I have two younger sisters. They're twins."

"Twins?" Regina wrinkled her nose. "What does that mean?"

"He means that his sisters are like Jana and Jacob," Amanda said. "They were born at the same time."

"Except my sisters look almost exactly alike," he teased. "Somehow I don't think Jana and Jacob do."

"They don't. One's a boy and the other is a girl."

"It's good they look different then, *jah*?"

"Are you close to them?" Amanda asked.

He grinned. "If you knew them, you'd know that I had no choice but to be close to them." His expression softened. "But seriously, they're great. They're only one year younger than me, so we grew up together. My *mamm* used to say she felt like she had triplets, not twins. One of them, Viola, just got engaged to a missionary."

"And the other? Is she married yet?"

He shook his head. "*Nee*. I don't know if Elsie will ever marry."

Amanda was waiting for him to tell her more when Regina tugged on her apron.

"Mamm?" she whispered, with a pleading look in her eyes.

Offering an apologetic look Roman's way, she bent down. "What is it, dear?"

"Do they like *eis rawm*, too?"

With a soft chuckle, Amanda turned to Roman. "I'm sorry. My Regina has something of a one-track mind."

"Regina, you didn't want to ask me about that yourself?"

"As I said, sometimes she can be a little shy."

"Oh. Well, *jah*, Regina. My sisters do like ice cream, very much," he said seriously. Just as if Regina's question meant the world to him.

Once again, Amanda felt that little, unexpected pull toward him that caught her off guard. What was it about him that made her feel so comfortable with him? That made her trust even Regina to be around him?

Luckily, she didn't have to ponder that because they had just arrived at the counter. "Ah. Here we are."

"Are you going to get vanilla with sprinkles as usual?" Roman asked with wink.

"Probably . . . "

"You're not feeling adventurous?"

"Not in my ice cream," she replied. Then realized that that had become the case with a lot of things lately. It used to be that she had loved to try new things and meet new people. But after Wesley, even deviating from her regular routine had felt daring.

As Roman leaned down to talk to Regina, Amanda realized that he wasn't merely pretending to be interested in her daughter. He actually was at ease with her. She also couldn't help noticing that Regina didn't seem to be displaying any of the typical reticence she usually did when she was around men.

Did Regina sense in Roman the same thing that she did? That there was something about him that was safe . . . and terribly attractive?

And if she *was* attracted to him, what did that say about her? She knew better than to ever put her heart in danger again. Especially not with someone with whom there was no hope of a future.

"Amanda, do you want your usual small cup of vanilla?" Cheryl, the chatty red-haired *Englischer* who owned the Swirl asked.

With a start, Amanda realized that they were holding up the line. "Sorry," she said with a blush. "I guess my mind wandered."

Cheryl's smiled broadened. "The heat must be getting to you today." Picking up a small dish, she raised her pencil-thin brows. "So, the usual?"

"You know what, I think I'm going to get a medium chocolate-and-vanilla swirl in a cone today." She paused, then added, "And I'll have it dipped in chocolate, too."

Cheryl's brows went even higher. "Well, I'll be. Wonders never cease. I'll get that for you in a jiffy."

As Regina gaped, Roman grinned widely. "Care to tell me why your order is such a big deal?"

"I've been coming here for years. Every single time, I've always gotten the same thing. A habit, I guess you might call it."

"But today it was time for a change?"

"*Jah*. Today, it was time for a change." Of course, the ice cream was the least of it—not that he needed to know that. She shook her head in embarrassment. "That doesn't say much about me, does it? I mean a change in an ice cream order shouldn't be such a big deal."

"I disagree," he murmured. "I think it says a whole lot about you. And I think it's all good, Amanda."

After handing Amanda her chocolate-covered cone, Cheryl turned to him. "And for you?"

"It's time for me to live dangerously, too. I'll have the same," he said.

"And me, three?" Regina asked.

"*Nee*," Amanda said with a shiver. "That is far too much for you. You may have your usual."

"Oh, all right."

When Cheryl handed out Regina's cone, Roman pulled out his wallet. "I've got this."

"Roman—"

"It's my idea, my treat."

"But—"

"It's ice cream. Let me."

"*Danke,*" she said, deciding to give in gracefully.

After they were all armed with more napkins, Regina having her favorite—the small orange swirl—they walked to a bench and sat down together in a row, each of them enjoying the treat and seeming to enjoy the company and the sunny day just as much.

Amanda kicked her feet out a bit, liking the way the sun heated her ankles. Liking all of it.

Until she spied her mother-in-law looking at her across the way. "Uh-oh," she murmured before realizing that she had spoken out loud.

Roman turned to her in concern. "What's wrong?"

"It's nothing wrong, but things might be a little uncomfortable," she whispered. "That's my mother-in-law, and I'm afraid she's going to be mighty surprised to see me with you."

"Just tell me what you want me to say."

"You can say whatever you want . . . just don't be surprised if she peppers you with questions."

The moment Regina spied her grandmother, she stood up and ran to her, chattering all about the beach and Pop-Tarts and Roman and the ice cream.

As Marlene listened to her, her expression became more and more concerned.

With a sinking feeling, Amanda stayed where she was. If she was going to have to explain herself in front of all of Pinecraft, she preferred to do it from where she was. She was determined to stand her ground, even if she was, well, sitting.

When Regina finally took a breath, Marlene took Regina's free hand and walked over to them. "Hello, Amanda.

You said you were going to stay at the *haus* today. And that Regina was going to be with a friend."

"Some of our plans changed, though we do still hope to see Lindy later today. Um, Marlene, please meet Roman Keim. Roman, this is Marlene Yoder. My mother-in-law."

Roman was already standing up. "Nice to meet you."

Cool blue eyes looked him over before nodding, and then deliberately ignoring him. "Amanda, what in the world is going on?"

"We're eating ice cream."

"That is not what I meant." Her lips pursed, then she continued. "Why don't you and Regina come with me to lunch?"

"*Danke,* but no. As you can see, we're eating ice cream," she protested lightly. "Plus, we have other things planned."

"We do?" Regina asked. "What are we doing?"

"We have a play date with Lindy, of course."

As she'd hoped, the news brought a bright smile to her daughter's face. "I like Lindy."

"And she likes you, dear." Turning to her mother-in-law, she said, "It was nice to see you, Marlene, but I'm afraid we're going to continue with our plans."

"Plans."

"*Jah.* We're going to be fairly busy the rest of the day," she said firmly. Getting to her feet, she said, "Roman, let's go ahead and take that walk to the park you told me about."

Luckily, he nodded, like he had any idea what she was talking about. "Whatever you want is fine with me. It's a great walk." Bending slightly, he smiled at her daughter. "Regina, are you ready?"

"Uh-huh."

Amanda liked how he called her daughter over. Even more, she liked how Regina answered with a happy smile.

For a moment, they looked like a family. And though it hurt to think that she could be in a family without Wesley, it didn't hurt quite as badly as she had thought it would.

"Amanda, I will call you this afternoon. We'll talk then."

"If I'm home, I guess we will. Good day, Marlene."

Roman blinked, then reached for Regina's hand. "Let's go to the park."

"Yay!" Regina exclaimed, just as if they did this all the time.

Amanda found herself smiling, too, as they walked down the boardwalk, the three of them a little unit. It felt nice. Almost perfect.

All she had to do was not think about how much she'd just upset her mother-in-law.

And how for just for a moment, she hadn't cared.

chapter six

"Viola, another letter came for you today," Nancy called out when Viola entered the staff room at Daybreak to have lunch. "I put it on the corner of my desk."

"*Danke.*" Eagerly, Viola ran to the front office and snatched up the letter that was, indeed, waiting for her on the receptionist's desk. Though her family thought it was silly, she'd begun to ask Edward to mail some of his letters to her at Daybreak. Otherwise, every letter she received was commented upon. Sometimes she just wanted to read Ed's letters in private.

Because no one was there to see, she ran her finger over her neatly printed name and address on the envelope, thinking how Edward had written it all just days ago.

Then, feeling giddy and more than a little self conscious, she quickly walked to one of the cozy conversational areas down the hall to read his latest note from Belize.

The irony of her actions didn't escape her. For almost a year before she and Ed had met in person, she'd been practically forced to listen to every one of Ed's letters. His father, Atle, had received each one with pride, and had eagerly shared his son's news with everyone and anyone—whether they'd expressed a desire to hear about Edward's mission work or not.

But while Atle had glowed with pride about his son's work, Viola had inwardly seethed. Accustomed to managing everyone and everything around her, she'd been sure Ed should have put his father's needs first and stayed in Berlin. For some reason, everything that Ed had written about his hard work in Nicaragua had struck her as selfish.

Now, she realized that she'd taken a bunch of misconceptions about Ed and had wrapped them in a tight ball of self-righteousness.

But a funny thing had happened when she and Ed had met—sparks had flown between them, right about the time that she'd realized that she'd jumped to conclusions that weren't right at all. Before long, she'd fallen for his good looks and charming ways.

The next thing she knew, they were trading barbs and flirting with each other. And not too long after that?

They'd been falling in love.

No one had been happier about the new developments than Atle, of course. The gregarious, opinionated old man loved his son and wanted him happy. He'd thought all along that the two of them would make a good couple, and it looked as if he'd been right.

He'd loved pointing that out, too.

Now she and Ed were engaged. After much discussion, they'd agreed that, though it would be difficult, they would have to live apart for six months. That would give Ed time to concentrate on his new job as director of Christian Aid Ministries Association's mission in Belize.

It also gave her family time to plan the wedding she'd always dreamed of, and, of course, it gave her time to get used to the big changes that were happening in her life. In just a few short months, she, too, would be traveling to another country. This time, as a missionary's wife. It was thrilling and nerve-wracking, too.

Moving far away from her whole family scared her. And, in the middle of the night, when she rolled over in bed and spied her twin sister Elsie across the room on her own bed, Viola wasn't even sure if her heart would be able to stand living so far away from her sister. They were closer than close, and added to that was how much Viola worried about Elsie's illness. Elsie's sight was steadily becoming worse, and Viola knew it was just a matter of time before Elsie was going to be blind.

Sometimes Viola doubted every decision she'd recently made. She wondered how she was ever going to be able to leave her family for the brand-new love of a man who she'd really only spent a few weeks with.

But then she'd get a phone call or a letter from Ed and all her worries would fade away and she'd realize that what was happening was meant to happen. She and Edward were meant to be together, and she couldn't prioritize everyone else's happiness above her own.

Satisfied that she was completely alone, she opened the envelope and carefully unfolded the letter.

Dear Viola,

Have I told you about the pretty sunsets over the ocean?

She'd just begun to smile when Gretta, Ed's little dachshund that was now the retirement home's unofficial mascot, trotted over. As if she read Viola's mind, she curled around Viola's feet . . . just like she, too, was anxious to hear more about her former owner.

Happy to have Gretta's quiet comfort, Viola scooped up the dog and set her next to her on the couch.

Gretta wagged her tail, obviously pleased with the special treatment.

"Just imagine, Gretta. In a week, I'll be going to visit Ed and we'll be watching the sunsets over the ocean together. Won't that be something?"

With a dreamy sigh, she continued to read.

I've begun walking to the beach on Friday nights with two other men from the mission. We rush to make it there just before the sun begins its descent. Once there, we take off our work boots and roll up our pant legs and walk on the sand, letting the warm grains underfoot ease our tired, sore feet. Then, we step into the warm, salty water and enjoy the sensation of complete relaxation.

When the sun starts to set, we sit on an old cement embankment. It's cracked and worn, but makes a perfect perch to watch the sun slowly glide into the sea, marking the end of another day. And another week.

Viola grinned and rubbed the dog behind her ears before continuing to read.

It's moments like that when I miss you the most, Viola. When I have time to breathe deep and count my blessings. It's then that I realize that having you here will only help me—and the people we serve, too. You've become a part of me that I miss when I'm without you.

Once the sun sets and the orange and red waves turn dark again, we hike back to the mission's compound, feeling refreshed and ready to tackle whatever comes our way again. I know when you are here, too, I'll even be feeling more at ease. I feel certain that we'll have a wonderful life here together, V. I promise I'll do everything I can to make it so.

Viola felt her eyes become damp with unshed tears as she once again contemplated what her life would have been like if she'd never given him a chance. If she'd never given herself the opportunity to learn and grow and change. If she'd only let her common sense guide her . . . instead of her heart.

But, of course, it was no secret what would have happened. She would have continued to be alone and self-centered. But most of all, she would have been fighting off the feeling that there was something more for her out there . . . if she wasn't afraid to go out and look.

"I'm so lucky and blessed, Gretta. So lucky, so blessed."

And with that, Gretta snuggled closer and closed her eyes, reminding Viola that the little dog had been abandoned and was living alone outside in the elements before Edward had brought her into his life.

Funny, though Viola had been living with her family, she too, felt as if her life had become better under Edward's care. He'd become her comfort, her own particularly vibrant ray of light.

Regina had fallen asleep while playing with her stuffed animals on the floor. Amanda lightly covered her with a thin blanket, then quietly tiptoed outside, leaving the glass sliding door ajar in case Regina woke with a start and needed her.

As was her habit, she brought out her crochet hook, intending to work on her latest project—a shawl for Wesley's grandmother's birthday. But she couldn't seem to persuade herself to pull out the yarn.

No, all she seemed to want to do was sit in the sun and spend a few moments enjoying the solitude.

"Which is what a vacation is for, you goose," she murmured to herself. "You're supposed to read and relax. Not work on your to-do list."

Hearing her own voice, Amanda winced. When had she begun to talk to herself, anyway? When she got engaged? Pregnant with Regina?

It had been when she'd been sitting by Wesley's bedside in the hospital, of course.

When he'd fallen into an uneasy slumber—on account of the many medicines he'd been given to combat the pain of the disease—she'd begun talking to him. Telling him about her day. About every little thing that Regina did.

Then, just to have something to talk about, she'd start telling him stories about her childhood. Over time, she'd begun to talk aloud just to help herself deal with all the sadness that had welled up inside her. She'd felt like she had to talk about everything; otherwise, it would get stuck inside and make her sick, too.

And she'd already been so very tired and heartsick.

Wesley's decline had lasted for months. Long enough for her chatty vigils to become a habit. After his death, she'd taken to talking to herself when she'd known she was alone. The habit felt comforting to her in a strange way. It was now something she was used to.

But living without Wesley? That was something she wasn't used to at all.

Now, she realized with a start, things had changed again. After two years, the daily emptiness that had been her constant companion had slowly abated. Oh, the pain was still there, but it wasn't as sharp or obtrusive as it used to be.

Now, missing Wesley wasn't the first thing she experienced in the morning, or the last thing she thought of before she went to sleep. She no longer thought about him every waking moment, instead thinking of him at odd times. His memory no longer brought her to tears, and she'd begun to remember their life together in a distant, almost melancholy way.

Though this transition wasn't something she was altogether comfortable with, Amanda certainly welcomed the relief. For so long she'd felt like a woman twice her age.

"Being a widow isn't for the faint of heart," she told herself. On the heels of that, she remembered an old saying of her aunt's: There is no strength where there is no struggle.

That saying had a lot of truth to it.

But sometimes, even the truth didn't bring the sort of comfort she craved.

Oh, but she hated these bouts of depression! What she needed to do was think of her blessings.

"You have Regina," she said out loud. She had Wesley's family, too. And even though Marlene was determined to keep Amanda wrapped in grief, she'd always been there for her, and that was a blessing.

Her own family was still back in Pennsylvania. And though she loved them, they'd been distant witnesses to everything she'd gone through with her husband. Never had she considered moving near them.

But now, for the first time, she wondered what she was giving up by embracing only her past with Wesley.

"You should call and write your family more often. And while you're at it, pray about your fear of moving on, Amanda," she told herself sternly. "Every time you try to give up another part of your life with Wesley, it's brought you to tears. Why, it took you six months to even take his clothes out of the house."

The memory of boxing his clothes still made her cringe. It had taken her almost three hours to pack one large box, and almost another one to carefully seal the box with packing tape.

Just when she was about to scold herself a little more, she noticed Roman walking on the beach with a dog, of all things. The shaggy yellow dog was darting along the shoreline, sniffing the sand, scampering into the water, then rushing out with surprising speed.

Intrigued, she walked to the white picket fence and leaned her elbows along the top of it.

Roman held the dog's leash with one hand, but gave the animal enough leeway so that he could race around exuberantly. He'd run to the waves, then dart back out and shake vigorously, spraying water everywhere, like a wayward sprinkler.

Then, next thing she knew, the dog was back in the waves, dipping its nose in, darting here and there, barking happily.

He was a furry, soggy, noisy mess.

And Roman looked as if he was enjoying every minute of its company.

She was mesmerized by the dog playing in the water and by Roman's lack of concern about getting wet or sandy. Suddenly, she ached to be so carefree, so unbound by rules of propriety, or by responsibility. She yearned to be completely happy—exuberant. If only for a moment.

She realized with a start that it didn't matter if her conscience told her to be more careful with her heart—she simply wanted to be happy.

As Roman stopped almost directly in front of her, Amanda also realized she'd become attracted to Roman Keim. Why else would her heart have started beating a little bit faster . . . just because he was around?

In fact, she was so mesmerized . . . she was struck silent. Fancy that.

When the dog barked again, then darted after a crab, Roman laughed. Standing there watching, Amanda chuckled, too.

Roman looked her way, paused, and raised a hand.

Without thinking, she called out, "You've got yourself quite a dog there!"

"You don't know the half of it!" he called back with a grin, then got yanked as the shaggy dog practically galloped into an approaching wave.

"Watch out!" Amanda cried out with a laugh.

And managed to wake Regina up from her nap

"Momma?" she asked as she sleepily sat up. "Who are you yelling at? And is that a dog barking?"

"I was yelling at Roman. He's walking a dog. Well, it's kind of walking him."

Scrambling to her feet, Regina walked to the open door and peered out to where Amanda was looking, then gazed at the pair in wonder.

"Momma, how did he get a dog? Where did it come from?"

"I have no idea." As the dog scampered back into the water,

then shook himself, making the coarse-looking golden fur stand on end, Amanda said, "But it sure looks like a happy dog, doesn't it?"

"Uh-huh." With wide eyes, she added, "Mamm, do you think we could go see it?"

"If you want."

Her hand on the gate, Regina asked, "Do you think Roman will let me pet it?"

"It's all wet. Do you want to?"

"Uh-huh."

"Well, it doesn't hurt to ask if we can," Amanda said as she smoothed back her hair and shook out her teal dress. "Are you ready to go see them now? Would you rather have a snack first?"

But that was a silly question, of course. Because no sooner had she half offered the invitation than had Regina clicked open the gate and trotted toward Roman, her bright pink dress flying up around her ankles. "Roman! Roman, hi! It's me, Regina!"

Amanda was so shocked, she almost called out to Regina to come right back. But the scene that unfolded before her rendered her almost speechless.

There was her quiet Regina running to Roman, a big, bright smile on her face.

And there was Roman turning to her and greeting her with a broad grin.

And then, to Amanda's surprise, Regina held out her hand for Roman to take. Roman took it easily, then looked for Amanda. When he spied her, that warm gaze was like something out of a silly daydream. It was heated and earnest, sweet and sincere.

All directed at her.

It took everything Amanda had not to sigh. Instead, she forced herself to walk toward Roman and Regina and that rambunctious golden dog as sedately as she could.

After all, it wasn't as if anything could ever happen between the two of them. He was a farmer from Ohio. And she?

She was Wesley's widow.

chapter seven

For two days Marie had stewed about her conversation with Lovina. For two days, she'd contemplated keeping quiet. To allow her in-laws to keep the story about Aaron's first wife and son to themselves.

But then she realized that they could never go back to how things used to be. The proverbial cat was out of the bag and it certainly wasn't about to sneak back in.

Which was why she found herself standing outside the barn, working hard to gather her courage before confronting her father-in-law. Even though things were going to be mighty uncomfortable, it was time to really talk.

With a new resolve, she entered the barn, where Aaron was currying Chester.

"I wondered when you were going to come inside," he said over his shoulder. "What have you been stewing about out there?"

"I wanted to talk to you about your first wife and son."

After a brief pause, he set down the curry brush and turned to her. "Marie, it's really none of your concern."

"I think it is. Aaron, I've been a part of this family for over twenty years."

"Yes, but—"

"Aaron, you foisted this news on my family, then left, like we deserved no explanations."

chapter seven

For two days Marie had stewed about her conversation with Lovina. For two days, she'd contemplated keeping quiet. To allow her in-laws to keep the story about Aaron's first wife and son to themselves.

But then she realized that they could never go back to how things used to be. The proverbial cat was out of the bag and it certainly wasn't about to sneak back in.

Which was why she found herself standing outside the barn, working hard to gather her courage before confronting her father-in-law. Even though things were going to be mighty uncomfortable, it was time to really talk.

With a new resolve, she entered the barn, where Aaron was currying Chester.

"I wondered when you were going to come inside," he said over his shoulder. "What have you been stewing about out there?"

"I wanted to talk to you about your first wife and son."

After a brief pause, he set down the curry brush and turned to her. "Marie, it's really none of your concern."

"I think it is. Aaron, I've been a part of this family for over twenty years."

"Yes, but—"

"Aaron, you foisted this news on my family, then left, like we deserved no explanations."

propriety, or by responsibility. She yearned to be completely happy—exuberant. If only for a moment.

She realized with a start that it didn't matter if her conscience told her to be more careful with her heart—she simply wanted to be happy.

As Roman stopped almost directly in front of her, Amanda also realized she'd become attracted to Roman Keim. Why else would her heart have started beating a little bit faster . . . just because he was around?

In fact, she was so mesmerized . . . she was struck silent. Fancy that.

When the dog barked again, then darted after a crab, Roman laughed. Standing there watching, Amanda chuckled, too.

Roman looked her way, paused, and raised a hand.

Without thinking, she called out, "You've got yourself quite a dog there!"

"You don't know the half of it!" he called back with a grin, then got yanked as the shaggy dog practically galloped into an approaching wave.

"Watch out!" Amanda cried out with a laugh.

And managed to wake Regina up from her nap.

"Momma?" she asked as she sleepily sat up. "Who are you yelling at? And is that a dog barking?"

"I was yelling at Roman. He's walking a dog. Well, it's kind of walking him."

Scrambling to her feet, Regina walked to the open door and peered out to where Amanda was looking, then gazed at the pair in wonder.

"Momma, how did he get a dog? Where did it come from?"

"I have no idea." As the dog scampered back into the water,

then shook himself, making the coarse-looking golden fur stand on end, Amanda said, "But it sure looks like a happy dog, doesn't it?"

"Uh-huh." With wide eyes, she added, "Mamm, do you think we could go see it?"

"If you want."

Her hand on the gate, Regina asked, "Do you think Roman will let me pet it?"

"It's all wet. Do you want to?"

"Uh-huh."

"Well, it doesn't hurt to ask if we can," Amanda said as she smoothed back her hair and shook out her teal dress. "Are you ready to go see them now? Would you rather have a snack first?"

But that was a silly question, of course. Because no sooner had she half offered the invitation than had Regina clicked open the gate and trotted toward Roman, her bright pink dress flying up around her ankles. "Roman! Roman, hi! It's me, Regina!"

Amanda was so shocked, she almost called out to Regina to come right back. But the scene that unfolded before her rendered her almost speechless.

There was her quiet Regina running to Roman, a big, bright smile on her face.

And there was Roman turning to her and greeting her with a broad grin.

And then, to Amanda's surprise, Regina held out her hand for Roman to take. Roman took it easily, then looked for Amanda. When he spied her, that warm gaze was like something out of a silly daydream. It was heated and earnest, sweet and sincere.

All directed at her.

It took everything Amanda had not to sigh. Instead, she forced herself to walk toward Roman and Regina and that rambunctious golden dog as sedately as she could.

After all, it wasn't as if anything could ever happen between the two of them. He was a farmer from Ohio. And she?

She was Wesley's widow.

"And you think you do deserve one?"

She forced herself to meet his gaze directly. *"Jah."*

After guiding Chester back into his stall, he walked over to where she stood and sat down on a hay bale. "What is it you want to know?"

"I just want you to talk to me. Just tell me a little of the story." She was so tired of the way they'd been communicating lately, as if every little bit of information was something to be stingy with, and whoever revealed the most would be the loser.

His eyes narrowed, then he brushed his hands over his eyes. "I met Laura Beth when I was fourteen. She and her family had recently moved to our church district. Almost immediately, I knew she was the girl for me." He paused, then finished simply. "We married at eighteen."

"That was young."

Something flashed in his eyes. "Perhaps it was. It didn't feel that way at the time, though. You know how it is . . . when you're that age."

She nodded. "When you're eighteen, you don't feel young. You feel ready for anything." Smiling slightly, she added, "And now that I'm in my forties? Some days I feel like I don't know anything."

"The Lord gives us pride instead of experience when we're teenagers." He met her smile, then looked beyond her, as if he were peering into another time. "A year after Laura Beth and I married, we had Ben. I thought my life was perfect . . . and that it would always be that way."

"Then they died?"

He nodded. After a pause, he said haltingly, "Laura Beth was driving in the buggy in some sleet. Something happened, no one knows what. Maybe she lost control, maybe the horse got spooked? But she lost control and was hit by an oncoming car." He swallowed hard. "The doctors said she and Ben died instantly."

Marie felt tears prick her eyes. It was such a sad story, such a waste. "Aaron, why all the secrecy? It was a heartbreaking accident, for sure, and I would think you would want your new family to honor your past and your first family."

A muscle jumped in his cheek as he visibly reined in his emotions. "Not everyone thought it was an accident."

"What do you mean?" She hated to press, but Marie instinctively knew that if she didn't get the full story now, it would be a long time before Aaron would ever talk about Laura Beth and Ben again.

"Some folks thought it was my fault," he said.

"Yours?"

Abruptly, he stood up, turning his back to her. "Laura Beth was in that buggy because of me. We'd had words. I'd said some foolish things. I . . . I let my temper get the best of me."

She couldn't imagine such a thing. "Aaron, I've never seen you lose your temper."

He gazed at her, his expression soft with regret. "I was different back then, Marie. I used to be something of a loose cannon."

"Who blamed you? Her family?"

"But of course. Her brother promised he'd never forget her death . . . and that he would make sure I never forgot it, either."

"What did he mean by that?"

He blinked. And just like that, Marie knew their discussion had drawn to a close. He'd told her as much as he wanted to. "I'll see you at supper, Marie. I have a lot to do since Peter and Roman ain't here. You understand, I am sure."

She nodded as she watched him retreat from the barn, headed toward the fields. Well, she'd gotten the answers to her questions. But instead of relieving her mind, it had only served to spark more questions and worry.

Lost in thought, she walked back to the house, and wondered if she was going to be able to ever let this new development go.

The moment Goldie spied the crab in the water, the shelter dog seemed determined to make it her own. Though Roman had tried to warn her about making friends with the creature, the dog refused to heed him.

"Have it your way, Goldie," he said. "But if your nose gets pinched, don't come crying to me."

Over and over, she'd spy the small critter, dig furiously for it, then jump away the moment she came face-to-face with an angry claw. She'd look at Roman in wonder, he'd shrug and tell her he told her so . . . then it would begin again.

"Careful, Goldie. That crab ain't going to like you disturbing it for much longer. Pretty soon it'll be the one chasing you!"

As he'd expected, the dog barked, promptly ignored his warning, and pounced.

And this time came out the loser. The crab snapped at her and its swipe stung Goldie's nose. With a yelp, she jumped back and looked at Roman in confusion.

"It's the way of it, *hund,*" he said kindly. "Each of God's creatures has ways of keeping themselves safe. That would be the crab's."

The shelter dog seemed to take the warning to heart. After a moment, she once again seemed happy to trot by his side.

Until Regina approached.

The minute Goldie saw the little girl scampering toward them, her bright pink dress pulled up to her knees, a bright smile plastered across her face, Goldie seemed mesmerized. Even the sea crab was forgotten.

"She's had the same effect on me, pup," Roman murmured. "But of course, it's her mother who makes me stop and stare even when I shouldn't. She's a pretty thing, for sure. Ain't so?"

"Roman, Roman it's me, Regina!"

"I would know you anywhere, silly," he said as he greeted her. "What brings you out to the beach?"

"Mamm and I were watching you and your *hund*. She's pretty."

Roman looked at Goldie again. The dog was wet and scruffy and covered with a good coating of sand and salt water. "She's a mess, that's what she is." After making sure Goldie wasn't about to jump or be too rough, he motioned Regina closer. "Want to say hello to her? Her name is Goldie."

"Uh-huh."

"Come on then." Carefully, he showed Regina how to let the dog smell her hand. After a few exploratory sniffs, Goldie was ready to play. She nudged Regina's hand. With a smile, Regina petted the dog.

He'd just showed Regina Goldie's dog tag when Amanda caught up. "Did you get yourself a dog, Roman?" she asked.

"*Nee*. Just borrowing one. I discovered that there's an animal shelter here that will let you take walks with the dogs for a few hours at a time. I decided to take them up on the offer."

"I've lived here all my life and never knew there was such a thing."

"Perhaps you weren't missing your own animals like I was," he said easily. Plus he had to admit to having a soft spot for an animal with no home. Every creature needed a place to live, he thought.

Amanda bent down and scratched Goldie between her ears. Goldie showed her appreciation by tilting her head just enough to give Amanda a swift, wet lick.

Amanda lifted her hand and wrinkled her nose. "Ick!"

Regina giggled. "She likes you, Mamm."

"I guess so."

To Roman's surprise, she bent a little and gave the dog a quick hug. "You're a sweet thing, for sure."

"You're going to get all wet and sandy," Roman warned.

Amanda looked fondly at her daughter. "I'm a mother. One gets used to becoming a mess."

"I can't imagine you ever being a mess," he blurted before he could stop himself.

Amanda smiled, but immediately a faint blush colored her cheeks.

"I'm sorry. Sometimes I speak without thinking. But I do, ah, think you are pretty."

"*Danke.*" She stood up and turned away.

Roman decided he had better retreat a bit and keep things light. "So, would you girls like to walk with us? We've been walking and chasing sticks and annoying crabs."

"We can for a few minutes, but then Regina has a play date with Lindy."

Roman noticed his cousin Beth and Lindy sitting on their back patio, obviously waiting for Regina. "How about we walk you over to Lindy, Regina?"

At the mention of Lindy, Regina whispered to Amanda, then after giving her a brief hug, ran toward Lindy.

He and Amanda watched as Beth and Lindy ran to meet Regina halfway, gave them a little wave, then retreated inside.

Roman was surprised at how quickly Regina had left her mother's side. "That was quick."

"She's usually not so eager to leave me, but I do believe they're going to play house. Regina loves that."

After another few moments, he gestured to Goldie. "Would you still like to stroll?"

Amanda looked doubtful. "If I do . . . "

"I promise, we'll keep things easy. I won't tell you again about how pretty I think you are."

"Roman!"

"I'm sorry. From now on, we'll only talk about what you want to talk about."

"Or not talk at all?" She smiled when she said it, so he wasn't sure if she was testing him or not.

But he didn't care. She was the first woman he'd ever not been able to stop thinking about. She was the first woman who'd intrigued him enough to want to push aside all the boundaries he'd erected in order to keep others at a distance.

With her, he didn't think he could ever get too close. Just thinking about where his mind was going made him feel even more off-kilter.

But no matter what, he was willing to pass all her tests.

"It's okay not to talk at all," he murmured. Deciding to get them going, he started walking, Goldie happily trotting by his side.

After a second's pause, Amanda followed.

Ah. He'd just gotten his way. Roman had never tried so hard to hide a smile.

Walking by Roman's side, Amanda chastised herself. She'd heard his compliment. She'd seen the look in his eyes. Wesley had once looked at her like that, as if he was smitten.

But she certainly was not. She had no business encouraging Roman's flirtations. She'd already found love. She'd already had courtship and romance and marriage. No person should expect more in a lifetime.

Especially since she had a daughter, too. Regina was almost the spitting image of her father, with her dark wavy hair. Watching Regina every day was a constant reminder of Wesley, and that was a good thing. A wonderful thing.

So why did she seem unable to ignore Roman?

Roman was being true to his word. He'd stayed silent, content to watch the dog's antics.

But now Amanda realized she was ready for something more. "So, what possesses a man to want to borrow animals?"

He shrugged. "At home, I work in the fields, of course, but my favorite chores involve the animals." He looked at her. "Perhaps you think that's strange?"

"Not at all, though I have to admit that I don't have much experience with farms. Actually, I've never had a pet."

"Not even a cat?"

"Not a one."

When she noticed his grin, she felt slightly defensive. "What do you find so amusing?"

"Only that in my experience, it's rare to find an Amish woman who's not used to farm life. Back in Berlin, most people live on farms. Those that don't work in an offshoot of a farm—like a cheese shop. And almost all of us have a horse or raise chickens or at least have a barn cat."

"If you lived here, you'd meet a great many women and men who are the same as me. The Amish lifestyle is different down here. But it's not like I've never been around animals. I did grow up in Pennsylvania."

"I don't mean to sound critical," he replied, looking a bit contrite. "It's just unusual to me. That's all."

"Tell me about Berlin. I suppose it's much different in the winter."

He laughed. "It's about as different as night and day! Right now, it's terribly cold and snowy in Ohio, even though it's the beginning of March. We still get lots of snow into April there. Right now, you'd be hitching up your sleigh in heavy snow, and bundling up in coats and cloaks and scarves and mittens."

"And?"

"And it's hilly there." He looked out into the distance, just as if he were staring at a giant postcard in front of him. "Really hilly. The roads are winding, and there are lots of trees. In the fall, the leaves turn orange and yellow and gold. Tourists come from all over, just to look at them."

This time, she couldn't hold back a smile. "Tourists come to see leaves?"

"They come for more than that, I reckon. It's peaceful. Quiet. Out in Holmes County, the pace is slower, and not simply because we're Amish. You have to live more slowly because we're dependent on the Lord's seasons and His weather."

"The leaves are all gone now, right?"

He nodded. "Yep. The trees are bare, but that's okay, because you can see the red cardinals that much better. Or winter hares. And deer."

"You have deer?"

"We sure do. But not as pets of course . . . they just wander around. Sometimes I'll be out in the barn with our horse, cracking the film of ice that's formed on the water troughs, when I'll look up and see a pair of bucks. It's a lovely sight."

The picture he'd painted captured her interest, spurring her imagination. "Maybe one day I'll go up and see this Berlin."

"You should. You and Regina can come up on the Pioneer Trails bus and stay with us."

"Stay with you?" she blurted, taken aback.

"I live in a pretty big *haus*, my family's lived there for quite a while. Anyway, when you come, me and my family could show you around. You can visit my aunt Lorene's place of work—the cheese shop." He winked. "We'll even drive you out to Walnut Creek and Sugarcreek. There's a lot to see."

She laughed, because they were only pretending that she'd ever go up north. That she'd ever see him after he left. "You almost sound homesick."

He slowed down and looked at her more carefully. "Not at all. I like home, but I needed a break. I like it here, too. I think you're a lucky woman, to live this close to the ocean."

Amanda flinched. He was the first person in years to mention that she was lucky about anything. Most people looked at her in pity.

"Oh. I guess I stuck my foot in my mouth again, haven't I? I realize, of course, that you've lost your husband."

"Actually, I was just thinking how grateful I am that you

reminded me of my blessings. Sometimes, it's very tempting to only think about what I've lost and how different my life is from how I'd hoped it would be."

He glanced at her for a long moment, his eyes serious, his gaze tender. Finally, he said, "It sounds like you had a good marriage."

"I did. The best."

Something flashed in his eyes, right before he looked forward again. "I am sorry about your loss."

"*Danke*. My Wesley, he was a good man. He would have been a wonderful husband to me forever, I think. But I have Regina and Wesley's family."

"His family?"

"Oh, yes. As I said, it's their condominium that I'm staying in." Feeling a little braver, she said, "This is the first time since my husband died that I've done something on my own."

"Doing something for the first time is always hard. Were you scared?"

"Honestly? A little bit. Before I was married, I was part of a big family. And spoiled enough to be born number six out of eight children."

He raised a brow. "I've never heard of anyone calling themselves spoiled because they were from a large family. Usually that means they are used to sharing."

"I'm used to sharing, but that's not what I was thinking of. Instead, I was thinking of the gift of privacy. And of being alone. If I had been the eldest girl, I'm sure I would have had to watch over the other *kinner*. But because I was one of the younger siblings, I didn't have to do much of that. So I developed a healthy taste for being alone. By the time I was twelve, one of my brothers and two of my sisters were already married. See, when you're always surrounded by siblings, half of who've been asked to always look out for you . . . it can be confining."

"I know what you mean, to a point. Being the only boy, I was able to get time alone." He seemed to want to say more, but instead he looked down at his feet and chuckled. "It looks like Goldie here needs a rest."

The dog was sprawled across his feet, panting heavily. Amanda pointed toward a spigot. "If you have something to hold water, we could fill it up."

Roman looked around, found someone's abandoned paper ice cream bowl wedged under a rock, and pulled it out. "This should do, if we rinse it out."

"I think so," she said, taking it from him. "I'll be right back."

"*Nee*, I'll do it," he said quickly. "This dog is my responsibility. I should be getting the water."

"I don't mind. You stay here with Goldie," she said over her shoulder as she walked briskly to the public water fountain.

As Roman looked after her, looking more than a little chagrined, she heaved a sigh of relief. That man might be thinking she was all about being helpful, but she knew the truth. At the moment, she was only thinking about herself. She needed a few seconds to catch her breath and come to terms with how she was feeling.

Though she was enjoying the conversation with Roman, she didn't like how comfortable she felt with him. The feeling was far more scary than staying at the condominium by herself.

Though she knew better, she couldn't help but feel like she was betraying Wesley.

She knew deep down that wasn't what Wesley would want. When he was ill, and she was trying so hard to be brave and stalwart, he'd told her time and again to never stop living.

Of course, at the time, she'd had no inkling of what he was talking about. All she'd been able to focus on was the fact that one day very soon her husband would be going to heaven, and she'd never be able to look into his smiling brown eyes again. The pain of watching him suffer, coupled with the knowledge that she was losing him, had prevented her from thinking of anything else.

She'd pushed aside his efforts to talk about her future, about a life spent without him. For her, it was too painful to consider. For Wesley, it had been all he wanted to think about.

"You've got to move on one day, Mandy," he'd murmured one evening when they'd been all alone and she'd been so tired she hadn't even bothered to light a candle. "One day, you're going to need to find someone else."

"I'll be fine. And Regina will, too." She'd been thankful for the dark room, hoping he wouldn't notice how she was lying. Because, really, how was she ever going to be fine without him?

"One day, you're going to be tired of being alone."

"Nee—"

"And I want you to know that I'll be watching you from heaven, smiling," he'd said, just as if she hadn't interrupted him. "I don't want you to mourn me forever."

Back then, she couldn't imagine doing anything but mourning him. He'd been her world, her daughter's father.

But perhaps he'd been right.

Because at the moment, mixing with the guilt she felt

about even thinking about Roman Keim in a romantic sense was a small sliver of exhilaration, too. She'd felt his interest.

And she'd felt interested, too. Reminding her that though she was a widow and a mother, she was also a woman.

It was only lately that she'd forgotten.

chapter eight

Even when she didn't understand why things happened the way they did, Lovina believed with all her heart that the good Lord always had a plan. Furthermore, she believed that His plan was the right and best one. When she was tempted to despair, she simply prayed harder.

She'd grown up believing that was true faith.

Her faith had gotten her through some of the toughest moments in her life.

She'd tried to pass this on to her children. Whether she'd been successful or not, she did not know.

For the life of her, she couldn't understand why God had decided that all of their secrets needed to come tumbling out, one right after the other, all at this time in her life. It seemed to her that His timing, while always impeccable, was somehow off the mark this time. All He was doing was causing havoc in their lives and making the lot of them very unhappy indeed.

But perhaps the Lord had been giving her the chance to make changes in their lives? Maybe He was now making everything a jumbled mess so they'd all be forced to make some changes?

Thinking about the brief conversation she'd had with Marie while sewing, Lovina looked across the small living room at her husband.

Either she could avoid things a little longer . . . or finally push her husband to make things right.

Feeling as if the Lord was at her shoulder, giving her strength, she knew there was only one option. "Aaron, what should we tell the family about Laura Beth and Ben?"

Half asleep in his ancient easy chair, he didn't even bother to open his eyes. "Nothing."

"Well, why did you mention it to the family, then? You opened up a wasp's nest when you revealed you had another wife and child."

One eye opened. "Lovina, it ain't their concern. All that happened long before they were born. It doesn't affect them. Not one bit."

As Lovina smoothed out the pale yellow fabric she was making napkins out of for Lorene's wedding, she pursed her lips. She wasn't surprised by his answer. For over forty years, he'd been adamant that they only worry about the present, not the past. Time and time again he'd told her that nothing could be done to change what had already happened.

Mostly, his opinion had made sense. It certainly had kept their lives calm.

She'd done her best to abide by Aaron's wishes, to be the good and dutiful wife he'd wanted her to be. She'd even gone so far as to pretend that she wasn't curious about his first wife. Or his child.

The smart thing to do would be to say nothing and let this disagreement fade.

But it seemed she wasn't all that smart after all.

Or maybe she was just tired of being told what to think.

"Well, Elsie told me that their kitchen phone has been ringing nonstop. Our *kinner* are talking to each other. Before you know it, they're going to push us to talk about this. I know that is what Marie wants."

Both eyes were now open. Sitting straighter, Aaron hardened his voice. "Marie has more to worry about than my marriage. Her husband is in some center because he's too weak to deal with his addictions on his own."

The way he'd said "my marriage" stung. But what hurt even more was his lack of sympathy for their son. "Peter is not a weak man, Aaron. For the last twenty years, we've watched him farm this land, increase its value, be loyal to his wife, and raise three children. He is a good man who is going through a difficult time."

Aaron lumbered to his feet. "I refuse to feel sorry for him, Lovina. He brought his problems on himself, and he should be able to solve them that way, too. I did."

Her husband was as agitated as she'd ever seen him. His shoulders were stiff, and his expression was strained. And his voice . . .

His voice held a true note of sorrow in it. As if what had happened with his first wife and child was still a great source of pain for him.

Even though that accident had happened so very long ago.

Her heart went out to him. Because she loved him dearly, she pushed a little more. She knew from experience that the only way to heal a wound was to doctor it . . . not to merely cover it up. "You are being unfair to Marie, as well. She's our daughter, too, Aaron. The daughter of our hearts."

He raised a hand and made a brushing motion. "Oh, you know what I mean. And you know also that Marie shouldn't be focusing on our problems when she has so many of her own. Why, you'd think she'd be spending every free moment she has praying for Peter's health and for him to return home."

"Peter is getting help, and his well-being is in the Lord's hands now. That is why Peter left us, I am sure of it. The Lord guided him to this treatment center. I have a feeling we'll be glad he sought help."

Now his expression matched his tone. "If he gets better, it is because the Lord wanted him to get better, Lovina."

Of course the Lord had a lot to do with his improvement. But she also thought that the Lord had guided Peter to seek help, and that the Lord had given the doctors and therapists the tools to provide that help.

But Aaron would never understand her point of view. "Of course you are right," she said instead.

She waited a moment, folding the edges of one of the napkins and pinning it down. Her hands were trembling a bit and she pricked herself.

She walked to the bathroom, got out a bandage, and neatly fastened it on her finger so that she wouldn't accidently stain the cloth.

Staring at her finger, she walked back to her chair. Yes, covering up cuts was good. Necessary. But trying to cover up their past? Their memories?

Their marriages?

She was beginning to think that that was one of the biggest mistakes she and Aaron had ever made.

It was time to bring things out in the open, to force the conversation, even if it was painful. Marriage was about having the difficult conversations, wasn't it?

She vaguely recalled her mother telling her that, back when she'd been in high school.

Back when she'd had such a crush on Jack and thought she was the luckiest girl in the world.

Grabbing her courage, she pressed. "You know, you never even told me much about Laura Beth and Ben."

"We just talked about them."

"No, we talked about why you didn't want to talk about them to the rest of the family. There's a difference."

Starting to look resigned, he said, "I already gave you the chance to ask me anything you wanted."

He'd given her one evening. She'd been eighteen and knew nothing about marriage and raising children. All she'd been aware of was how different Aaron was from Jack.

"You didn't say much then, or maybe I didn't really ask the right questions. I mean, what were Laura Beth and Ben like?"

His eyes widened. "What were they like?"

"*Jah*. I mean . . . was she a kind woman? Was she young? Pretty? Silly?" A thousand more questions bubbled up inside her. Lovina wanted to know a hundred details. Had she been shy or outgoing? Had she laughed a lot or been moody? And how had they met? And Ben? What kind of boy had he been? Was he the quiet type like Jacob, gregarious like Aden? Or was he more dutiful like Peter?

More than that, she wanted to know how happy he'd been with his first wife. How happy had his life been before they'd passed away, and he'd married her? Though it had all happened more than forty years ago, she worried that his memories were still as sharp, and that after all this time, she still couldn't compare with them.

After all this time, she ached to know her competition.

Lovina stared back at Aaron, begging him silently to tell her everything she wanted to know. To give her reassurance that she'd never been a poor copy of his first wife.

She wanted Laura Beth to suddenly become a person to her instead of a woman who she could never measure up to.

"Laura Beth . . . she was . . . " His voice cracked, as if even saying her name was a difficult thing. "My Laura Beth . . . she was everything. That's what she was," he finished. He stood up.

"And Ben?" She forced the question even though she was sure she didn't want to hear the answer.

"Ben?" A line formed in between his brows. "My Ben was my first-born son, that's what he was. The three of us . . . we were a family. A perfect, happy family."

His words couldn't have been any more hurtful. Her pain couldn't have been sharper if he'd slapped her.

And the reality couldn't have been more clear.

Never had she been first in his heart. Never had he even attempted for her to be. She'd only been a substitute.

A copy of the perfect Amish woman who would always remain perfect in his heart.

She was still staring at him when he turned away and walked quietly out the back door.

Then she leaned forward and carefully folded the fabric into neat rectangles.

And realized that something else had happened. She'd never imagined she'd feel worse about herself than the night she'd come home from her homecoming dance.

But oh, she had been so terribly wrong.

chapter nine

Roman's time in Pinecraft and at Siesta Key had flown by. Every day, he'd spent time at the beach, going into town with his cousins, and spending time with Amanda and Regina.

On some days, they'd done little but talk briefly on the beach. Other times, though, they'd spent far longer in each other's company.

One evening Amanda and Regina had come over for a barbecue. Just that morning, he'd made sand castles with Regina while Amanda had pretended to read a book and relax.

Now, he felt as if he were as different inside as his tanned skin looked on the outside. He felt more relaxed, better prepared to deal with the pressures of home.

He was just watching the sun make its initial descent when Beth stepped out onto the patio.

Roman had been about to greet her when he noticed—with some alarm—that she had a certain "look" about her. The one that said she had much on her mind.

He stifled a groan. He'd learned from his sisters that whenever they approached with such an intent look it was time to prepare to explain himself—even if he'd done nothing wrong.

With Viola or Elsie it was usually some imagined slight. With Beth? He guessed she was preparing to talk to him about a certain neighbor.

Truth be told, he wouldn't mind discussing his feelings about Amanda. His insides knotted at the thought of never seeing her again after he got on the bus tomorrow. Those knots were warring with his usual levelheaded reasoning. He and Amanda couldn't live farther away from each other. He knew that meant they couldn't have much of a future.

But he didn't want to have to think about that right now. All he really wanted to do right now was enjoy these last precious moments of peace before they boarded the Pioneer Trails bus and headed home in the morning.

How could his vacation pass so quickly? He wasn't ready to head north. To be cold again. To say goodbye to Amanda.

Finally, Beth spoke. "Roman, you're not asleep, are you?"

"You've been hovering by my side for at least eight minutes," he said dryly. "If I had been asleep, I'd be awake by now."

"Oh."

He turned around and noticed that she looked a little dejected, as if she were carrying a great load and couldn't find the right spot to set it down.

So he decided to focus on his cousin. "What has you so spun up?"

"Oh, nothing. I mean, nothing's really wrong. . . ."

"What is on your mind, then? Is it something to do with Paul? Or the *kinner*?"

"Not at all. I mean, they're all *gut.* Paul and Lindy and Caleb are great."

"Then what is it? And don't say nothing again because I'm tired of talking in circles."

With a thump, she took the chair beside him and scooted closer. "It's just that I noticed . . . I mean, we all noticed, even Mamm and Daed, that is . . ."

Now this was even worse than dealing with his sisters. They at least didn't have a problem speaking their mind. "Beth. Noticed what?"

"That you and Amanda have spent quite a bit of time together."

Roman wasn't surprised she'd noticed. He'd done nothing to keep his feelings secret. And though he wouldn't have minded talking to Beth about his worries about a long-distance relationship, he didn't appreciate her tone with him. It sounded vaguely accusing, vaguely maternal.

And since he was twenty-three, not thirteen, he didn't appreciate it.

"And?"

"And I, um, just want to talk to you about that. If you don't mind."

"All right." After one last look at the ocean, he turned slightly, sat up a bit, and rested his palms on his knees. Looking her right in the eyes, he said, "What did you want to say?"

She looked abashed, then finally blurted, "I'm afraid you are leading her on."

"What do you mean?"

"I mean that they've already been through so much. The last thing either of them needs is to be hurt again."

"Beth, are you worried about me hurting Amanda?"

"A little. I just was thinking that you're getting ready to go back home. And she's here."

"Believe it or not, I had figured that out, too."

He knew his tone was sarcastic and harsh. But what did she expect?

Beth glared at him. "Roman, I just think you need to maybe talk to Amanda."

"We've been talking. As you pointed out. Over and over."

"No, I mean really talk."

"And say what?"

"I don't know. Maybe that you have true feelings for her?"

He was becoming embarrassed. "We are not having this conversation, Beth."

"I'm sorry if you're uncomfortable, but I know what my brothers are like. They're not always all that serious about the women they date. I mean Evan is seeing three girls at the same time . . ."

"I'm not Evan."

"I realize that. I just don't want her to get her feelings hurt. And I'm especially worried about her daughter's feelings," she said quickly, steamrolling over his protestations. "Amanda shared that Regina has only recently stopped asking about her father."

Roman sobered. He couldn't imagine what that poor girl thought was going to happen next. Four years old was too young to understand the concept of death. He'd purposely tread lightly around Regina. The last thing he wanted to do was create trouble for that little girl.

But then he remembered just how capable Amanda was, and what a good mother she was to Regina. And he remembered the smiles Regina had gifted him with. The way she'd acted around him, like their affection for each other was mutual.

"Shouldn't we be letting Amanda worry about Regina's emotions?" he said lightly. "I think she is a wonderful mother. I'm sure she can take care of her daughter without our interference."

"I agree, but . . ."

"I didn't do anything besides enjoy Amanda's company,

Beth. I never tried to be more to Regina than her friend. I understand your concern, and I appreciate that. But I promise it was never my intention to hurt either of them. And I've been well aware that Amanda is a grown woman who's been through a lot in her life. I think she deserves to make her own choices about her relationships. She doesn't need our help."

Beth slumped, as a dawning look of agreement flared in her eyes. "Perhaps."

"If Amanda and I never see each other again, it's really none of your concern. And if we do continue to stay in contact, then I'll let you know how we're all doing emotionally."

She finally looked shamefaced. "I guess I should've kept out of this."

He nodded. "I know you meant well, but yes."

"Sorry."

"I have two sisters; I'm used to meddling women. But don't create problems where there aren't any, cousin. And please think, if you would, how you would feel if the shoe were on the other foot. Would you really want my unasked-for advice regarding you and Paul?"

"This is different."

"We're still talking about feelings," he said softly. "Private ones."

"I'll remember that." Just as Beth rose to give him a brief hug, Roman noticed Amanda step out onto her patio next door.

With a rush of pleasure, he watched her instantly look over her shoulder his way just as Beth closed the door behind her. And then smile when she caught sight of him.

"Hi, Roman."

"Hi." He got to his feet. "Care for some company?"

"*Jah,* if you don't mind staying close. Regina fell asleep while playing with her farm animals on the carpet inside. I need to wake her up soon."

"I don't mind. Should I come over to your patio?"

She pointed to the pair of beach chairs sitting just beyond her condominium's white picket fence. They were in the spot he'd first seen her sitting on that very first morning.

"How about there?"

With some surprise, he realized that there was still time to make new memories. Hope filled him.

"Looks good." Truthfully, she couldn't have picked a more perfect spot. He knew he'd always remember his first sight of her sitting there, with the sun rising in the background.

Now in the glow of early evening, it felt especially fitting.

As he opened the little wooden gate for her, he felt as if every sense was heightened. Maybe it was because he was so close to returning to Ohio and his regular routine. But never had he expected that a vacation could pass by so quickly, or that he would feel as if he needed to hold each moment tightly, as if it were about to slip through his fingers like a drop of water.

He was going to miss this place.

As they walked, Amanda seemed to wilt a bit as they got closer to the chairs. Finally, she spoke. "So, you're leaving tomorrow?"

"We are. When do you go back home?"

"We'll go back sometime tomorrow or Monday. It's time, I suppose."

He noticed that she didn't seem all that enthusiastic about it. She seemed just as intent on memorizing the beauty of the moment as he did.

"What's wrong?"

Blue eyes searched his. "Are you sure you want to hear? I'm afraid it's a little bit maudlin."

"Of course." He wanted to know everything about her, to hear everything she was thinking. One day, he hoped they'd be close enough so that he could tell her that.

For now, he did his best to keep things light.

"What's on your mind?" he asked as he sat down in the bright blue Adirondack chair and relaxed.

She perched on the white chair next to his. "Well, something about getting away from my traditional routine has made me realize something. After spending the week here, away from my in-laws, I've realized how much I've been living in the past. I've been only thinking about Wesley, and my life with him."

Her hands clenched together in her lap, making her look almost as if she expected him to find fault with her statement.

But how could he ever fault a woman who had loved her husband dearly? "That seems only natural," he finally said. "Your vows were meant to last a lifetime."

"I thought so, too, but God had other plans. And Roman, even though I had promised Wesley I'd move on, I didn't."

"You were mourning his loss. There's nothing wrong with that."

"I was in mourning," she agreed. "But I must admit that I never intended to mourn for years. More importantly, I had promised myself that I wouldn't do that to Regina."

He didn't want to interrupt her, but he thought she was being a little hard on herself. Surely there was no right or wrong way to deal with a spouse's passing. What a person expects to happen and what actually does are two different things. She'd loved her husband so much that she wanted to continue to honor his memory. There wasn't anything wrong with that.

Unfolding her hands, she continued. "Lately—I mean this week—I realized that I truly do want to move forward, Roman. It's time."

"Good for you." He smiled.

"*Jah*. Good for me." She bit her lip. "Now all I have to do is find a way to get Wesley's family to agree to that."

"What are you worried about? You've told me that they can be attentive . . ."

"They are that. But they can be possessive, too." The moment she said the words, she looked horrified. "Don't get me wrong, they are wonderful people. *Wunderbaar!* They truly are! But I fear that they've forgotten that I am in my twenties. And that as much as I loved Wesley, I certainly cannot live the rest of my life as only his widow."

Roman reflected on his own community in Berlin. Because she was a widow, with a daughter to raise, in his world, some would think it was almost her duty to eventually find a husband and a father for Regina. "Do you really think they expect that?"

"I think they do. But it's not their fault. I'm afraid I've led them to think that that was what I wanted, too. But now I'm beginning to see that I'd rather look to the future than the past."

As he thought of her, and how much he was going to miss her, he realized that he was already missing her. Missing what could have been between them.

Suddenly, he realized he didn't want to let Amanda go.

Here was his chance. His chance to tell her how he felt. "Amanda, I don't want to lose you."

A flash of pleasure appeared in her eyes before she visibly tamped it down. "What do you mean?"

"I want us to stay friends," he said, though he wished he had the nerve to say more. Leaning forward, he added, "I'd like to write you. Maybe call you on the phone sometimes."

An eyebrow arched. "Why would you want to do that?"

He knew she wasn't being coy. She was nervous and unsure of herself. He felt much the same way. Like a young teen, he felt his cheeks heat with renewed bashfulness. "Because I like you." Even as he heard his words, he felt his cheeks heat so much he would have sworn they were on fire. He wished he had more poetic words to say.

But perhaps Amanda didn't need flowery language? Slowly, her lips curved upward. "Truly?"

"*Jah*. I'm sure it's no surprise. My attention has been pretty obvious."

"A woman still likes to hear the words, I think." She took a breath, then let it out. "Roman, I like you, too," she said in a rush.

"That's *gut,* then." He gave thanks that he wasn't anywhere near his sisters, because they would most certainly be laughing at him mercilessly. He couldn't seem to stop smiling.

Her cheeks bloomed with happiness, but then she looked down at her dress and fussed with a fold in the white fabric of her apron. "However, I must warn you that my daughter is everything to me. I couldn't begin anything serious without you realizing that."

"I'm glad Regina means the world to you. It's one of the reasons why I admire you so much."

Her smiled deepened.

He cleared his throat. "So, may we continue to talk to each other and write?"

"I would like that."

"*Gut.*"

"Roman, do you think anything will come of this?"

"I don't know. I suppose this friendship of ours can turn into anything we want. Maybe one day we'll decide that we fancy other people instead. Or maybe one day I'll want to move out here with you. Or you'll want to move to Ohio."

"Talk like that makes my head spin."

"It doesn't have to." Little by little, his tentativeness evaporated. He knew what he wanted. "Amanda, I want to be the person in your life who you can relax with. My needs right now are simple—at least where the two of us are concerned. See, I only want what you want."

"That's it?"

"Pretty much. Well, I want us to continue to be friends, at the very least." Yes, he certainly wanted so much more than mere friendship from her, but he was willing to wait until she was ready for more.

She gazed at him. Studied his face. "All right. Yes, let's go where this takes us."

"You sound almost sure," he teased.

She chuckled. "I'm not sure about much right now—it's all such a surprise to me. But I do happen to know one thing I'm sure of, and that's that I don't want to stop figuring out what our future holds, Roman. Getting to know you, feeling what I'm feeling? It's been like a sudden ray of light in my life. Almost an awakening. I've gone from expecting every day to be muted and gray to expecting something new."

If she hadn't been through so much he would have held her close.

But because she wasn't ready for more, he kicked his feet out in front of him, rolled up his pant legs, and leaned back in his chair. He closed his eyes as he felt the cooling breeze dance across his cheeks.

He sensed her body tense in confusion. "Roman, what are you doing?"

"Fully intending to enjoy your company, that's what." He peeked at her through one eye. "Is that a problem?"

After a moment, she shook her head. "*Nee*. Not at all."

"*Gut*. See, Amanda, all we have to do right now is take things one step at a time. The Lord will guide us from there."

To his amusement, she copied his position. "Roman, being around you makes me happy. I'm going to miss you."

Gazing over at her pretty face, seeing the vulnerability and strength that made her who she was, he said, "I'm going to miss you, too, Amanda. Very much."

Already he was missing her. And already he was wondering when they could see each other again.

chapter ten

Viola had just set her suitcase on her bed when her grandmother wandered into the room and sat down on the window seat. In her hands were a pair of quilted pot holders. The front of each was decorated with a beautiful star pattern. Viola recognized much of the fabric—it looked as if her grandmother had been putting the scraps of fabric from the dresses for Lorene's wedding to good use.

"Hi, Mommi," she said politely. "I was just getting ready to pack."

"Elsie told me. I thought I'd come upstairs and see for myself." Glaring at the open suitcase, she said, "Our *haus* suddenly feels like a turnstile, the way you and Roman keep coming and going. Why, practically every time I turn around, it looks like one of you has a suitcase out."

Viola shook her head. Her grandmother was either exaggerating for no reason at all . . . or she was feeling a little left out.

"Mommi, we all know that I've never left Berlin and Holmes County before. It's time, don'tcha think?"

"Maybe. Maybe not." She looked at the pot holders in her hands, but said nothing about them.

The lackluster agreement inspired Viola to now stick up for her brother. "And Roman—he is only returning from his first vacation."

But instead of sounding more understanding, Mommi scrunched her brows together, making the lines in between her eyebrows deepen. "That is true."

Viola sighed. Her grandmother could be such a stickler sometimes. "There's nothing wrong with taking days off. Even God took time to rest, *jah*?"

"I suppose."

She decided her grandmother needed a change in subject. She thought about the phone call she'd received from her cousin Beth. It seemed Roman had developed quite a friendship with the woman staying in the condominium next door. Far closer than what he'd led them to believe in his letters.

Viola couldn't wait for his bus to arrive in Berlin so that she could talk to him about it. "I'm just glad Roman enjoyed himself. Beth said he had a good time, Mommi," she said almost patiently. "We all need good times in our lives, *jah*?"

"Well, of course," her grandmother grumbled. After a pause, she said, "What did he do with all his time?"

"Beth said he played shuffleboard and walked on the beach. Slept late. Ate at restaurants."

"Hmmph." She paused, then said, "It's sure to be different where you're going. Have you thought of that?"

"*Jah*."

"Belize sounds like a dangerous place," she said a little more softly. "I hope you'll be all right there."

Finally, Viola understood her grandmother's motivation for the visit. She was worried about her. "It sounds beautiful. I can't wait to go," she said firmly. So far, she'd pushed all of her worries about being in a strange country like Belize far out of her mind. All she was focused on was seeing Edward.

"You're the first person I've heard of to get a passport."

"Ed got one. All the folks at the mission have them, too."

Mommi folded her arms over her chest and peered at Viola through her bifocals. "Are you scared, child?" she asked at last. "Because it would be understandable if you were."

"I am scared. I mean, I am, a little bit." She wanted to pretend she wasn't worried about flying alone on an airplane, or visiting a foreign country. But she was. "I'm trying not to be. I don't want Edward to think I can't handle this."

"He seems like the kind of man who only cares about you being happy, Viola."

"He is that kind of man. But I want him to feel proud of me, too."

Her grandmother peered at her some more, then finally handed over the pair of pot holders. "I thought you might like to give these to the folks at the mission."

"They're beautiful."

"Oh, they're just from scraps I had lying around. But the folks down in Belize might like them."

"I'm sure they will, Mommi. *Danke*." Carefully, Viola set them at the bottom of her suitcase.

After a moment, her grandmother reached out a hand again. But this time, it was to enclose Viola's in hers. "There's no shame in being afraid of something that's unfamiliar. It's to be expected."

"You truly believe that?"

"I do," her grandmother said with a small smile. "After all, I've been in your shoes a time or two, you know."

Never had Viola recalled her grandmother speaking so cryptically. "Are you speaking of when you became Amish?" she asked.

After a pause, her grandmother nodded. "I suppose I am." Her eyes widened, and then, to Viola's astonishment, she chuckled. "After all these many years of keeping my past a secret, I now have the strangest urge to talk about that time. It's like I just let the genie out of the bottle."

Viola didn't know what she meant by that, but she let it pass, eager to get more information before her grandmother changed her mind. Her grandmother was one of the most private people she'd ever known. "Why did you leave your English life and become Amish, Mommi? Was it because you fell in love with Grandfather? What did you miss? What did your parents say?"

"One question at a time, Viola!"

"Well then, tell me why you became Amish."

"It was because of Aaron." She bit her lip, then added, "At least a big part of the reason was because of him."

"What were your other reasons?"

Mommi looked around the neat room, then finally smoothed a hand along the intricate quilt on Viola's bed. "Before I met your grandfather, I made some mistakes in judgment. I, um, had gotten my heart broken."

"You did?"

"Very much so. This boy, well, he upset me." She opened her mouth, looked like she was going to continue, then pursed her lips instead. "It was a long time ago, of course."

"Was this boy an *Englischer*?"

"Don't act so surprised, Viola. *Englischers* fall in love, too." With a wince, she added, "And fall out of love, as well."

"It must have been mighty exciting."

"It didn't feel like that at the time. It, ah, was a dark time for me."

"I'm sorry. That was rude."

"*Nee,* you are only being honest. Believe me, I'd rather us be honest with each other than not. Keeping secrets and spouting lies didn't serve me well."

Seeing the faraway expression in her grandmother's eyes, Viola forgot all about her own problems. "So, who did you love, Mommi? Was he handsome?"

Mommi chuckled. "He was handsome, indeed." Her grandmother's expression softened. "At least, I thought so."

"Then how—"

"Quiet, child. This is my story, and it happened quite a long time ago. Let me tell it my way."

"Of course. I'm sorry."

Looking a bit amused, her grandmother gazed out the window, then said, "Well, it all started when I decided to help with the football players float."

"What's a float?"

"For us, it was a trailer bed that you would hook to the back of a big truck. We'd decorate it with balloons and crepe paper. Then people would stand on it during a parade. I liked one of the football players, so I made sure I was helping with their float for the parade."

"And?"

"And it was great fun. There was lots of laughter, and flirting with the boys . . . and then Jack started talking to me."

"Jack was the boy you liked."

"He was. I'd liked him for some time. Then, one day, he liked me, too." She took a breath, but just as she was about to say more, Viola's grandpa came in.

"What are you talking about, Lovina?" His voice was hard with disapproval.

With a look of warning in her direction, Mommi shrugged. "Nothing too important. Was there something you needed?"

"Supper."

"Goodness, I hadn't noticed the time." Immediately, she got to her feet. "Viola, we'll have to talk another time," she said, then quickly disappeared out the door with her husband.

Viola felt like she'd been left on the side of a hill and she didn't know whether to climb up or down. Or to hold tight where she was and hope no strong winds came along.

Frustrated, she glared at the door and wished with all her might that her grandfather had decided to enter just a few minutes later.

But then she realized that her grandmother's story had done a very good thing. Now she was no longer only thinking about how scared she was.

Instead, she was wondering how her grandparents had become the people they were, and what experiences in her life would shape her character. Make her the person she would one day be. Would moving to Belize change her for good?

chapter eleven

The gray skies seemed grayer in Berlin. Roman frowned in annoyance as he looked out the window of the bus. It felt as if the dreary color was draining all of the life right out of him with each passing mile.

Depression lurked on the edge of his heart as he spied the familiar landmarks.

He'd be home soon—which meant he'd be even farther from Sarasota, Florida. And though he'd made every effort to think positively about his future with Amanda, Roman knew those dreams were going to be almost impossible to turn into reality.

She had a life in Pinecraft, and he had a load of responsibilities right here in Ohio. His father was in a rehabilitation center. His mother was at her wit's end. One of his sisters was almost blind, the other was days away from visiting her fiancé in Belize. Therefore it was up to Roman to take care of the majority of the farm.

And do the majority of the work as well.

Roman didn't begrudge the work. He'd never minded working in the fields and helping to make his family's land more prosperous and profitable. But at the moment, the responsibilities weighed on him something awful.

For the first time in his life, he wanted something different from what he had.

He glanced out at the clouds again and noticed they'd darkened even more. Snow was likely on the way. He sighed in frustration. Of course it was.

The man sitting next to him noticed. "You've been on this bus ever since it left Pinecraft, haven't ya?"

"Yes." The bus had made several stops along its way north. More than a few people had boarded in Cincinnati, while others had switched buses there, some heading west toward Indianapolis like his cousins. But he'd been on it for the entire long journey.

The older man grunted in satisfaction. "I thought so. You're wearing that look."

"What look is that?"

"The one that says the beach and bright sunlight are now months away," he said with a cackle. "Don't feel bad. I was wearing that same expression three weeks ago."

"So it fades?" He didn't bother describing the feeling. The man had already pegged it perfectly.

"In my case it fades because I'm always anxious to get home. There's no place like home, you know." He flashed a smile as he paused for breath. "You married yet?"

"*Nee.*"

"Don't want to impose, but my advice is to find a woman you fancy and soon."

"Is that right?"

The man didn't catch the sarcasm. "Oh, for sure. Son, get settled down in a place of your own. Have a houseful of *kinner.* That will keep you grounded. You'll be settled and happy wherever you are, because you'll have the people who matter to you most close at hand."

"I'll keep that in mind." To his surprise, he truly meant the words. Roman wanted to dismiss the words of wisdom out of hand, but he actually thought the advice made a lot of sense. "*Danke.*"

"Glad I could help." After stretching his arms a bit, he looked around his seat with a slight grimace. "I suppose I better start getting my things in order," the man said. "Before you know it, we'll be stopping in Berlin."

Roman glanced out the window. Saw the cheese house and the row of shops that lined Market Street. They'd be arriving at the German Village shops in less than five minutes.

There, Viola or Uncle Samuel would be waiting for him in the buggy. They'd ask him about his trip, and it would be his duty to tell them just enough to assure them that his vacation had been *wonderful-gut*.

But not let on how disappointed he was to be back home. Letting them know that truth wouldn't help anyone.

Since he had nothing to organize, Roman stared out the window again and watched the automobiles pass by. Watched an Amish woman walking beside her man, both of them bundled up against the weather.

Noticed a pair of English teenagers dressed in jeans and thick coats and holding hands.

And realized for the first time that he didn't mind the idea of marriage and children anymore. Perhaps it was because when he thought of marriage now, he thought of brilliant blond hair that glinted against the bright rays of sunlight. And when he thought of children, it was in the form of a dark-haired little girl with a fondness for ice cream and animals. Who'd claimed his heart when she'd held out a soft, pudgy hand.

With a bit of regret, he realized it wasn't the lack of sunlight he minded, it was the lack of Amanda and Regina.

Unfortunately, he was far more likely to see the sun than them anytime soon.

It was always harder to pack up to go home than it was to prepare to arrive. Somehow they always left with twice the amount they arrived with.

Standing in front of a pile of sand toys, Amanda shook her head. "Regina, where did all of this . . . this stuff come from?"

"The stores, I think?" Regina said, completely serious.

Which, of course, made Amanda chuckle. That's what she got for asking rhetorical questions of her very literal daughter.

"I think you might be right about that, dear. But I sure don't know how we're going to load everything in the van when the driver gets here."

"When is he coming?" Regina plopped down on the top cement step and daintily crossed her bare feet in front of her.

"In about thirty minutes."

Regina backed away with a fierce frown. "I sure wish he wasn't."

"Why is that?"

"Because we have to go back to our regular house."

Regina spoke so dramatically, Amanda couldn't resist teasing her a bit. "And you don't care for our house anymore? You have a lovely room at home."

"I like my room. . . . " she said slowly, then closed up her mouth tight.

There was definitely more upsetting Regina than the end of a vacation. "What will you miss here?"

"Goldie."

Ah, yes. That silly, adorable dog that had claimed all of

their hearts with her happy manner and insatiable need to chase crabs. "I'll miss Goldie, too."

"She needs a home, Mamm."

"I know. But . . . I just don't think we're ready to have Goldie at our house in town."

"But I miss her." Looking petulant, she said, "I'm going to miss the beach, too."

"Ah, well, we'll visit the beach soon."

"I'm going to miss you, too."

"Me?" Amanda looked at her in surprise. "Child, you're making no sense. I'll still be with you when we get home."

"I know, Momma." Regina turned away with a little nod, and a somewhat bleak, resigned look on her face.

Amanda couldn't let that go. Brushing a wayward curl from her daughter's forehead, she said, "Regina, tell me what you mean. I promise, I won't get mad."

"Promise?"

"I promise." She sat down on the step next to her little girl, thought about grasping her hand, but decided against it when she noticed how tightly Regina had her hands fisted together. "Please talk to me. Why do you think you won't have me at home?"

"When you are home, you get sad."

With effort, she attempted to hide the shock she felt. She'd tried so hard to keep her depression hidden. But obviously, she hadn't been able to hide much. "Not so much anymore."

Regina shook her head. "It's true. You do. And you don't laugh as much."

"Well, that is to be expected. I'm working and taking care of you and our home. That's a lot to do. But we're still together a lot."

"It doesn't feel like it."

Amanda was about to argue that point, but decided to hold her tongue. After all, she knew what her daughter meant. Things were different in their "regular" lives. She did work a lot, and she was pretty much tired all the time, too. "I'll try to be better."

"Uh-huh." Her daughter squirmed a bit. Poked at a roving ant with her big toe.

Amanda watched her, wondering what else she could say that would reduce her worries but wouldn't get her hopes up too much.

Because, well, things would be different when they got home again.

Looking bored with the ant, Regina sighed as she crossed her arms over her chest. "Momma, I liked Roman."

Amanda stilled. At first it felt like that comment came out of nowhere, but she was starting to realize that Regina was finally feeling comfortable enough to speak her mind, and this was what was on her mind. "I liked Roman, too. But he had to go back to his own home in Ohio."

"I wish he was still here."

"I know, dear." Amanda drew a breath, ready to end this barrage of wistful thinking.

But Regina interrupted her thoughts. "You smiled when you were with him. A lot. And he made me smile, too."

Yes, there were lots of things to like about that man. And many things she was going to miss, too. "Roman was a *verra* nice man."

"I miss him."

"We hardly knew him." But even as she said the words, she knew she was lying. She felt like she'd known him all her life.

Regina turned away again, telling Amanda without words that she disagreed with her mother.

Well, she had raised a smart girl.

Standing up, Amanda held out a hand. "Come now, dear. Let's stop wishing for things that we can't have."

Regina ignored her hand. "Momma, are we ever going to see him again?"

"We might. It depends if he wants to come back to visit."

Regina's eyes widened, then she pursed her lips and quietly nodded. "Okay."

"Regina, Roman was just a vacation friend. At least, that's all he is now." And perhaps one day she'd even believe that.

"Are you going to talk to Mommi about him when she calls?"

"Definitely not."

"I heard her say she wanted to ask you questions." Her bottom lip puffed out in between a set of tiny white teeth. "I heard that."

"I know she did. But Gina, that doesn't mean I have to answer them. I hope you don't start telling tales about Roman to your grandmother. No good will come out of that." The moment she heard her words, heard her tone, Amanda regretted saying anything. She'd managed to frighten her daughter—all because she was confused about her life and what she wanted.

Tears filled Regina's eyes.

Quickly, Amanda sat back down and wrapped her arms around her daughter's thin frame. "I'm sorry. I didn't mean to speak to you like that. Everything will be fine, you'll see."

"You think so?"

"I do. Before you know it, we'll be settled and snug in our very own house and we'll be glad we're not here any longer. I promise, that will happen."

After a moment, Regina hugged Amanda back, then stood up. "I'm going to go check my room again."

"All right, dear."

But instead of jumping to her feet and attempting to organize all of their things one more time, Amanda stayed seated.

And gazed through the screen door at the pile of clothes neatly folded by the door . . . to an empty box of Pop-Tarts in the trash, and the open window beyond. The breeze blew in the fresh scent of salt and ocean.

Funny, it now smelled like freedom.

chapter twelve

"Hold still, Lorene," Lovina said. "I want to make sure your dress looks perfect."

But, just like when she was still a child, her daughter twitched and wiggled. "Mamm, the dress already looks fine. It looked perfect last time I tried it on."

"Then stop squirming! I swear, you're as jumpy as a cricket."

"And twice as chirpy," Lorene finished with a grin.

Lovina couldn't help but smile as well. "Ach. That is an old joke, daughter."

"It still makes me smile."

This joking between them was new. Lovina hadn't thought she would have embraced the bright, teasing conversation, but she was finding a lot of pleasure from their new interactions. It gave her hope for their future.

Hope where she had imagined there would be no more.

"It is nice to see you happy, *maydel*," she commented, afraid to make too much of it, in case Lorene might just pull away from her again.

But instead of turning wary, her daughter simply smiled. "It's nice to *feel* happy. I'm excited to finally marry John. And in just two weeks!"

That simple statement cut deeply into her conscience. Smoothing out fabric, then kneeling at her daughter's feet to check the hem, she said, "Lorene, do you think you'll ever be able to forgive me?"

"What?"

"You heard me. I'm only asking so that I might prepare myself," she said quickly.

"There's nothing to forgive, Mamm. While it's true that you were the one who asked me not to see John, I was the one who agreed." She shook her head. "I didn't fight your decision at all . . . and then I let years go by before I attempted to reconnect with him. Years!"

Lovina knew what kind of parent she'd been. She wouldn't have put up with any disobedience of any kind. "Things were different back then," she said hesitantly.

"Not that different." Bitterness tinged her voice and though Lovina couldn't blame her for that, Lorene's words made her heart ache.

"I know you wanted to be an obedient daughter."

"I did. But now I realize that I was afraid, too. I was afraid to go out on my own. I didn't trust my heart."

"I see." She had her daughter spin so she could ensure every part of the hem was perfect and smooth.

"And after several conversations with John about this, I don't think he was as ready for marriage as he believed, either. God's timing is always right, Mother. You were right—even though I was certainly not happy about your opinions."

"Ach," she said. Because her daughter had surprised her once again. And because she, too, knew what it felt like to not be heard.

After all, her parents had made her feel much the same way.

"All right," Viola announced as she entered the room with a pair of yellow placemats and cloth napkins. "I just finished another set for the wedding reception. What do you think?"

As Lorene oohed and awed over Viola's handiwork, Lovina continued to kneel at her daughter's feet. As was her habit, she made a great show of concentrating on her task. But in truth, she was happy to let her mind drift back to another day, another year.

Another lifetime, really. Back when she'd gone to the Homecoming dance with Jack. The night when so much had gone so wrong. . . .

"You look real pretty, Lolly."

"Thanks." Lovina smoothed her satin gown over her knees nervously as Jack drew his car to a stop at the light. "Are you excited about the dance?"

It was a dumb question. The dance had been all her group of friends had been able to talk about for days. Who wouldn't be excited?

But he surprised her.

"I guess." He shrugged. "I was more excited to be alone with you, if you want to know the truth."

"Me?"

"Well, yeah. I mean, everyone knows your parents keep a tight rein on you. It makes seeing you a real challenge."

"I didn't think they were stricter than anyone else's."

"Maybe not. But it sure seems like it. I didn't mind though."

"You didn't?"

"Nah, I always get my way, sooner or later." His lips curved up into a devil-may-care grin. "I mean, look at us. I got you alone."

If he hadn't looked so delighted, she would have been nervous. But he was happy and so she felt wanted. Special. So she smiled back and tried not to fuss with the curls on the ends of her hair.

Moments later, Jack pulled into a parking place far from the gymnasium's entrance. Actually, it was far from most of the other cars.

"Why are you parking way out here?" she asked. "I've got my mother's heels on, you know."

"If your feet start to hurt, I'll carry you."

She laughed, though the image made her feel all tingly—like daydreams really could come true. "Are you worried about someone hurting your car?"

"Nah, no one's going to touch my car without getting hurt." He leaned closer. "It's for privacy, of course." He grinned as he pulled the key out of the ignition. "How am I going to get a kiss if we're in the middle of a crowd?"

Her mouth went dry as her mind went blank. She'd imagined kissing him, of course. In her daydreams, he'd ask her permission, then carefully press his lips to her cheek. Maybe, just maybe, after the second or third date they'd kiss on the lips.

But what was on his face was something far different. The first tingling of nerves filtered through her. Biting her lip, she contemplated telling him that she wasn't ready for what he was talking about.

But how did a girl say such a thing to the boy of her dreams? Too worried about her feelings and the tingling going on in the back of her neck, she chose action instead of words. With a steady breath, she opened her door and got out of the car.

He scrambled out of the car, shouting after her. "Lolly, what are you doing?"

"I don't want to be late for pictures."

"Pictures? Oh, yeah. Sure." He caught up to her, reaching for her hand when they were almost at the entrance.

Other girls hurried over when they neared. They commented on her dress, her shoes. Her hair. Lolly did the same thing, it was only polite.

Jack's friends spoke to her, too. Their expressions were differ-

ent, though. Almost as if they were privy to a private joke. Jack joked around with them, then tossed an arm over her shoulders, his hand dangling around the top of her bare arm. Every so often she'd feel the warm pads of his fingers graze her skin.

After they posed for pictures, the group of ten of them strode into the decorated gym like they owned the place. Then, one of Jack's friends pulled out a flask and poured something into one of the cups for punch.

Jack shoved it at her. "Here, Lolly. Drink up."

It was liquor, the smell sharp and pungent. Wrinkling her nose, she attempted to move away. "Um, I don't think—"

"It's no biggie, Lolly," Jane interrupted. "Everyone's having some. You'll be the only one who doesn't if you refuse."

When Lolly still hesitated, Jane's voice turned urgent. "Come on."

And so she did. Because she'd felt like she had no choice. And because she didn't want to cause a scene.

Jack smiled. "Good girl."

At the moment, she felt like the opposite of a good girl. She felt wicked, and more than a little disheartened. She was with the most popular boy in her class but everything about the situation made her feel uneasy.

But it wasn't like she had a choice.

With that first sip, her spirits deflated. And she'd known that everything she'd imagined happening had been nothing but childish daydreams of an innocent, naïve girl.

"Lolly, want to dance?"

Raising her chin, she looked into his dark eyes, saw desire and satisfaction in his expression. That was everything she'd thought she wanted. "Of course," she said, smiling as he took her hand.

And let him guide her into his arms.

And pretended she wasn't shouldering a very new, very real sense of foreboding.

As the memories spilled forth, Lovina grimaced. She'd been such a fool that night. So silly. So misguided. If she'd only been a little bit braver or a whole lot smarter, she could have saved herself a great amount of pain. Could have saved a lot of people from a great amount of pain.

"Mamm?"

Lovina started. "Hmm?"

"Mamm, I asked you a question," Lorene said. "Did you hear me?"

"I'm afraid my mind went walking. What did you ask?"

"I was asking if you thought it was wrong for John and me to want to go on a honeymoon trip to New York. I know no one else took one."

"Lorene, I think you should do whatever you want. Time passes too quickly to always worry about what others may think."

Surprise, then pleasure, lit her daughter's features. "*Danke,* Mamm. Hearing you say that means a lot."

"It's only my opinion. That's all," she said quietly.

She knew better than anyone that her judgment wasn't always good. In fact, it was sometimes very, very bad.

chapter thirteen

When the phone rang, Amanda practically ran across the kitchen to answer it. Before he'd left, she and Roman had made plans to speak today, just to make sure they'd both gotten home all right. All day long she'd been wavering between excitement for the upcoming call—and nervous apprehension that he would forget.

"Hello?" she asked, wincing as she heard the breathlessness in her voice.

"Amanda, it's Roman."

"Hi, Roman." She leaned against the white laminate counter, smiling from ear to ear. Not only did he call, but he sounded exactly the same as she remembered.

"Hey. I thought today would never come. I've already tried to call you several times this week. You're a difficult woman to get ahold of."

He'd been calling? "I've been working a lot," she said in a rush. "I guess I've been missing some phone calls."

"You might consider getting an answering machine."

Roman sounded so cross, she smiled, standing alone right there in her kitchen.

"That would be a *gut* idea, for sure," she agreed.

But even so, she knew she'd never get one. Even if she had known he'd called, she knew that she wouldn't have called him back. It would seem too forward. Too eager.

"I'm glad you're home now. Tell me what you've been doing. And how you are. And how Regina is. And tell me about the weather, and the beach, too."

She chuckled at his enthusiasm, loving how it mirrored her own. "That's all?"

"*Nee*. I want to know what you've been eating and reading and if you've seen our dog."

To her surprise, her eyes teared up. "You've been thinking about Goldie, too?" For some reason, that he would remember how much she had liked that shelter dog meant the world to her. It meant that he remembered what was dear to her.

"Goldie was a fine dog."

"I thought so, too," she said just as her mother-in-law wandered into the kitchen. "I miss her," she added. To her surprise, a tear escaped and she wiped it away impatiently.

Across the kitchen, Marlene noticed. "Amanda, what is wrong?"

"Nothing."

"Nonsense. You are crying." Eyeing the phone like she feared it was about to bite Amanda, she said, "Who are you speaking to?"

Covering the mouthpiece of the phone, she said, "Merely a friend."

"Who?"

"Roman."

"I don't recall a man by that name."

Just as Amanda was about to call her mother-in-law's bluff, Regina popped in. "He's the Roman from Ohio," she said helpfully as she joined them in the kitchen. "Mommi, he was our neighbor at the beach."

"Why are you speaking with him?" Marlene asked, just as

if Amanda was keeping company with a dangerous man. Just as if everything in Amanda's life was her business.

And she did that probably because, Amanda realized, until this very moment, she had let Marlene have that much access. She froze, staring at Marlene, her prying mother-in-law.

Amanda felt her heartbeat quicken as she felt the gap between her former life and her future one becoming wider. Yet, at the same time she wondered what she was doing. Was a momentary infatuation with a man who lived in Ohio worth jeopardizing everything she had with Wesley's family?

Roman's concerned tone of voice filtered through her thoughts. "Amanda? Amanda, are you still there? Can you still talk to me now?"

At least she knew that answer! "*Jah*!" she chirped into the phone. "Just give me one second. . . ."

As she glanced at Marlene, who was still eyeing her with interest, Amanda knew it was time to make some changes. Now.

There was no way she was going to be able to speak to Roman while being watched and monitored by her mother-in-law.

"Marlene, would you mind leaving the kitchen with Regina for a few moments?"

"So you can talk to a man on the phone?" Marlene raised a condemning brow. "To that stranger?"

Roman was anything but a stranger. But Amanda sure didn't feel like spending another second fending off her mother-in-law's pesky questions. "Yes, please."

"I will leave, but I don't know what to think about this, Amanda."

Oh, but she did. Amanda was sure of it! She didn't care for it one bit.

"*Danke*," she said. Then she turned her back on any response, and took a fortifying breath when she heard Marlene take Regina from the room. "I'm sorry, Roman," she muttered. "I had to ask someone to leave the room."

"I heard you say Marlene. Isn't that your mother-in-law?"

"It is. I mean, she was." What was Marlene's relationship to her now, with her husband up in heaven?

"Is my calling causing you trouble?"

She appreciated that he cared. She appreciated that he remembered her mother-in-law's name.

But because of that, she knew she was willing to risk getting into trouble with Marlene. There was something about hearing Roman's voice that was making her feel alive again. Instinctively, she knew if she cut off her ties with Roman, a part of her would die again.

And since she'd already died once with Wesley, she wasn't willing to go through that again. Once had been enough.

"You won't cause any trouble. At least, not too much."

"All right." But he sounded doubtful.

Hoping to change the subject, she attempted to keep her own tone sounding positive. "I want to hear what you've been doing since you got home."

To her delight, he chuckled. "Then I won't make you wait another moment to hear about my exciting life."

"Do go on."

"First of all, it's been terribly cold here," he quipped, his voice thick with humor. "We've had a bit of snow, too. At least a foot."

"Snow?" Forgetting about their joking, Amanda closed her eyes and imagined a hilly Ohio landscape, covered with a thick carpet of freshly fallen snow. It sounded so lovely, and she could only imagine what Regina would have thought about such a winter wonderland! "I'm jealous. It sounds *wunderbaar*!"

"I don't know about that. Living with snow isn't the same as watching it fall from the warmth of a kitchen. It's been icy and cold out. Every morning I have to go to the barn and break the ice on the horses' water troughs."

"I had no idea the water in their troughs could freeze."

"The horses don't appreciate it none, that's for sure." After a pause, he continued. "I've also been keeping busy by mending fences and building a new chicken coop for my mother."

"A new chicken coop, hmm?" There in the solitude of her kitchen, Amanda allowed her smile to grow. "That sounds mighty interesting."

"You think so?"

"I do. And it sounds difficult, too."

"It's only difficult if you've never built a structure like that before."

"And you have?"

"Too many times, I'm sorry to say. And, I promise, the chickens are only interesting if you've never spent much time with them. They're nasty creatures."

"Maybe they're not so bad."

"Enough about the chickens. Now, tell me about you."

"Me? Well, I worked one day this week at the bakery, I ran errands, cleaned out two closets, and Regina lost her favorite toy dog. See, not much of interest here with me either."

"That's where you're wrong. I want to hear all about Regina losing her dog."

Amanda chuckled, sure he was teasing.

"So, did you ever find the dog?"

Her mouth went dry. "You really are interested, aren't you?"

"Yeah."

His voice was quiet. Roman wasn't joking. He really did

care. Amanda realized what was happening between them was special.

More than that, really. It was rare.

Roman hadn't called just to say hello. No, he called because he really did want to hear about her life.

Even if it wasn't anything special or fancy.

He cared because it had to do with her, and that's what was important to him.

She was important.

Focusing on the novelty of her feelings, she grabbed one of the kitchen chairs, pulled it near the phone, and sat down. And carefully went about telling him all about the search for the missing stuffed animal. Felt warmth from his interest.

And then, at his urging, she talked some more.

Far too soon, she heard Roman groan. "Listen, Amanda, I had better go. I just looked at the clock and we've talked a long time. This call is surely costing a pretty penny."

"Truly?" With a touch of dismay, she realized that they'd been talking on the phone for a whole thirty minutes. "Oh, *jah*. You're right. Thank you for calling."

"Will you be home tomorrow afternoon? About the same time?"

"I should be." Although at the moment, she couldn't think about much beyond the way talking to him made her feel.

"Then I'll call. If you don't think it's too soon?"

He was giving her space. Letting her be the person to tell him no.

"It's not too soon. I'd like to hear from you."

"Amanda, we're going to have to be careful, don't you think?"

His words warred with the smile she heard in his voice. "Why do you say that?"

"If we continue this, we're going to have to plan to see each other again."

"Would you come back to Pinecraft?"

"I could try. Or, maybe you could come up here. You and Regina could see our snow in person."

"Oh, I don't know about that. . . ."

"Why not? I think you'd love Berlin. And I know Regina would love to make a snowman."

"She probably would. But I'm just not sure if she's ready for a long bus trip."

"She might be." He chuckled, the sound making her feel warm all over again,. "Don't sound so worried," he said, his voice at once comforting and slightly chiding. "It was just a thought. I'll talk to you tomorrow, Amanda."

"Bye." When she hung up, his words rang in her ears. Would she one day be brave enough to get on a bus and go see him in Ohio? Or would she only be comfortable asking him to visit her?

What would it mean if they progressed to such cross-country visits? Would it mean that they'd become serious?

She shifted in the chair, and stared across the kitchen, not seeing a thing. Not believing all the feelings coursing through her. Did it all mean that she was actually thinking about marrying again?

And if she was, what did that say about her?

Why, just a few weeks ago, she'd been sure she'd always mourn Wesley. And now . . .

Tears pricked her eyes as she felt his loss all over again. It mixed in with her confusion about herself and her future and hurt, grating on her insides, scraping her raw.

"Are you off the phone now?" Marlene asked as she walked back in.

Amanda realized it was a rhetorical question. No doubt she'd been waiting, hovering just outside the kitchen, to hear the click of the receiver. Who knows? Perhaps she even overheard some of Amanda's conversation, too.

"*Jah*," she said quietly. "I'm done."

After a moment, Marlene walked to her side and tentatively rested her hand on the back of the chair. "Amanda, may we talk?"

"Of course. Where's Regina?"

"She's coloring in the other room." After a pause, Marlene pulled out a chair and sat down across from Amanda. "My dear, what is going on?"

Marlene's gaze was direct and forthright. Amanda answered her in the same way. "As you know, when Regina and I were staying at the condominium, I met a man from Ohio. His name is Roman Keim, and he is a farmer. We spent some time together."

"He lives in Ohio?"

"*Jah*. Berlin. Holmes County."

"Do you know anything else about him?" she asked, letting Amanda know that not only did Marlene know more than she was letting on, she'd also asked Regina questions.

With effort, Amanda pushed away the burst of irritation that coursed through her. She hated when Marlene asked her things she already knew the answer to. "Well, he's New Order, just like us. But more importantly, he is a good man, a caring man. He still lives with his parents and twin sisters. His grandparents live in their *dawdi haus*."

"Do you think there is something special between the two of you?"

"I don't know." After some thought she added, "All I know

is that when I'm with him I only think about the future, not the past." Amanda felt her skin heat. Her words sounded so hopeful, so earnest.

Marlene folded her hands tightly on the top of the table. "He must like you if he's calling you on the phone, Amanda."

"I guess he does, then."

"I wish you'd talk to me. I want to know what's going on in your life."

"I'm not trying to be evasive, I simply don't know what's happening between the two of us. You can be sure that I didn't go looking for another man in my life."

"It's only been two years."

Only two years. "I know." She'd been alone one hundred and four weeks—730 days. Too many hours to count. How long, she wondered, was long enough?

"And . . . and my Wesley was your husband."

My Wesley. "Yes, he was." There was nothing more to add, was there? He had been her husband, and she had certainly planned to be his wife until her last dying breath.

But he died first, when she was only twenty-three. "I still miss Wesley. I'm not trying to replace him."

"I hope not. I can't imagine that he would have wanted to replace you so quickly."

The words stung, and Amanda knew that Marlene had meant them to hurt.

Over the years, she'd been the best girlfriend and wife she'd been able to be.

She'd borne Wesley a beautiful daughter and had planned to have a whole house of *kinner.*

And then, when he'd gotten sick, she'd done nothing but stay by his side and nurse him.

And now, for two years, she'd done her best to be his good and proper widow. She'd honored his memory and cried more tears than she could ever measure.

But she was lonely . . . and she'd promised Wesley that she wouldn't spend the rest of her life grieving. Promised him more than once when she'd sat by his bedside, when she'd held a hand that was no longer strong, when she'd cared for a man who was no longer vibrant. Who slowly became almost unrecognizable except for his beautiful brown eyes that always seemed to see too much.

"Marlene, you're not being fair to me or to Wesley."

"I'm only watching over his memory."

"He didn't want me to mourn him forever."

"Yes, but it hasn't been forever, Amanda. Only two years." Her mother-in-law murmured as she stood up and turned away. But that wasn't fast enough to hide her quivering lip.

Amanda tried to remember that Marlene was mourning her son, too. "Marlene, I am sorry if I've hurt your feelings. I don't mean to make you upset. I don't mean to be disrespectful."

With her back still to her, she said, "Amanda, I think I will go home now."

"You don't want to help me with the casseroles?" They'd volunteered to make several meals for some families in their community, and Amanda had only volunteered for the job because Marlene had wanted to do it with her.

"Not today. I'm sorry," she said over her shoulder as a bit of an afterthought.

When she heard the front door slam shut, Amanda sat back down. Heard Regina talking to herself while she colored.

And realized she'd never felt more alone. Without even

meaning to, she'd finally severed the past and it couldn't be fastened back together.

Even if things returned to how they used to be, there would always be the memory of her phone call. As well as the knowledge that for thirty minutes, she'd once again been giddy and happy and flirty.

She'd once again been the woman she used to be . . . all for a man who wasn't Wesley Yoder.

chapter fourteen

The Keims were just leaving the Millers' home after church services and a light luncheon of sandwiches and salads when Bishop Coblentz stopped Roman as he was slipping on his black wool coat.

"It was a nice service, Bishop," Roman said politely. "Once again, I find myself uplifted from listening to the Scripture's words."

"*Jah,* the Lord always has the right words, ain't so?"

"Always." He flashed a grin. "Enjoy your nap this afternoon." It was well known that the bishop appreciated an hour's rest after church on Sunday.

"Oh, I shall." His blue eyes crinkled at the corners. "I guess my habits are no secret."

"Good ideas are always talked about. I'm thinking of taking things easy this afternoon as well. We all need a day of rest."

He started to turn away when Bishop Coblentz stopped him with a firm touch to his shoulder.

"Before you begin that rest, may I speak to you for a moment, Roman?"

"Of course." Looking around, he saw Elsie and his mother still chatting with Mrs. Miller and her newly married daughter. About a dozen other folks were either talking in small clusters, cleaning up the last remnants of the luncheon, or attempting to gather their children.

Only the back cement patio was deserted. "Why don't we head over here?" he said after motioning to his mother that he needed more time before leaving.

The bishop nodded. "That's a good spot."

Roman led the way to the Millers' back patio. In spring and summer, an iron table and chairs sat squarely in the middle, the whole arrangement framed by the sweet scent of blossoming apple trees and the beauty of more flowers than he'd ever be able to name.

Now, in the dead of winter, the area was rather desolate. Flowering plants lay dormant under the covering of snow, and the apple trees were bare, their spindly arms lifted toward the sky like misshapen scarecrows.

Without any foliage to block the wind, Roman thought the air seemed even colder. But it also felt crisp and bracing, and he gave thanks for it, since it seemed he was going to need a clear head to talk with the bishop. The older man looked like he had something important on his mind to share.

"Is everything all right?" Roman asked. "Is there something I can help you with?"

Bishop Coblentz folded his weathered hands neatly on top of one of the black wrought-iron chairs he was standing behind. "I am fine, Roman, and I thank you for asking. Actually, your well-being was one of the things I was hoping to discuss with you."

Though the bishop's words were stated, he'd lifted the end of his sentence, as if he were asking a question.

Roman started to feel uneasy. "My well-being?" he echoed.

"*Jah*." The older man cleared his throat. "How are you,

Roman? I imagine you're having quite a time, what with your father in the treatment program and all."

"I am all right. Just fine." With some surprise, he realized he was speaking the truth. Just a few weeks before, he would have given almost anything to make his life easier. He'd been disturbed by his grandmother's news about her past life and had dearly wished for his father's alcohol abuse to go away. Sometimes, late at night, he'd even stayed up and worried about what was going to happen with Elsie. With Viola getting married, he'd felt that it was his duty to accept more responsibility for Elsie's future care.

Now, everything still seemed difficult, but not insurmountable.

He knew the reason, of course. Ever since he'd returned from Florida he'd been so consumed with thoughts about Amanda that all the problems in his family had ceased to keep him up at night.

After staring at him intently for a moment, the bishop nodded. "Roman, I do believe you are all right. That is *gut*. It makes this a little easier."

Roman was starting to have the feeling that he'd walked into the middle of another man's conversation. "It makes what a little easier?"

"Henry Zimmerman came to see me two weeks ago. He's in poor health and has to step down from his preaching duties. The job has become too much for him, especially what with his farming and his failing health."

"I see."

"So, we asked for suggestions for a replacement from the congregation at the last church."

"I heard. I'm sure the congregation chose several good men for the lot."

"They did." As the bishop paused for breath, a slow, sinking feeling settled deep in Roman's chest.

Suddenly, he realized why the bishop had wanted to speak to him. "Was my name mentioned?"

"*Jah*." The bishop nodded. "Your name was chosen for the lot, Roman. It got one of the most votes."

"I see." Their church district had three ministers, who took turns preaching every two weeks. Whenever it was time for a vacancy to be filled, the congregation voted, then the top vote getters would be entered into the lot. Of course, every man who had been baptized into the church was eligible. Then, a Scripture passage was slipped in a stack of hymnals. If a man picked up the hymnal with the verse inside it, he would be the congregation's new preacher.

There were precious few reasons for a man to not accept the burden. Serious illness was just about the only viable excuse that would be accepted. It was their belief that the Lord chose the next preacher.

Roman believed that completely. However, it didn't make the heavy burden any easier to bear.

If a man drew the hymnal with the chosen verse inside, he would be required to serve in the open position. For the rest of his life, or as God saw fit.

It was a good system, a fair one. And one that their community had honored for as long as he could recall. Every man he'd known who'd been chosen had approached the process with both seriousness and a heavy sense of responsibility.

But now, selfishly, Roman realized that he'd been taken by surprise. He didn't know if he was ready. He felt too young, too immature for such a large job.

And he certainly wasn't ready for the change that would take place in his life. When a man realized he'd been chosen by the Lord to be a preacher, he knew he was going to have to preach in front of their whole church district for years. In addition, he was going to have to be available to guide and counsel other men and women in their community.

But how did a man refuse? Roman had never heard of anyone not living up to his obligation. Moreover, he'd promised the bishop when he was baptized that he would be willing to accept the process, if he was ever considered a suitable candidate.

"Are we choosing a new preacher today?" he asked, mainly to buy himself another minute of time.

"*Jah*." Bishop Coblentz's gazed sharpened. "We had hoped to only announce it today, so that the men could all pray about the opportunity. But I'm afraid in two weeks many folks have plans to head south for vacation or to visit family to celebrate Easter." He shrugged. "So, we're doing it today. It's God's will anyway, ain't so?"

"*Jah*," Roman said quietly. Bishop Coblentz was right. This was all under God's control, and because of that, it made little difference when the new preacher would be named.

The bishop pressed a hand onto Roman's bicep. "*Gut*. I wanted to speak to you first, to be sure you were able to accept God's calling if He sees fit." Softly, the bishop added, "I'm sure we would all understand, Roman, if you thought that your father's troubles were weighing too heavy on you to accept His call at this time." He shrugged. "Life has a way of taking twists and turns for everyone. If you don't feel ready for the responsibility, I'm sure there will be another opportunity to serve."

Roman sighed in relief.

He didn't have to say yes. Bishop Coblentz would understand. Perhaps the other men in his community would, too.

But forevermore Roman knew that he would feel guilty if he refused the calling. It wasn't the Amish way to push things aside because they felt too hard or scary. More important, it wasn't his way. "If God wants to use me, I am willing and able to try my best."

"You are sure?"

Now, Roman didn't even hesitate. It was as if the Lord was behind him, prodding him forward. Helping him be the man he wanted to be. "I am sure."

Slowly, the bishop's lips curved above his long, graying beard. "Roman, I am happy to hear you say that. I promise, a willingness to be used by the Lord is all that anyone can ask for." He clapped a work-weathered hand on his shoulder. "*Jah*, I am most pleased. Well now, the four other men are already gathering in the barn. Let's get on with it then."

He turned and walked back toward the barn. Strode forward with steady, even steps, never pausing or looking over his shoulder to see if Roman was following.

But of course, there wasn't any need for that. Roman had given his promise.

Silently, Roman followed, nodding to John Miller and another couple of men who were standing around, watching to see who would be part of the lot. A few women looked up as he passed, then turned back to their conversations after giving him encouraging smiles. It was obvious word had already spread that a new preacher was about to be selected.

As he entered the dark barn and met the gazes of the other men assembled, Roman secretly told himself that his chances to be chosen were slim. He was the youngest man by a good eight years.

Surely God would choose a better, more experienced man than him? Someone who wasn't so confused about his life and his family? Who wasn't half in love with a lady in Florida?

That made him pause. Was he already "half in love"?

Was he *already* in love? Did he love Amanda Yoder?

Yes.

The answer came to him as clearly as if the Lord himself had just whispered into his ear.

He loved Amanda Yoder.

His mind spun as Bishop Coblentz walked to the front of the barn and gestured toward the neat stack of hymnals. "The Lord speaks to each of us in His own way," he began to the group of them. "It is up to each of us to open his heart to God's will."

Levi, the man on his right, murmured his agreement.

As Bishop Coblentz spoke, talking about responsibility and commitment, Roman let his mind drift to the one person he couldn't stop thinking about. He wondered when he could get away to see Amanda again. Perhaps he could go see her in three or four weeks, even if just for a few days. It would be a hard trip, of course, and his family would probably be displeased about him going away again so soon.

But Roman knew he could ask the other men in the family to watch over things . . . and after all, it wasn't like he had always shirked his duties.

No, he'd never shirked his duties. . . .

"Roman? It's your turn," Levi muttered.

"Huh?" With a start, he realized that the other men held hymnals in their hands. "Oh. Sorry," he muttered, as he walked up to the stack and picked the next one. He held the book with both hands.

Silence settled over them as each man seemed to tense slightly in anticipation.

"It is time," Bishop Coblentz said. "Open your hymnals. Inside one is a verse from First Corinthians."

In unison, the five men did as the bishop directed. Some flipped through their hymnals quickly. Others were like him, letting their nervous fingers flip through the paper-thin pages carefully, trying not to rip the pages.

As men found nothing, they shut their books with firm hands. And Roman's heart began to beat a little faster. Realizing he was borrowing trouble, he mentally berated himself. There was no way he would have the Scripture verse. In just a few seconds, he would be closing his hymnal, too. Then he could go back to thinking about Amanda, and making plans to see her again.

Visions of their reunion calmed him. Before he knew it, he was imagining her in a blue dress on their wedding day.

Yes, it was fanciful to imagine her as his wife, but the daydream was doing what his reality hadn't been able to do. He was feeling calmer, more at peace.

More slowly, he thumbed through his hymnal, looking for a loose slip of paper. Little by little, he realized that the other men were now sitting quietly.

And that everyone's eyes were focused on him

Then he saw what he'd been dreading—and what he'd thought he wouldn't actually see. Beside him, Levi nodded.

Swallowing hard, he felt his options for the future slip away. With a heavy hand, he lifted the paper. "It is I," he said.

Bishop Coblentz stared at him intently. "Roman Keim, will you accept God's will?"

"I will accept," Roman said solemnly, not daring to look at John Miller or his uncle Sam or his grandfather. He didn't want to see the sympathy in their eyes. Not even the warm glow of pride.

Instead, he looked straight ahead and kept his back stiff.

And tried not to think at all.

Bishop Coblentz nodded. "His will is done."

He'd managed to avoid most of the family until supper time on Monday night.

But as Roman sat down across from Viola, felt Elsie's gaze on him, and saw the knowing glance of his grandfather, he realized he had no choice but to talk about his new responsibilities in the church. It was obvious they'd all heard. And just as obvious that they were trying their best to let him be the leader of the discussion.

He knew they were curious. But for the life of him, he couldn't bear to talk as if he was ready to be one of their district's preachers.

Even though he'd already told all the men that he'd accepted God's will.

Which, of course, made him feel even more confused and upset.

Tucking his chin, he forked another bite of green bean casserole and chewed. Anything to delay the inevitable.

For the last twenty-four hours, the feeling of following God's will warred with his own selfish wishes. In the middle of the night, he'd felt so torn, he wasn't able to fall back to sleep and had lain there, restlessly struggling with the news.

"Please pass the sweet potato casserole, Roman," his mother said. "And while you're doing that, perhaps you could at last speak to us about what's happened."

Feeling like the glass dish weighed three tons, he lifted it and passed it clumsily to Elsie. "Here."

She took it without a word, but he could almost feel her frustration with him. And he saw clearly that she'd had to shift her hands quickly in order to not drop the dish on the table.

Which made him feel worse than he already did.

"Yesterday after church, Bishop Coblentz told me that I was one of the men who had received the most votes from the congregation for the open preaching position. The five men who were nominated drew hymnals. Mine was the chosen one," he said matter-of-factly. Because after all, those were the facts.

As he'd expected, no one burst into praise. Or shouted a congratulation. All knew it was a heavy burden to carry, especially in a man his age. Preachers were expected to carry out all sorts of pastoral duties, the same as in any other Christian denomination. However, in the Amish community, the preachers were not supported by the church.

Therefore, men kept their regular jobs, then added the new duties. For some men, it could be too much, especially over a long period of time.

"Well, what do you think about it?" Viola asked.

Roman met his grandfather's gaze. Roman had seen him sit quietly in the back of the barn when the hymnals had been drawn. To his credit, he hadn't said a single word about what had happened, either.

Instead, he'd let Roman have the time he needed to come to terms with what lay ahead.

"There is nothing to think about," Roman declared. "What's done is done. Besides, it's the Lord's decision."

"*Jah*, that is true," his grandfather said with a nod. But he didn't look entirely in agreement with his words. "Accepting

God's calling is not always easy to do, but it is necessary. A man who accepts God's will without complaint is a man to be respected."

Just as his grandmother nodded, Viola shook her head. "Hold on. I understand that you had no choice but to be in the lot, and that you've accepted the Lord's calling."

He raised a brow. "But?"

"But you must have some opinion about it. Are you excited? Nervous? Upset? Confident?"

"It doesn't matter what I think." Roman shifted uncomfortably, wishing he could ease out of the room and sit and stew in private.

"Of course it matters what you think," Elsie blurted. "As a matter of fact, I think it might matter a lot."

Elsie's comment drew more than one startled glance. "How so?" their *mamm* asked quietly.

"Well, the Lord's will may be final, but that doesn't mean we have to agree with His decisions."

"Elsie, you can't mean that," their grandmother exclaimed.

"Sure I do," Elsie countered. "I mean, I've accepted that one day I won't see . . . that one day I will no longer enjoy the sunrise or spring pansies or the sight of your faces. I've accepted that will be my future, but I'm not happy about it."

Around the table, everyone lowered their heads, anxious to change the subject as almost always happened when Elsie mentioned her disease.

But instead of remaining quiet like she usually did, she glared. "Ignoring things doesn't make them better. But sometimes talking about how we feel can make our burdens easier to bear."

To Roman's surprise, it was their grandmother who spoke up. "That is true, Elsie. You are right. We should all be talking about things that are on our mind. Roman, I know your father isn't here to advise you. Have you found someone to talk things through with?"

There was no way he was going to share his private thoughts around the dinner table. He could hardly imagine what they might say about his love for Amanda Yoder and his fear about preaching in front of the whole church.

"There's no need to discuss anything, Mommi," he said sharply. "I gave my consent to be considered to the Bishop, I drew that hymnal, and I've accepted the Lord's choice."

His grandmother didn't look cowed in the slightest. "But what about the girl in Florida?"

He set his fork down. "Amanda?"

She looked impatient. "Of course I mean Amanda. I've seen you on the phone in the kitchen, Roman. Hasn't she been the girl you've been talking to?"

"I've been calling her. And writing," he admitted somewhat grudgingly. Because, well, his phone calls weren't his grandmother's business.

"Well, then? What are you going to do about her?"

His temper broke. "Well, then?" he echoed. "Well, I have no idea. I hadn't planned on being a preacher, and especially not anytime soon."

Now that he'd begun, he could hardly stop; it was like another person had taken ahold of his tongue. "Actually, I'd been hoping to see her again, but now it looks like the Lord has made other plans for me."

Standing up, he pushed the chair out behind him with a noisy scrape. "I'm sorry, Mamm. I'll clean up my plate in a moment. But for now, I need to get out of here."

Like a sulking child, he tore out of the room, pulled open the back door, and raced outside.

Only when the cold wind whipped against his cheeks did he realize he was crying.

And only then did he speak the awful, awful question that had been brewing in his stomach from the first moment Bishop Coblentz had asked him to chat. "Why me, Gott? Why me? Why now?"

chapter fifteen

While the rest of the family sat stunned, staring at the closed door, Viola stood up. She couldn't simply sit and worry, and she certainly didn't feel ready to debate Roman's behavior with her mother and grandparents. "I'm going to start clearing the table, Mamm."

Her mother looked at her in surprise. "Oh. Well, all right . . ."

"I'll help," Elsie said just as quickly.

More than ever, Viola was thankful for her twin. Elsie was the one person she never needed to hide her feelings from. It was usually because she was feeling the same way. After picking up both her plate and Roman's, she walked to the kitchen. Elsie followed with her own plate in her hands.

Once they were together in the privacy of the kitchen, they put down the plates on the counter and stared at each other in wonder as they began to fill the sink to drown out their voices.

Elsie broke the silence. "Have you ever seen Roman like this before?"

"You know I haven't," Viola answered, adding soap to the water. "Gosh, Elsie, I didn't even think Roman knew *how* to be angry. All he's ever done is hold his temper and calmly discuss things."

"He's always been the one to remind us to be patient."

"And to pray and follow the Lord's way," Viola added. When they were younger, Roman's patient, preachy ways had driven her crazy. He'd never understood her need to act on things impulsively, and had made no bones about sharing his opinions.

Elsie lowered her voice. "I think he really is missing that woman. I know he misses Daed, too. And now he's been given this new responsibility. I can't even imagine what he's feeling. I bet he's worried and frustrated and hurting."

Elsie always did have a way of reading other people clearly. "I bet you're right."

"I sure don't know how to help him, though."

"Elsie, there's got to be a way to make things better. He's a *gut* man, and a *gut bruder*. I want him to be happy."

"I know, but he's got to come to terms with the reality. He's pining for a woman who lives over a thousand miles away. Sometimes it doesn't matter how much you want something. Sometimes you have to understand that there are things you simply can't change."

Viola felt her heart clench, knowing that Elsie was referencing her disease. "I agree, but maybe Amanda could come here? Then Roman could see Amanda without leaving the farm and his new church responsibilities."

"I don't know if Roman will feel comfortable asking that. A woman likes to be pursued. Plus she has a daughter. Roman said she had a nice life out there in Florida."

"We could ask."

Elsie's eyebrows rose. "You mean *Roman* could ask her."

"No, I mean *we* could give her a call and ask her if she'd be interested in visiting. If she says yes, then we can let Roman know."

"He won't like that."

"That's true, but that's also what sisters are for, I think. To meddle in places where their brothers don't want them involved." As Elsie shook her head slowly, Viola couldn't help but grin. "Oh, come on, twin. It will be like we're *kinner* again."

"No, following him around on the playground at school would be like we were *kinner* again. This is interfering with his life, Viola."

"It's in his best interests." She pushed away Elsie's protests by gesturing to the dining room. "We better finish clearing the table before Mamm asks what we are doing."

"I know what you're doing, you know," Elsie said. "You're hatching a plot that I'm going to have to put into play—and have to deal with the consequences of."

"What do you mean?"

"While you're in Belize, I'll be here, dealing with the repercussions."

Viola felt slightly guilty. But not guilty enough to back down. "You're always telling us you're stronger than we think, sister. Now you can prove it."

And with that, she strode back into the dining room and picked up her grandparents' plates. They were deep in discussion with their mother. Not one of them even looked Elsie's and Viola's way as they finished clearing the table.

And just like that, Viola felt every bit of her exuberance fade away. Her family was feeling the burden of change more than ever.

When they returned to the kitchen, she noticed that Elsie's playful manner had faded as well.

After scraping the plates, Elsie walked to her side, a dishcloth in her hand. As Viola washed each plate, Elsie silently dried it and put it in the cupboard. It was a task they'd easily done a hundred times before, and the familiar comfort of the chore brought a peace that an hour-long conversation never could have done.

When their stack of dirty dishes was gone and the left-overs neatly put away, Elsie turned to her. "Viola, you are exactly right. Something needs to be done for Roman. It's not in his nature to push for something he wants. He's always been the member of the family to stand aside while the rest of us get our way." She paused. "Roman deserves happiness. We all do." Taking a deep breath, Elsie added, "If you don't have time to call Amanda, I will."

"Are you sure? Tomorrow I can get Amanda's phone number from Beth."

"I can do that, too, Viola. Actually, calling Amanda will make me feel good inside. Useful."

"*Danke*, Elsie," she said quietly, feeling her sister's resolve.

More than a week had passed since Amanda and Regina had returned to their regular schedule. But even though they were now settled only a few minutes away from the beach, everything felt different. Gone were the Pop-Tarts and beach towels. In their places were eggs and oatmeal and rain boots.

For some reason, the sun had decided to begin a vacation when they left the beach. Their usual sunny days were now filled with rain clouds.

"Mamm, when will it ever stop raining?" Regina asked from her spot at the window.

"When the time is right, I suppose," Amanda said to her daughter as she finished packing Regina's lunch.

She slumped. "I'm tired of the rain."

"I know."

"It's ruining our day."

"Well, it will make us wet," Amanda corrected. "But I'm not so sure if it's been ruining our day." As she watched her daughter continue to stare at the rain out the window with disappointment, she brightened her voice. "You know, it's a good thing we aren't too sweet, Regina. Otherwise we'd melt in the rain."

"I don't want to melt."

Of course, Regina had taken her statement seriously—she took all her statements seriously. And there was no reason she would have ever heard her grandfather's saying about melting in the rain before. Living in Pennsylvania, Amanda's parents hadn't had the opportunity to spend much time with Regina. "I was only joking, dear. I meant that a little rain never hurt anyone. It's not a terrible thing."

"I still feel sad."

"And why is that? Does the rain make you feel gloomy?"

"*Nee.* On rainy days, Mommi only wants to look out the window and talk about Daed."

Amanda winced. Soon she was going to have to find a different situation for Regina. Her mother-in-law's perpetual state of mourning wasn't healthy.

"I am sorry about that. We could pack you some books to look at while you're with your grandmother."

"All right." Regina scampered off to her room to retrieve the thick canvas book bag that held her dozen library books.

Fighting off the feeling of guilt that was nagging at her, Amanda carefully closed up Regina's lunch bag, smiling as she did so. About four months ago, while grocery shopping at the store, Regina had seen a bright purple nylon lunch sack with Velcro on the ends of it. Decorating the sturdy fabric were yellow and orange starfish and red polka-dotted seals.

Amanda had privately thought it was an ugly, garish design, but Regina?—she'd fallen in love.

For weeks she'd complained about the sturdy basket lined with pretty cloth napkins that Amanda used for her lunch. It was too heavy. It didn't keep the food cold. Amanda had tried to hold firm, but then didn't see the harm in a new lunch bag for her daughter. They'd gone to the store and bought it together. Ever since, Regina had carried it with pride.

Funny how something so small could matter so much to a little girl.

She was still thinking about that when the phone rang, jarring her thoughts. "Hello?"

"Is this Amanda Yoder?"

"It is," she said hesitantly. She didn't get many telemarketers, but this woman didn't sound like she was selling anything.

"My name is Elsie Keim. I'm Roman's sister."

Her heart leapt to her chest. "Is Roman hurt? Is something wrong?"

"Hurt? Oh goodness, no. He's fine. Well, kind of fine. He could be better."

Well, if that wasn't the strangest comment! "I'm afraid I don't understand."

"I'm, uh, calling to invite you and your daughter to Ohio. To Berlin. Would you like to visit us?"

Instantly the pictures Roman had created in her mind tumbled forth. She started thinking of snowmen and crisp, cold air. Pine trees and scarves and mittens. "Thank you for the invitation. But why are you asking me instead of Roman?" And furthermore, she chided herself, why was she even considering such a thing?

"Well," Elsie began, "my brother has recently been called

to be our district's newest preacher. It's a heavy responsibility, you know."

"Yes?"

"Anyway, we all know that he wants to see you, and was hoping to plan another trip to Florida, but now he canna get away."

"I see." That told her many things, but not why Roman wasn't the one asking her to visit.

"No, I don't think you do," Elsie replied, just as if she could read Amanda's mind. "See, my brother is the type of man who doesn't care to make waves for anyone. When he learned of this new responsibility, he decided to work hard to honor it."

"I still don't understand why you are calling and not him."

"Because he is stubborn. We all know you and your daughter mean a lot to him, but we also know that he's the type of man to put everyone else's wishes and needs before his own. He wants to see you, but doesn't want to let that interfere with his duties at the farm."

"Elsie, do you mean to tell me that you are inviting me without his knowledge?"

"Actually [illegible] that would be true."

Amanda could tell that Elsie was getting impatient with all her questions. But while Amanda knew that she longed to drop everything for a surprise visit to see Roman, she certainly could never do that with Regina's heart on the line. Never could she risk taking Regina to a place where she wasn't wanted. Her little girl had already been through so much.

"I appreciate the invitation, but I cannot accept. It wouldn't be right."

"No, it would be right. Roman will love that you're here. I promise you that."

"I'm not thinking of him, I'm thinking of my daughter. She is who I must concentrate on."

After a pause, Elsie spoke again. "Yes, I suppose so. Well, I'm sorry for the phone call. I hope I haven't offended you."

"Not at all. I can only imagine what it must be like to have a *shveshtah* who loved me so much."

When she hung up, she noticed Regina lurking at the edge of the kitchen.

"Who was on the phone, Mamm?"

"Roman's sister Elsie."

"Why did she call?"

"Merely to ask me something."

"What did you say?"

"I said I didn't know the answer," she said quickly. Clearing her throat, which seemed suspiciously tight all of the sudden, she said, "Now, daughter, it is time to get on our way." She held up the lunch tote. "You need to get to your grandparents' house and I need to go to work."

"Even in the rain?"

"Yes, dear. Even in the rain we must do what we are supposed to do."

Always. Even when she wished to do otherwise. Even then.

chapter sixteen

It was raining. "Could there be anything worse than rain in March?" Roman asked his horse as he double-checked the lines on the buggy that he'd just attached. "Our journey to the store is going to make us both a wet, soggy mess."

Chester tossed his head as if in agreement . . . or maybe it was annoyance. Roman figured the old horse was probably as irritated by the bit in his teeth as the cold rain soaking his coat. Of late, Chester had become quarrelsome. "Sorry, *gaul*," he murmured, rubbing the horse's neck. "We've all got our jobs to do. Pulling me in the rain is yours today."

Chester looked away and pawed the ground with a hoof.

He was still smiling at his horse's strong personality as he strode into the barn and saw Elsie standing next to one of the stalls. "*Gut matin*," he said. "What are you doing out here so early?"

"I have something to tell you."

Elsie was wearing a look he knew well, one that said she was ready to chat for hours. Well, the horse wasn't the only one in the barn impatient to get on his way. "Can it wait? I've got to get into town before the weather gets worse."

She shook her head. "I don't think so."

"Go ahead, then. What is it?" he asked as he shrugged into his coat.

"I called Amanda this morning."

Roman froze. He wanted to ask a million questions. Ask if she was talking about *his* Amanda. Ask how she'd even gotten Amanda's telephone number.

But instead, he asked the question that mattered the most. "Why would you do that?"

She tugged on the edge of her apron. Crinkled it into her fist. "Well, Viola and I got to talking . . ."

"And?"

"And, we were discussin' how you've been mooning over her . . ."

"Lord, save me from twin sisters! Elsie, you and Viola had no business talking about me like that."

Releasing the apron, her chin rose. "You're our brother. Of course we're going to talk about you." She pressed on, her words tumbling out of her mouth in a rush. "It was easy enough to get her number. Cousin Beth had it."

He breathed a sigh of relief. He supposed it was good that the pair of them hadn't gone through his room, looking for the small scrap of paper in his desk drawer that held the precious information. "What did you say to Amanda?"

"Oh, not much. I introduced myself. Told her about me and Viola . . ."

"Elsie, get to the point."

"Well, actually, after we talked for a bit . . . I invited her and her daughter to come visit."

He could hardly believe his ears. She'd picked up the phone. Called up Amanda. And asked her to come to Ohio. That's all. "It's Regina," he said.

She blinked in confusion. "Hmm?"

"Her daughter's name is Regina," he repeated, mainly to buy himself some time to rein in his growing temper.

"So, what do you think?"

He thought he had the two most interfering sisters on the planet. That's what he thought.

"I'm not sure why you care what I think, Elsie," he snapped. "Seein' as how you've taken it upon yourself to get involved in my life and all."

"It wasn't just me."

"You. And Viola."

"So you're mad at us?"

"You could say that," he bit out. "Honestly, did you two really think I'd be grateful for your interference?"

After a moment, she nodded. "*Jah.*"

"You two are more trouble than a pair of goats in love."

She blushed. "I think not." Stepping a little closer, she said, "It's been my experience that family members usually meddle with the best of intentions."

"Just because someone doesn't mean to cause damage, when they do, things still need to be repaired. You should have minded your own business." He could only imagine how horrified Amanda must have been, receiving a call from his sister.

"Nothing is hurt, Roman. Nothing needs to be repaired."

"Oh, really? What am I supposed to do now?"

"Call her and say you want her to come."

"Is that right?" He snapped his fingers. "I'm sure it's just that easy."

"It sounded to me like it was."

He stared at her, forgetting about the rain, about his ornery horse, about his irritating younger sisters. "Did . . . Did Amanda sound like she wanted to come north? To see Ohio?"

"Well, she sounded like she wanted to see *you*, Roman."

"She said that?" With effort, he tried to keep his body and

expression cool and detached. Inside, however, he was raising his fist in the air in triumph.

"More or less." Amusement lit her voice. "Amanda said she would look forward to speaking to you about it. So that sounded positive to me. But then again, I don't know her like you do."

Roman couldn't help but smile. He liked the thought that he knew Amanda, that he understood her. But then he gathered his resolve again. He had a sister who couldn't see him softening. "Elsie, you don't know her at all."

"But I'd like to. She sounded really nice. She sounded fond of you, Roman. Which, of course, makes me like her a whole lot more. I do want to meet this Amanda in person. Viola and I both do."

His sister was so earnest, so sincere, he couldn't stay mad at her for long. "Have I ever told you that you're my favorite twin?"

"Last month, just days after you told Viola the same thing. Right before you said we were going to be the death of you."

"I didn't mean that."

"But this time?" She raised a brow.

"This time I think it's true."

She chuckled. "Call Amanda sometime today, Roman. What can it hurt?"

"I might just do that," he said grudgingly. "*Danke*, Elsie. I owe you."

"Don't worry, one day you can help me when I'm being courted. Viola's going to be of no use, since she'll be in a foreign country and all."

"Of course I'll help you," he called out as he watched her carefully make her way back to the house.

But as he watched her stumble on the edge of a stone step

and straighten her glasses, Roman wondered when Elsie was ever going to come to terms that she would most likely never have a husband.

As he trudged out to the buggy, he couldn't help but shake his head. It truly was a shame, he realized. Because in many ways, she was the best of the three of them. Continually happy, eternally poised. A hard worker and patient.

She would have made some man a wonderful wife.

A wonderful wife.

Pushing off thoughts of his sister, he let his mind drift back to Amanda and the upcoming phone conversation. And to his surprise, he wasn't dreading it at all.

Turning back to Chester, he said, "Well, boy, let's get this trip to town over with. It looks like I have much to do today. So much, I might not even mind the rain."

The disdainful look Chester gave him in response was priceless.

And pretty much made him grin most of the way into town.

It seemed everyone wanted to go to the airport with her. "I told you, Mr. Cross said he'd be happy to take me and make sure I got on the plane just fine," Viola said to her siblings, her grandparents, her mother, and—unbelievably—Mr. Swartz. "He took Edward."

"I'm sure Mr. Cross is a *verra* nice man. But he ain't family," her mother said briskly. "And he is most definitely not your *muddah*."

"That is true," Atle said with a gleam in his eye. "It's been my experience that no one can take a mother's place when it comes to fussin'."

As they piled in the van that her grandfather had hired for the day, Viola held her purse tightly on her lap, and double-checked her papers and plane itinerary again. And then slowly opened her passport and glanced at the photograph of herself.

Not for the first time, her grandfather held out his hand and examined the blue booklet carefully, running his finger over her signature.

Though he'd never actually said so, Viola felt that of everyone in the family, he'd been the one who was most unhappy about her choices. "Are you terribly upset, Grandfather?"

"With what?"

"With me, because I'm getting on an airplane and going to Belize."

"To see your man? *Nee*. I'm not upset."

"Then you understand?"

"I understand what it's like to miss someone you love. And I understand what it's like to take a chance on something new, too. You forget, when your *mommi* and I moved to Ohio, we didn't know anyone at all. It was a scary adventure." He glanced to his right. "Wouldn't you say that, Lovina?"

She chuckled softly. "Well, I would have to admit that that time is all a blur to me now. I was newly married, and had just become Amish."

This was the first time her grandmother had ever mentioned her transformation in such a casual way. Viola wished Elsie was sitting nearby so she could give her a nudge.

But perhaps Elsie had already read her mind. "Mommi, what was it like, moving with Dawdi?"

"Scary. I didn't want to let him down."

That seemed like a strange comment. Viola looked at her grandmother in surprise. "Why would you have been worried about that?"

"Because I was always doing things wrong." She shook her head in a guilty manner. "I could hardly speak Deutch."

"I didn't expect you to know everything." Her grandfather looked at Viola then and grinned—a very cheeky, very male grin. "It didn't matter so much to me, anyway. She was the prettiest woman I'd ever seen."

This time it was her mother who spoke up. "Is that right, Aaron? You were taken in by a pair of pretty brown eyes?"

"Yes, I was." He cleared his throat in a gruff way as he handed the passport back to Viola. "And that will be the end of this talk."

They all laughed. The mood in the van was light and comfortable, bringing back memories of times when things weren't so confusing and hard at home.

Viola gave thanks to God for reminding her that while things weren't perfect in the Keim family, it wasn't completely broken, either. It was the first glimmer of hope she'd felt in weeks—just as she was leaving town.

"Everyone is going to have to tell me how Roman looks at Amanda," she said just to keep the conversation light. "Because we all know Roman won't tell me about the visit."

"I'm sure there will be nothing to tell," Roman said.

"I'm sure there will be lots to tell," Elsie teased. "After all, you called her just days ago, and now she's on the bus to Ohio. That was quick."

"She got a special price on the tickets, that's all," Roman said.

"I'm putting my money on the girls, Roman," his grandfather said with a wry look.

Roman scowled. "When she gets here, no one better be looking at the two of us."

Viola raised her brows at Elsie, conveying silently that Elsie better plan to give her a full report.

Her mother and grandmother chuckled.

As did Atle. "Come now, Roman. Are you really so backward that you don't think everyone's going to be watching you together?" he asked. "I'm counting on getting as many reports as possible at Daybreak."

To their amusement, Roman's cheeks turned red. "I don't want Amanda to feel awkward," he sputtered. "Plus, she will have her daughter with her, you know. Everyone needs to take care around her."

"Whose name is Regina, I believe," Elsie said. "Isn't that right, Roman?

Roman groaned.

Viola bit her lip to refrain from commenting on that. Around her, she felt the rest of the group's efforts to hold their tongues. Roman was a private man. If they teased him too much, there was no way he'd ever say another word about Amanda again.

Luckily for her brother, their driver soon announced they were approaching the Cleveland Hopkins International Airport. Now she had no thoughts except for her worries about traveling alone to a foreign country . . . and an almost breathless anticipation about finally seeing Ed again. Their six-week separation had felt at times like an eternity.

She only hoped when they were together again that their reunion would be as sweet as she'd imagined. What would she do if Ed acted differently toward her in Belize?

What would she do if she hated Belize? If she found that no matter how hard she tried she couldn't live in a foreign country?

Or if she realized she didn't want to be a missionary's wife?

Or, worst of all, if she didn't think she could work with the people that Edward served? She would be so embarrassed.

And Edward would be so disappointed!

As they stopped in front of the terminal, she felt a calm hand on her shoulder. "Don't," her grandfather murmured, just for her ears.

"Don't what?" she whispered right back.

"Don't start fretting and worrying." When her eyes widened, he said, "Your thoughts are written as plain as day, all over your face." Moving his hand from her shoulder to her chin, he raised it slightly. "Have faith, Viola. Have faith in yourself and in Edward, and in the Lord. I feel certain that he isn't leading you down this path just to feel pain."

Her grandfather's words were just the boost she needed. Feeling better and more confident than she had in days, she led the procession out of the van and inside the airport.

The moment they were in the brightly lit, noisy building, no less than three airport personnel rushed to their side. Viola guessed their Amish clothing stuck out like sore thumbs.

When she told them what airline she was flying on, and to where, they guided her—and the whole family—to a check-in booth.

Ten minutes later, her suitcase was on a conveyer belt, she had her travel documents in hand, and another person was offering to walk her to the airport security station.

"But your family can't come with you, miss."

Though she was trying to be brave, tears pricked at her eyes as she glanced at Elsie. "I guess I better go. All by myself."

One by one, everyone hugged her. In between hugs, her mother asked her about money and snacks and if she had her new Karen Kingsbury novel to help pass the time.

Her grandparents reminded her to pray.

Roman teased her about being such an independent woman.

Last of all, she was in Elsie's arms. "I'm going to miss you so much," she whispered into her twin's neck. "I don't know what I'm going to do without you."

This time, it was Elsie who was the strong one. "Of course you do, twin. You're going to be yourself and enjoy every minute of your adventure."

Finally, she admitted her greatest fear. "And if I decide it's all not for me?"

"Then you will know that it isn't," Elsie said with her usual patient manner. "You need to know for sure, Viola."

A lady in a security uniform cleared her throat. "Miss, it's time to go. You're holding up the line."

"*Jah*. Okay." Biting her lip, she waved to them all, then turned and walked toward the many people in their blue uniforms.

And tried not to listen for her family as they walked away.

"You've got a great family, miss," her escort commented. "It's been a long time since I've seen someone get such a sendoff."

"Yes. They're *wunderbaar*, for sure." Had she ever truly realized that?

Still dwelling on her family, she handed the security person her passport and plane ticket, then walked toward the screening station.

Before she started putting her things on the conveyer belt, she turned, trying to catch one last glimpse of her family.

But they were already out of sight. She was completely on her own now. Completely on her own, for better or worse.

chapter seventeen

The Pioneer Trails bus had traveled through the night, with frequent stops along the way. Through it all, the rest breaks and the naps and the snippets of conversation, Amanda had felt as if she were in a daze. Well, she would have been if Regina had not kept her on her toes.

While others slept through the stops, Regina had insisted on getting out and exploring the truck stops, waffle houses, and McDonald's. Each one was a new experience for her, and Regina seemed determined to enjoy every locale to the fullest.

While others complained about greasy food or uncomfortable seats, Regina asked for seconds and cuddled close. When some men grumbled about the colder temperatures, little Regina had beamed when Amanda placed her new pink cardigan over her dress, saying that the cooler weather necessitated it.

Yes, Regina Yoder was a champion traveler, happy and excited. Her mother, on the other hand, was tired.

Mighty tired! Only Regina's obvious excitement kept Amanda from turning cranky. But sometime around two in the morning, when Regina was cuddled next to her, sleeping deeply, and most of the other folks on the bus were sleeping, too, Amanda realized that she was just as excited as her daughter.

And thankful to have something new to look forward to.

After all, it wasn't every day that a woman took a fifteen-hour bus ride north to see a man she'd only spent five days with. And to bring her daughter along, too?

She was a little embarrassed about the trip. Well, not embarrassed as much as hesitant to tell the strangers on the bus about her private business. So she kept to herself more than usual, and was thankful no one pushed her for information when she answered their questions in a vague way.

Sure enough, dawn had come, the rising sun bringing with it yet another chance for a quick breakfast, and an excellent way to see the countryside. She and Regina had passed the last two hours looking for different state license plates.

Now they were only twenty miles away from the Berlin German Village Market, where Roman had said he would be waiting for them in his buggy. Nervous flutters had begun to dance in her stomach as soon as they'd entered the state of Ohio. Now that they were so close, she wondered how she was going to appear calm and relaxed when she and Roman came face to face again.

Or when she met his whole family!

What would they think of her? she wondered. Would they be eager to meet her? Or instead wish that Roman was interested in someone a little younger, or at least a woman who hadn't been married before?

Or maybe even they wished he was seeing someone who didn't have a child.

Knotting her fists, Amanda frowned. One would have thought she would have outgrown such nervousness. After all, she'd already been married and had buried a husband. It's not like she was an anxious teenager.

Regina tapped her on her arm. "Mamm, did you see all the snow outside?"

Craning her neck over her sweet daughter's white *kapp* and black bonnet covering a pair of braids that had long since started to fray, Amanda gazed at the huge expanse of hills and valleys covered with a thick blanket of snow. "It's pretty, indeed. Why, it looks just like the clouds have come to visit us."

As Amanda hoped, Regina giggled. "Do you think we're going to get to play in the snow?"

"Of course. I'm sure Roman will let you play in it as much as you want."

"I can't wait to roll around in it. And make a snow angel."

Her daughter had been fascinated by snow angels ever since she'd seen a picture book of Amish children playing in the winter. "I'm sure you will make a mighty fine snow angel."

"And then I want to see Roman's horses."

"You will. He's coming with a van and driver. We'll get to his farm quickly."

"I want to see his cows, and the chickens. Oh! And the pigs, too."

The older couple they were traveling next to laughed. "Just wait until you smell the farm animals, Regina. That's when you might change your mind. And snow is cold. You might not like that much at first. It takes some getting used to."

"I'm going to like it all," Regina stated confidently. "I'm sure of it."

Amanda felt Regina would like it. She had always been a happy girl, and eager to try new experiences—or at least she had until Wesley had died. Her father had been like that, Amanda recalled. He'd been an easygoing man. The very best of husbands.

"Look," Anna, the Mennonite lady next to them said, pointing out the window, "We're almost there."

Once again, Amanda craned her neck. Then gulped as she saw the green sign stating that they were now in Berlin.

"You're going to love it here," Anna said.

"We're only here for a short visit," Amanda replied quickly. Though she wasn't quite sure if she was assuring Anna or herself.

Regina started bouncing up and down in her seat. "Settle, child," Amanda cautioned.

Then, all too soon, they had arrived at the German Village Market. For the next few minutes, Amanda busied herself with gathering all their belongings and making sure Regina was bundled in her scarf, black bonnet, and thick wool coat.

"Let's go," she finally said. Leading the way down the aisle, into the sunny day that beckoned through the doorway of the bus, they were met with a burst of cold air.

"Brrr!" Regina said.

"Indeed, child," Amanda replied with a tight smile. "It is cold and snowy and sunny. All at the same time."

"Amanda? Regina?"

She turned to find Roman striding toward them, an intriguing combination of smiles and confidence.

Her pulsed started racing as Regina pulled away from her hand and scampered to Roman. She told herself it was simply because she was no longer holding on to her daughter.

Roman picked up Regina and spun her around. Regina squealed happily.

And then Amanda felt short of breath. Surely that was due to the fact that it was so cold her breath was a puff of vapor in front of her lips.

But when he settled Regina on the ground again, then started forward, looking at no one else but her, Amanda knew she couldn't fool herself any longer.

She was foolish and delighted and excited and happy—all things that had been absent from her life for much too long.

She held the feeling tight and hoped it would stay deep in her heart for a very long time.

Or at least for a few hours.

"Peter, I need you home again," Marie said into the phone, wishing—not for the first time—that they had to go to a phone shanty like the Old Order Amish. Though she was grateful not to be out in the cold, she privately thought that having a phone in the kitchen sometimes created more problems than it helped. It was a struggle to have a private conversation in the busiest room in the house.

"I know my being gone is hard on you, but the therapists say I need to stay here a little while longer. No one wants me to have a relapse."

She was so frustrated she felt tears prick her eyes. "So you're sure you have to stay?"

He sighed. "You know coming here wasn't an easy decision for me. I don't want to leave until they say I'm ready."

"I know you don't," she said around a cough.

"Marie, are you sick?"

"It's just a little cough. It's nothing."

He paused. "Marie, you have to know I wouldn't wish this on you. I know you're having a difficult time. But I have faith in you. You are a strong woman, and I have a feeling that you are doing a *gut* job keeping everything together—even with a cough," he teased.

She smiled in spite of herself. "I'm doing my best. I don't know if it's good or not."

"I'm sure you are doing great."

His confidence in her felt good, but Marie ached to lean on him. Usually, they'd end each day going over things, rehashing discussions they'd had with the kids or with friends or other family members. She'd grown to rely on that time to reflect on the way she or he handled things. "I hate complaining to you."

"Complain all you want," he murmured. "You've earned that right."

Just because she was strong didn't mean she wanted to be strong all the time. And just because she knew it was all right to complain and whine, well it didn't make her feel any better. If anything, it made her feel like she was living a lie. Here, everyone in the family thought she was being supportive and kind. . . .

But inside, she was harboring a multitude of secret complaints. The worst of which was that she resented Peter for leaving her to deal with everything.

His voice as smooth as silk, Peter prodded her to open up more, "Why don't you tell me what's going on?"

"Roman is picking up the woman he met in Florida right now. And Viola left for Belize."

"How was she when you dropped her off?"

"Excited, but nervous."

"That sounds like our Viola."

She smiled, enjoying his comment. Then, she steeled herself. "And, ah, it turns out your father was married before and had a child."

"What?"

"Oh, yes. He only met your mother after they passed away. Peter, did you know about any of this?"

"*Nee!* Not at all."

"Well, it was news to all of us, too," she said.

"What happened? Did he say?"

"He didn't tell us much, but I went and asked him for more information. And," she added proudly, "after a bit of hemming and hawing, he told me a bit more." Briefly, she told him about how Aaron had met Laura Beth and Ben, how they died . . . and about how Laura Beth's family blamed him for her death.

"Maybe that's why he married Mamm and moved away."

"Maybe so."

After a pause, he said, "What else is going on?"

"Nothing besides preparing for Lorene's wedding."

He whistled low. "That's enough, I think."

"Indeed." She twirled the telephone cord around her finger and chuckled, enjoying their conversation.

"How are the livestock? Have the seeds come in that I ordered for spring planting?"

"I don't know."

"What do you mean? Marie, that's our livelihood."

Sometimes men were so dense. "Come now, Peter. You know I haven't had time to think about plants. You'll have to ask Roman or John or Sam about that."

"Please ask them and let me know next time I call."

"I'll try. But please, try to come home soon." Closing her eyes, she felt full of regret. She didn't want to be this kind of person. But it was as if the devil had gotten ahold of her and was making her say things where before she'd only thought them.

A clatter jangled outside the kitchen window, followed by Elsie's happy cry. "They're here!"

"I must go, Peter."

"Oh. Well, all right . . . I'll try to call you again soon."

"Don't worry about calling. Just get better," she snapped,

then immediately felt contrite. "I'm sorry. I don't mean to sound so terrible. I'm just feeling overwhelmed."

"I know. Hey, Marie?"

"Yes?"

"*Ich liebe dich*."

Her heart softened. "I love you, too."

"Soon, this will all be in the past. Try to remember that."

"I'll do my best," she said wearily. She knew he was right. But she feared she was just about at the end of her rope.

She needed her husband. She needed her partner, her helpmate back. Quickly.

Lord, what was happening to her? Opening her eyes, she looked across the room and spied Lovina lurking in the doorway. It was obvious that she'd been eavesdropping.

Marie wished she would have been surprised. "I guess you heard me talking about Aaron and Laura Beth and Ben?"

Twin spots of color lit her cheeks. "I . . . I did."

"Peter needed to know," she said in a rush.

"I agree. If I've learned anything over the last few weeks, it's that some secrets come back to haunt us. It's better to talk about things."

As they heard the van doors close, Marie pointed to the door. "I better go out there."

"*Jah*. I . . . I think I'll wait here. No sense in us all descending on poor Amanda."

Feeling wearier than ever, Marie turned away and started walking outside. Ready to greet their houseguests . . . and to pretend that everything was a wonderful as it ever was.

chapter eighteen

As Lovina stood in the shadows of the hallway, listening to Roman introduce his mother and Elsie to his guests, she knew she'd made the right decision.

It really was best to wait to say her hellos.

To her ears, Amanda and Roman sounded a little reserved, a little nervous around each other. Marie sounded hesitant but friendly.

Elsie, on the other hand, seemed especially exuberant and excited.

Lovina smiled at that. Elsie's happy, honest personality helped just about every situation.

As the stilted conversation continued, Lovina leaned her head against the hall wall and smiled softly. It all sounded so ordinary. So right. So like what a "normal" family should sound like.

Lovina heard the kitchen chairs scraping against the wood floor as they were pulled out. She heard the clinking of Marie's good china as she poured coffee and served blueberry coffee cake. Every so often, she heard the high-pitched voice of Amanda's daughter. Questions about the bus trip floated her way, as well as gentle teasing about the daughter's fondness for junk food.

When she heard Amanda chuckle, and then the deep voice of Roman combine with hers, Lovina smiled fondly.

Ah! Young love. There was nothing like that first bit of excited nervousness, she mused. Even when she was ninety, she didn't think she'd forget how giddy she'd been around Jack.

Or how nervous she'd been when she'd first met his parents. She'd probably sounded much like Amanda did now, Lovina decided.

But, of course, she'd been nervous for far different reasons.

She hadn't met Mr. and Mrs. Kilgore in their kitchen. Instead, she'd been drunk and on the side of the road. Ambulances and fire trucks had lit up the street, decorating the dark, narrow road with shades of flashing red and orange.

The garish colors had matched the blood on her hands, the blood that stemmed from the gash on her head. And the blood that had covered Jack. The windshield had cut them both when he'd lost control of his car, then slammed it into a fence on the side of the road.

It was a night of horrors. First had been the alcohol that she'd never wanted to drink. Then, she and Jack had gone way too far in a corner of an empty classroom, which had led her to dissolving into near uncontrollable tears and demanding he take her home.

Jack had agreed, but then Billy Thompson had asked for a ride, too. If she'd just said no to Jack's advances, she wouldn't have needed to leave. And if Jack had just said no, Billy wouldn't have been in the backseat of the car.

Then Billy wouldn't have been thrown from the car. He wouldn't have been . . . dead.

She flinched at the memory, of seeing Billy broken and bleeding.

When Jack's parents had arrived, she'd looked at them groggily, in a daze. Fear and grief and disbelief had mixed with the last bit of alcohol in her system and had caused her to be rendered mute. When they'd leaned over her, she'd only stared back at them through foggy vision.

They'd glared at her as if she'd caused the accident. Then they'd surrounded Jack, comforting him as the paramedics loaded him into an ambulance.

She'd gone in the other ambulance to the hospital for X-rays and fifteen stitches.

Her parents had met her at the hospital. But they'd looked confused by the police reports, not sympathetic. No, far from it.

They'd been disgusted by the smell of alcohol on her breath. And bothered by the stunned look of guilt and sadness she couldn't quite hide.

And, of course, shocked and upset by Billy's death.

She'd been released right away, but her parents had refused to let her go see Jack. "He's in surgery, and his parents said he's in no condition to talk to anyone. He's very upset about Billy. Billy was Jack's best friend, you know."

"I know," she said weakly. She'd ached to tell them that of course she'd known that Jack was upset. She'd ached to remind everyone that she wasn't just some girl. After all, she'd been Jack's date for the dance. She'd almost been his girlfriend.

But she'd been too upset to argue. So she'd gone home, carefully unzipped the pretty dress she'd been so proud of, and stepped into the shower.

There, in the privacy of the small space, she'd cried hot tears under a cold spray of water, keeping the water cold on purpose, almost feeling the need to torture herself some more. She'd welcomed how its sting felt like needles on her skin.

Shame and sickness had warred in her stomach, making her realize that it actually was possible to hate herself.

No, she hadn't been able to stop Jack from agreeing to take Billy home. And no, she didn't try to take the blame for Billy's death.

But she had been there. She'd done things she wished she hadn't. She'd learned the difference between the sharp, anxious strike of infatuation and the slow, warm flow of contentment that came with compatibility and love.

When she was dry, she wrapped herself up in a long flannel nightgown, brushed out her hair, and curled into bed.

Then promised herself then and there that she would become someone different. Someone everyone would admire.

And if not admire? At least respect.

A few weeks later, she'd gone out to the country for a day at the farmers' market, and started visiting with a few of the Amish. Later, she'd gotten a job as a teller at the bank. Then, one day Aaron Keim had come to her window and he'd struck her fancy.

Jack's life had changed, too. Because there were rumors that Mr. and Mrs. Thompson were thinking about pressing charges against him, Jack's parents encouraged him to volunteer for the army.

The army had been anxious for volunteers for the conflict in Vietnam.

Stunned that she could still cry about those days after all this time, Lovina wiped the tears from her cheeks and forced herself to concentrate on the Lord instead. How He directed them always to the right place, even when it didn't seem like it at the time. Looking back on all that had happened forty years before, Lovina wondered how she could ever have been so naïve.

She'd been a bright girl—but for a brief moment in time, she'd had her head turned by the smile of a too-handsome man. She'd let her usual common sense get turned on its side for the chance of excitement.

Then she'd realized that it hadn't been excitement that she'd craved.

Instead, it had been the need to feel wanted. Maybe even special.

Never wanting to be in such a position again, she'd given up that craving, just like an alcoholic gave up the taste for liquor.

But, perhaps like the alcoholic, that craving had never completely left her. It had only been tamped down.

Ignored.

"Mommi? Mommi, where are you?" Elsie called out.

Pushing away from the wall, Lovina pinched her cheeks, then smoothed a wrinkle from her dress. Then she stepped forward with smile, just as if she'd only just entered the main house. "I am here, Elsie. What is wrong?"

"Not a thing. Not a single thing," she replied, all smiles. "I was wondering where you were, that's all."

"I haven't been far. I never am."

"I'm glad about that. Oh, Mommi, come on," she encouraged, grabbing her hand. "You've got to come meet Amanda and Regina."

Lovina curved her hand around Elsie's but didn't let herself be dragged down the hall. "Before we go, tell me what you think. How are they?"

"Pretty and sweet," Elsie said immediately. "You're going to like them." Then she lowered her voice. "But the best part is Roman. Oh, Mommi, you should see how he acts around them," she commented, her voice bright with amusement. "He is smitten!"

"You think so?"

"He's completely head over heels! He can hardly take his eyes off Amanda. I bet he hardly even realizes that we're in the room."

Remembering those feelings, of aching for just a few moments of privacy, Lovina chuckled, "I bet he realizes that."

"Barely." Elsie tugged. "Come on, Mommi. I promise, you've never seen anything like it."

Lovina laughed. "Yes, I must see this smitten boy."

Two minutes later when she saw his face, Lovina knew Elsie had hit the nail on the head. Roman Keim was completely smitten.

In love.

But her favorite granddaughter was wrong—she *had* seen the like. It had been how she'd looked when she'd been taken in by foolish wishes and wants, only to pay the price for it in spades.

And after all that?

Why, she'd made sure she never dreamed about such things ever again.

Belize was beautiful, perched right on the Caribbean Sea. Viola spied turquoise blue waters and white sandy beaches as the plane made its approach to Belize City. It looked like nothing she'd ever seen before.

Definitely very, very different from snowy Berlin, Ohio.

Only as the plane was about to land did Viola see an assortment of shacks. Pressing her nose to the window, she saw more disturbing sights. Dirty, cramped narrow streets. Worn-out vehicles and skinny children.

She knew Edward was there because there were people

in need. But now, for the first time, she wondered if she was ready to be faced with people whose lives were filled with such hardship.

When she stepped off the plane and followed the rest of the passengers along the tarmac and into the main airport, she felt as if all her senses had come alive. Belize felt hot and humid and smelled of sand and salt and humanity. She noticed both smiling faces and the wary, watchful eyes of men.

She felt small and insignificant. For twenty-two years, she'd been content to manage herself and her family in her small town. She'd felt brave and independent when she'd taken a job at Daybreak. She'd felt vaguely maternal toward her twin, always ready to step in and help her life run smoothly.

But this? It put everything in her past into a new perspective.

A little shiver snaked its way up her spine as her unease grew. What if she wasn't ready to live here? What if it was too big of a change from what she was used to?

How was she going to be able to tell Edward that? And how was she going to live with the knowledge that she wasn't nearly as strong as she'd thought she was?

She kept her head down and followed the officials' directions as best she could. As she walked through the airport, she felt as if her black stockings and heavy winter dress were slowly suffocating her.

Already her neck was sweating, what with both her *kapp* and black bonnet covering her hair.

She felt like such a fool. Ed had reminded her that it was warm and muggy in Belize. But for some reason she hadn't put that information to good use. Instead of packing lots of lighter dresses, she'd merely packed the three that were hanging in her closet . . . each one warmer than the next.

"You okay, Viola?" Karen asked.

Karen had sat beside her on the plane, along with Karen's husband of one day, Bob. Karen and Bob had flown down to Belize for their honeymoon and seemed as intrigued by Viola's reasons for traveling as she was about the *Englischers'* fancy wedding stories.

Karen, especially, had acted delighted when Viola told her about her recent engagement, and Edward's mission. They'd chatted the whole way to Belize, and Viola had been so thankful for their company.

But they weren't friends, of course. There was no way Viola could mention any of the doubts she was experiencing.

"I'm okay."

"Nervous?" Karen asked.

"I am, but excited, too," she admitted.

"We'll stay with you until you find your guy," Bob said as they continued through the customs area.

"Oh, that's not necessary . . . but thank you." She really didn't want to be by herself in the unfamiliar country.

At last, the three of them were walking toward the main part of the terminal.

"We're almost out of here," Karen teased. "I bet you can hardly stand the butterflies in your stomach."

Viola smiled, but was too nervous to acknowledge just how correct Karen's words were.

What if Edward wasn't outside waiting for her? What would she do then?

But then she didn't have to worry any longer because Ed was right there, waiting for her with a broad smile on his face. "Viola! Over here!" he called out.

"Is that him?" Karen asked.

"Oh, yes." For a moment, all she could do was stare at

Edward. Yes, he was still as handsome as she'd remembered.

Bob laughed. "I think you're in good hands now. Enjoy your reunion, Viola."

"*Danke*. And God bless," she said quickly before practically racing away from the couple.

She only faintly heard their soft laughs as she skirted around a number of people, then finally got to his side.

"Edward, I made it!" she said with a smile.

"You did. Oh, Viola, I'm so happy you're really here."

He was beaming. Everything inside her wanted to launch herself into his arms, to raise her chin for a kiss. But of course it wasn't seemly. She made do with smiling into his eyes, mentally comparing his appearance with the one in her memory. Thank goodness, he still seemed exactly the same.

As if Ed couldn't stand not touching her, he reached out and squeezed her hand. "I'm so glad to see you. How was your trip?"

"It was fine." In truth, her first plane flight wasn't nearly as scary as she'd anticipated. "A nice lady was sitting next to me on the first flight. She helped me switch planes in Miami. And then I was seated next to a honeymoon couple on the way here."

Scanning the area, she saw Bob hail a taxi. "That's them there."

"They look nice."

"Oh, they were. I heard all about their wedding. And then Karen wanted to know all about Amish ones. It made the time go fast."

He squeezed her hand again. "Viola, I knew you would be okay traveling. You're a strong woman."

She beamed. Maybe he was right. Maybe she was stronger than she'd thought, than she'd ever imagined. "You know what? Roman said the same thing. Of course, I thought he was teasing."

"I don't know if he was teasing or not. But I am proud of you." He reached down and grabbed the handle of her suitcase. "Let's get on our way, I can hardly wait to show you around."

As they walked to the crowded curb, the noises and foreign smells assaulted her again. "It's mighty different here. Different than what I imagined."

"That's because we're in the city. The mission is in the country, on the outskirts of the area. And I promise, the beach is beautiful. You're going to love going to the beach."

"I saw the ocean when we flew in," she admitted. "The water looked like the color of one of my teal dresses. Do you think one day we can go look at it?"

He scoffed. "Viola, we're going to go to the beach right now."

"What?"

"I made plans for us, for your first day here in Belize," he said with a broad grin. "The folks at the mission helped. Here's what's going to happen. Manuel is going to take your suitcase directly to the mission while we go do something else."

"That is possible?"

"Of course it is, silly. We're a family here. We help each other out. Everyone understands that I want some time with you all to myself. After all, it's been six weeks."

"It has been a long time. . . . "

"See? That's why we're going to play lazy tourists for a little bit. I'm going to take you to the beach. And after you get your toes sandy, I'm going to take you to a nice little restaurant and have lunch. After that, we're going to go out to the edge of the rain forest, so you can see what I was talking about when I wrote that the rain forest was the most beautiful place, ever." He winked. "Maybe we'll even see a parrot."

She was taken aback. "I didn't think we'd ever have days like this."

"No?"

"I thought we'd be working." She shook her head, irritated by her word choice. "I mean, serving."

"Viola, we do lots of good works here, and we work hard, truly we do. But even missionaries need to enjoy life, and you're only here for a few days. I want you to see how pretty it is here—Belize is a beautiful country. So, what do you say? Would you like to go walk on the beach, barefoot?"

"Um, all right." Wearily, she glanced at her stocking-covered legs. She was going to have to visit the ladies' room and take them off soon. Oh, why hadn't she thought about the heat when she'd been packing?

At her rather unenthusiastic reply, Ed's grin faltered. "Is that okay with you? Did you have something else in mind?"

Now she felt stupid. Here Edward was attempting to make her first hours in Belize wonderful, and all she was doing was acting upset because she was dressed wrong.

"I didn't have anything in mind," she said weakly. "You caught me off guard. For some reason I assumed we'd go straight to the mission first. I mean, I want to see it. I want to see the work you're doing. . . ." What *they'd* be doing.

"I'm anxious for you to see it, too. Of course I am. But once we get there, it will be all work, and we'll be surrounded by a dozen people at all times."

His gaze flickered over her lightly, almost like a caress, warming her insides and making her even more aware of the fact that there was much more between them than just friendship. "I want to spend a little bit of time with you first, Viola," he said, his voice hinting of love and desire. "I've missed you."

"I've missed you, too." She noticed that her voice had turned slightly breathless. Embarrassingly so.

Grinning, he took her hand again. Squeezed it gently. "I can't wait for you to fall in love with this place, Viola. I promise, I'm going to do everything I possibly can to make you fall in love with life here."

"Is that right?"

He nodded. "See, the alternative can't be considered."

"And what is the alternative?"

"That you never want to come back," he said simply. "That you decide that no matter how much you might love me, you don't love me enough. That I couldn't bear."

Don't love me enough. The phrase wasn't something she'd ever heard before, but it made sense. With all that had been going on with her family, she now understood that such a thing could happen. Relationships were all about balance. Balancing the good and the bad. What was easy and what couldn't be borne. What was worth everything . . . and what was worth nothing at all.

"I understand," she said.

Some of the hope fled from his eyes. She turned away, feeling slightly guilty. She knew she hadn't given him the unconditional approval he needed.

But she now knew better than to promise things she couldn't be sure of.

chapter nineteen

It had been years since Amanda had been a true guest in another person's home. Of late, life hadn't given her any time for things like that. First, she and Wesley had had Regina, and all the time constraints that came with a new baby. Not a year after that, Wesley had been diagnosed with cancer.

Her days had become a matter of survival instead of enjoyment. Each morning, she'd wake up with only thoughts about Wesley's health and Regina's needs filling her head. She'd jump out of bed and attempt to help them both as much as she could.

The only time she'd made for herself was for sleep . . . and some days, she'd only given in to that grudgingly.

She'd had no time for visiting friends or sipping tea or planting a garden or simply enjoying a good book.

After Wesley went to heaven, she'd been too overcome with grief to do anything but attempt to get through each day the best that she could. On some days, her main goal, besides caring for Regina, was to try to last until bedtime before dissolving into tears.

When the dark cloud of grief began to lift, she'd focused on Regina's needs. Her sweet little girl had been as traumatized by her father's death as Wesley's parents and Amanda had been. She'd become withdrawn and nervous. Amanda had soon realized that only a steady, reliable schedule would help her. Regina had needed structure like most other small children needed naps or a favorite toy. She'd craved the same foods, the same activities, the same schedule day after day. A way of life that had no surprises, nothing to catch her off guard or make her worry.

Amanda had been happy to oblige her. After all, that reliability had eased her grief, as well. Concentrating on filling a day hour by hour was far easier than contemplating a life without her husband.

Which was why she couldn't help but smile as she followed Roman's mother down the hall. Even eight months ago, Amanda would have doubted that they'd be able to travel to a far-off state, visit with strangers, or sleep in an unfamiliar bed.

To do all this because another man had caught her eye would've been unthinkable.

God was amazing in His glory. Of that, she had no doubt.

"This is your room," Marie said as she opened the second door on the left. "I hope you will find it comfortable."

Amanda walked inside, finding a wide queen-sized bed covered with a thick ivory quilt in a double shoofly pattern. A small little trundle bed covered in a pink, white, and yellow fan pattern stood right beside it.

Beneath her feet, wood floors glowed from years of care. And not a speck of dust could be found on the dresser or bedside table. Starched white curtains covered the window, and a pair of thick well-washed, soft-looking quilts lay over a rocking chair. The room smelled like lemon oil and Windex.

It smelled like someone had gone to a great deal of trouble to make things nice for them.

"This is a lovely bedroom. *Danke,*" she said politely.

Her daughter, however, was far more exuberant. "Ooh!"

Regina scampered to the small bed and clambered on top of it. "This bed is just right for you, Momma."

While Marie gasped, Amanda chuckled. "That is a *gut* joke, but I'll take the bigger bed, if you do not mind." Turning to Marie, she said, "We do appreciate your hospitality. I guess you can tell that staying here is a special treat for us."

"It's our pleasure," Marie said. "We were looking forward to meeting you."

She looked like she wanted to add something more—a whole lot more—when Roman appeared at the door. "Here are your suitcases."

"*Danke*, Roman."

After setting Amanda's in front of her, he comically crossed the room toward Regina, acting as if her little suitcase weighed a ton. "What did you put in your bag, Regina? Rocks?"

Her eyes widened. "*Nee*. Only my dresses and my nightgown. And my toothbrush, too."

"I was only teasin' ya, Regina," he said with a smile. Holding out his hand, he said, "Would you care to go to the barn with me?"

She stilled. "Can I see the *pikk*?"

"Of course. Sam the pig has been asking where you were."

"He has?"

Roman looked at Amanda and smiled. "He's been counting the minutes. Let's go put on your cloak and go see him. And Chester, too."

"Who's Chester?"

"You'll see. If you're ready."

In answer, Regina slid off the quilt and reached for his hand. "Bye, Momma," she said before walking with him down the hall.

"Bye," Amanda replied, feeling both relieved and somewhat at a loss. For so long, Regina had clung to her. It was a bit disconcerting to watch her daughter take another healing step forward into the world without her by her side.

Marie watched the pair of them depart with something that looked very much like the shock Amanda was feeling. "I've never seen Roman like this, Amanda. He's usually much more reserved."

"My Regina is, too."

"I'm glad they're getting along."

"Me, too. Regina is mighty fond of Roman, and has been ever since he asked her if she liked ice cream, too."

Marie laughed. "My son always did have a sweet tooth."

"So does my daughter." After sharing a smile with Marie, she added seriously, "I have to admit that I'm grateful for their friendship. Regina's needed someone in her life who makes her laugh and smile."

"I believe we all do," Marie murmured before sitting on the edge of the bed. "She is an adorable girl, Amanda. You must be so proud of her."

"She's my pride and joy," Amanda said, taking a seat on the padded chair next to the window. "With Wesley gone, I've kept asking God to help me raise her. I think He heard my prayers. I couldn't have done much without His help."

"I've raised children, too. And, though I've often given our Lord the glory, I sometimes selfishly like to think we mothers have to take some of the credit for wonderful children."

Regina smiled. "Perhaps. But truthfully, she is an easy child. She has Wesley's temperament. I got lucky in that regard."

At the mention of Wesley, Marie's easy expression sobered. "I imagine the two of you have had a time of it. Both of you were too young to lose a husband and a father."

"We have had a time of it," Amanda agreed. Softly, she added, "Losing Wesley so young was nothing any of us could have anticipated." However, she refused to dwell on it. Not any longer. "But we are doing better."

Marie stood up. "I'll let you have some privacy, but I did want to take this moment and ask that you please consider our home yours. Feel free to help yourself to whatever you or Regina might need, whether it be more towels or a late-night snack."

"That is kind of you."

"It's our pleasure. Roman is happy you are here, so of course we are happy, too."

"*Danke,*" she said as Marie walked out of the room. When she was alone, she closed her eyes and gave thanks to the Lord for bringing her on the journey, then lay down and rested her eyes for a few moments. Traveling with a four-year-old was not always easy, no matter how agreeable the child was.

And leaving her in-laws hadn't been easy, either. Marlene had tried her best to understand Amanda's need to visit Roman and his family in Ohio, but Amanda knew she hadn't understood Amanda's feelings at all.

Plus, Amanda had her own nerves to contend with. Over and over she second-guessed herself, and questioned her reasons for the trip.

Then, once she felt like she had gotten her head on straight, she'd find herself worrying about Roman's family. What if they didn't like her? What if Regina acted up and they thought she was a naughty girl and, therefore, Amanda a bad mother? Would they think she presumptuous to come visit a man she barely knew?

And then, just when she set her mind at ease about that, she'd start fretting about Roman. It had taken a huge leap of faith to take this journey all on the basis of a brief interlude and a series of long-distance phone calls and letters.

It felt almost foolish to let such a short relationship dictate such a big step.

Then, too, she'd feared Roman would seem different in his home surroundings than he had on vacation. She'd been afraid that he'd be cool to her. Distant.

But he wasn't acting distant, she reminded herself. *He's been warm and attentive and loving.*

Yawning, she let her mind drift back to their first sight of each other at the German Village Market. From the first moment their eyes met, all of her doubts drifted away. Right then and there, she'd felt his warm regard for her. And she'd felt drawn to his side, felt that ache inside her, the kind that she'd first felt with Wesley but had later pretended had been childish infatuation.

But now she knew better.

No, none of what she had feared had happened. Instead, everything was as good as it could possibly get. Surely nothing could go wrong now.

With that in mind, she drifted off to her first easy slumber in five days.

It was fun, seeing the farm through Regina's eyes. She was fascinated with everything in the barn, from the scent of hay to the plow and other farm implements to the pile of horse manure.

"That's stinky," she said, wrinkling her nose.

"I agree," Roman said.

"I'm glad we ride bikes or walk where I live."

"So even your grandparents don't keep a buggy and horses?"

"*Nee.*" Gazing at Chester, she said, "I like your horses, though."

"This is Chester, and I do believe he likes you, too."

Her little face brightened. "You think so?"

"I know so. Why, look at him watching you."

She lifted a hand about a foot, obviously wanting to touch the horse, but then thrust it back down to her side. "Is Chester soft?"

"His coat is. Do you want to pet him?"

"Will he mind?"

"Not at all. Chester is a sturdy horse. And, like I said, he wants to be your friend." Knowing that she'd like to pet his velvety nose best, Roman said, "Okay if I pick you up?"

"Uh-huh."

"Here you go, then," he said as he picked her up by the waist and held her securely against his hip. "Lean forward and give Chester a pat on his forehead." When he saw that she was being gentle, with his other hand, he gently rubbed the horse's muzzle. "See how I'm being careful here? Do you think you can rub him softly, too?"

She nodded.

"All right then. You try petting his nose."

Tentatively, she followed his example. He was rewarded with a beaming smile. "Roman, his nose is soft."

"It is indeed." Just then, Chester shook his head as if he were nodding. "Look at that, Regina. He's agreeing with ya, too."

She giggled, and the exuberant happiness warmed his heart, as did the realization that he was actually enjoying every minute in her company. He liked holding her and introducing her to his life.

"Ready to get down and see the pig?"

"*Jah!*"

He'd just put her down when his grandfather appeared at the door.

"I heard we had a guest, so I came to say hello," his grandfather said softly.

"Hi, Dawdi. This is Regina, Grandfather. Regina, this is . . ." What should she call him? Mr. Keim?

"Regina, you may call me Dawdi Aaron, if you'd like."

"But I already have a grandpa." Regina looked worried, like she was about to do something wrong.

"Lots of *kinner* have more than one grandfather," he said easily. "Or, you could call me Aaron. I'm fine with that."

Roman tensed as he waited for Regina to make up her mind about his usually stern grandfather.

"Do you know where the pig is, Dawdi Aaron?" she asked.

His grandfather's answering smile could have lit up the entire barn. "I know more about that pig than most anyone else. You want to see it?"

"Uh-huh. Roman says he's smelly, though."

"That's only because Roman needs to give him a bath."

Regina's eyes widened, then to Roman's astonishment, she left his side and scampered to his grandfather's. And to his greater amazement, his grandfather held out his hand to the little girl, and she took it like they'd been friends forever.

Then, away they went, Regina asking him questions and his grandfather answering each one carefully. Roman followed slowly behind, trying to remember if he'd ever been so comfortable around either of his grandparents. He couldn't remember a time, but surely there had been?

When they reached Sam's pen, Roman watched Regina grip Aaron's hand tighter. "He's a mighty big *pikk*."

"Yep."

"And he does smell."

"He does, but he can't help that, I'm sorry to say. It's a pig's way to smell. They're smelly by nature."

"My *mamm* makes me take baths. Sam needs one, too."

With a wink in his direction, his grandfather said, "You hear that Roman?"

"I hear you, Dawdi."

Sam, not used to so much attention, lifted his head and stared at Regina, his beady dark eyes looking like he was sizing her up for his next meal.

Sam was an enormous Yorkshire pig, and Roman prepared himself for Regina to back off quickly, maybe even be a little scared of him. As he walked to Regina's other side, he pressed a comforting hand between her shoulder blades. "Sam is big and smells, but he's not mean, Regina. He won't hurt you."

"Can I pet him?"

Aaron laughed. "I think not. He's not one for companionship, unless it's with the lady pigs. Would you like to see the hens now? I do believe we might find us an egg."

"Uh-huh."

"Roman, I'll take good care of her, if you want to see if your grandmother could make us some hot chocolate." Comically, he paused. "Do you even know what hot chocolate is, Regina, living down in the sun and sand like you do?"

"I know what hot chocolate is."

"Would you like to have a *cuppa* with my wife and me?"

"*Jah*."

Roman backed up a step. "I'll go talk to Mommi. Oh, and Grandfather?"

"*Jah?*"

"*Danke.*"

"*Nee,* Roman. I am the one who should be giving thanks. This little visitor of yours has brightened up my day."

As Roman noticed how Regina was beaming at Aaron, he said, "I think the feeling is mutual."

chapter twenty

Edward opened a thick, heavy wooden door with a flourish. "And this, Viola, is our main office and meeting area."

As she stepped into the cool, large room with the cement floor, Viola took care to keep a smile on her face. It took effort because inside she was feeling slightly dismayed.

Though she'd loved their visit to the beach and the rain forest, somehow, she'd hoped the exquisite sights would make her feel more comfortable and at ease . . . even though she was in a foreign country.

Oh, she had found a number of things awe-inspiring. Her first view of the ocean had been mesmerizing, and she'd been intrigued by the beautiful trees and flowers that had surrounded them.

But it had also been a bit overwhelming.

Actually, more than a bit. She was realizing that she'd been terribly sheltered, living her whole life in rural Ohio. Experiencing a new place was far different from reading about it.

What she really needed was a few minutes to cool off and rest her head. It had been so long since she'd seen Edward—part of her just wanted a moment to give thanks that they were together again.

But Edward, on the other hand, seemed more intent on showing her everything about Belize and the mission as quickly as possible.

She hadn't wanted to disappoint him, so she'd listened attentively and followed him as quickly as she could.

But the tour was starting to take its toll. She was overheated, and feeling a little nauseous—surely the result of a nervous stomach, mixed with the sights and smells of unfamiliar food.

Now, this room smelled of a curious combination of disinfectant and mildew. In the middle of it were two old couches and a pair of older looking metal desks. Against the far wall was a pair of doors with heavy locks on them. And though it was cooler, and they were blessed with two ceiling fans, it didn't feel cool enough. Under her apron, her dress was sticking to her skin. She ached to rip off her hot dress and stand underneath an ice-cold shower.

"Come over and meet everyone, Viola," Ed said.

She walked to where he was pointing. Several men and women were gathered near a table loaded with strange-looking food. Some of the people gathered were obviously Amish or Mennonite. Others were locals.

All of them were smiling at her.

She tried her best to smile back, but all she could think about were the trays of unfamiliar food. And of the skinned animals she'd seen in the street market.

And of how she was going to be expected to eat so as not to appear rude.

Her stomach gurgled. In an effort to keep her composure, she looked away from the food, toward the side of the room. There, a somewhat scrawny-looking orange cat was chasing a mouse. A lizard was climbing one of the walls.

All of a sudden, she felt a surge of resentment toward Edward.

Why had her fiancé never mentioned just how primitive

things were in any of his letters? All he'd talked about were sunsets and smiling, grateful believers. Never had he mentioned the dirt and the mice.

Or the lizards.

Or that the mission was surrounded by sharp, ominous-looking barbed wire. And that he'd had to hire guards to stand at the mission's entrance.

When he'd talked about his living arrangements, he'd mentioned the thick walls that kept the rooms cool. He'd told her all about the way he could smell the ocean breeze while lying down in bed.

Viola felt like her feet were glued to the floor. Each step forward felt like she was inching toward oblivion.

Everything inside her screamed to turn around. To rush back home, where she could be in control of things. Where she knew the language, and knew the rules.

Where she was comfortable and felt safe.

Where she wasn't so, so terribly hot.

Edward moved closer to her side, nudged her a bit farther forward. Then grasped her shoulders. "Viola, I'd like you to meet our team."

"Hello," she said, wishing that he would remove his heavy, hot hands. They felt like brands on her shoulders, pinning her in place.

"This is Viola."

She kept a smile pasted on her face like a porcelain doll as people introduced themselves. She muttered her thanks when they pushed a plate into her hands, full of food she didn't recognize.

As she stared at it in wonder, Ed's easy expression turned determined. "They made this in your honor," he whispered. "You've got to eat."

"I have no silverware."

Picking up a tortilla from his plate, he scooped up some of the strange-looking meat into it and brought it to his mouth. "Like this," he said, demonstrating easily.

Feeling sick to her stomach, she dutifully followed his lead, knowing she was being watched the whole time. But the food was spicy and she was exhausted and shaky. Nervous about making a good impression. And still full from their lunch.

And then, just as if she were right in the middle of an awful nightmare, her stomach began to churn and clench. In a panic, she thrust the plate at him and looked frantically for the bathroom.

But of course there wasn't one.

Standing up, she covered her mouth with a hand. Looking left and right, she searched for an exit. For anywhere to go.

"Here," a lady said, grabbing her wrist. In no time at all, she dragged Viola out back into the scorching sun, across a dirt yard, to a dilapidated outhouse. Once there, she yanked open the door.

Viola ran in and promptly threw up just as the door slammed behind her.

Tears stung her eyes as she heaved, then as she tried to regain some self-control.

And though it was dark and hot and the stench was terrible, she stayed inside. At least here she had some privacy.

At least here she could admit to herself that she wasn't okay.

Slowly, tears traipsed down her cheeks, dropping to the front of her dress.

She hated herself right at that moment. This wasn't the type of person she wanted to be.

Shame mixed with the heat. She'd just completely embarrassed Ed in front of everyone. She'd just been unforgivably rude and disrespectful to her hosts. Their first impression of her had been that of a flighty girl who couldn't take the slightest bit of discomfort.

And now she had to go out and face them all, without even being able to wash her hands or rinse out her mouth.

There in the tiny structure, she attempted to gather her courage. She needed to go out and apologize to everyone. To make amends.

And she was going to do that. She was. Just as soon as she was able.

But two knocks interrupted her plans. Yet again, she was causing trouble.

"Viola? Viola, are you all right?"

It was Edward. And he sounded concerned, not angry.

And, no, she wasn't okay. But how could she tell him that?

Taking a deep breath, she opened the door and walked out into the blinding sunlight. And tried to look anywhere but at him.

"Did you have a nice nap?" Marie asked when Amanda walked into the front parlor of the Keim house.

"I did. That bed was so comfortable, the moment I lay down and closed my eyes, I fell fast asleep. I didn't mean to sleep so long, though."

Roman's mother smiled kindly. "Please don't apologize. Traveling is hard work, especially with a child in tow."

"I think you're right, though Regina wasn't any trouble," she said, glancing around the quiet room. There were no signs of either Roman or her daughter. A mild undercurrent of panic bubbled in her stomach. "Marie, do you know where Regina is?" Hopefully, she added, "Did she fall asleep, too?"

"Oh no. She's been up the whole time. I believe she's currently having hot chocolate with my husband's parents."

"But she left my room with Roman." Had Roman already passed Regina off onto someone else? If so, her timid little girl was probably feeling lost and alone.

"Regina met my father-in-law when she was exploring the barn. Aaron invited her for hot chocolate. Aaron and Lovina live in the *dawdi haus*. You met Lovina in the kitchen earlier, remember?"

"*Jah*. But I didn't expect Regina to be with anyone but Roman." Of course, as soon as she said that, Amanda realized that she couldn't sound any less gracious.

"I promise, Regina's in good hands," Marie said, not appearing to be offended in the slightest. "If she wasn't happy, they would have brought her to Roman or you."

Thinking about how Marlene both enjoyed Regina's chatty personality but sometimes yearned for frequent breaks from the girl's exuberance, she frowned. "I hope she's not bothering them. Regina can sometimes be a chatterbox." That is, if she felt comfortable.

Marie waved off her concerns. "If she is a chatterbox, I'm sure they are enjoying every minute of it. It's been too long since we've had a four-year-old keeping us company. She's a sweet child, Amanda."

"*Danke*."

"Now, please sit down and relax. I'm eager to get to know you."

Hesitantly, Amanda sat down. She was used to being in charge of Regina, and it felt odd to accept a stranger's help.

Even more peculiar was coming to terms with the fact that Regina was happy with them.

That she didn't need her mother there to hold her hand.

But Amanda knew she should take the opportunity to get to know Roman's family as well. As she settled into an easy chair by the window, she wasn't sure what to say. She was used to people only asking about Wesley, or about being a single mother and widow.

Marie, of course, wouldn't be likely to ask her about Wesley. Not when she was here to see Roman. Which in some ways was a nice change.

So, what was she now, if not just a widow? It was disheartening to not be quite sure of that answer.

Marie gestured to a teapot wrapped in a bright green quilted tea cozy. "I brought an extra cup out in the hopes that you'd be able to share some tea with me," she murmured, her voice as soothing as Amanda was sure the hot tea would be. "Would you care for a cup of spiced orange tea?"

"That sounds heavenly," she said, relaxing. "*Danke*."

"You're welcome." After filling two cups with fragrant tea, she added a splash of milk and a spoonful of sugar to her cup. Then Marie sat back against her chair. "Before I forget to tell you, please let us know if you need to borrow some sweaters or stockings or anything. I imagine this cold weather is something of a shock to your body."

"It is chilly, but I think I'm all right."

"*Gut. Gut*, I'm glad. So, Roman tells me that you're not originally from Florida."

"No, I'm not. I was born in Lancaster County. So, I do have a little bit of experience with winter weather."

"I should say you do! Well, now, that is a pretty area. Are your parents still there?"

"They are. I moved to Florida when Wesley and I married. After he passed away, I found I wasn't eager to leave the sunny weather behind."

"I can only imagine. Roman seemed to enjoy the beach tremendously, and I know my husband's brother and his family do as well." Marie frowned slightly, as if she'd just said something awkward, but Amanda couldn't imagine what she'd said that was out of the ordinary.

"I like Florida," she murmured. Feeling a bit uneasy, she sipped her tea. "And Pinecraft is a wonderful community."

"I'd love to visit one day. So . . . is that where you intend to live? Always?"

Marie's questions were hardly subtle. But Amanda didn't mind. "I don't know," she said simply. She really didn't. Amanda was learning that life was filled with unexpected circumstances, and it did no good to make lots of plans, at least the forever type of plans.

"Ah," Marie said. Obviously she was waiting for Amanda to expand on her answer.

But what could she say? Instead of talking, she sipped her tea again.

Luckily, before the conversation got more stilted, the door opened and Roman came in. The moment their eyes met, she felt something inside her relax. His gaze was warm and loving.

"Hi," he said.

"Hi." Was she smiling as brightly as she thought she was? She felt her cheeks heat when she realized that she must look like a love-struck schoolgirl.

"Would you like to go find Regina with me?"

"I would like that very much." She practically jumped to her feet. "Thank you for the tea, Marie."

"I enjoyed our visit." Roman's mother smiled as she crossed her legs and made no secret that she was pleased by her son's new relationship.

When they walked out the kitchen door and stepped onto the chilly path that led to the *dawdi haus*, Roman's grin broadened. "So, was my mother grilling you? When I walked in, you looked like you would rather be anywhere but sitting in that room."

No way was she going to discuss *that* conversation. "Your mother couldn't have been more gracious. I . . . uh, I think I was still waking up."

"Ah, yes. That must have been it." Taking her hand, he folded both of his around it. "Are you feeling better now that you got some rest?"

"I am. I think I just needed a nap." Looking down at her hand in his, she once again felt a little burst of warmth flow through her. She'd missed Roman.

Running a finger along the back of her hand, gently tracing a line of veins, he said, "Don't worry, all right? No one has any expectations, least of all me. I want you to enjoy a few days in Ohio and for Regina to get a taste of the snow. If you two enjoy a few days off, then that's enough for me."

"Truly? Because, Roman, I don't know what I'm doing." There, that was as honest as she'd dared to be for the last few years.

"I'm glad you don't know. What is happening between us is something new for me, too. I want to enjoy every second of it."

And then, before she could think of anything else to say, he gave her hand a gentle tug and pulled her into the *dawdi haus*.

Any thoughts of quiet contemplation evaporated the moment she heard Regina's chatter.

"Mamm, I saw the *pikk,*" she called out, looking so grown-up from where she sat at the oak table she shared with Roman's grandparents. "His name is Sam and he smells. And I petted a horse's nose, and now I'm having hot chocolate."

Amanda smiled shyly at Mr. and Mrs. Keim. "It sounds like a *wonderful-gut* afternoon."

"It was *wunderbaar*!" Regina said. "I liked everything. I like it here, Mamm." Her daughter's eyes were shining, and for once, she didn't look stressed or worried or like she was trying to be happy when she wasn't.

After all this time, in a place that wasn't even home to them, it seemed Regina had become herself again.

Right there and then, Amanda felt all her doubts about the trip to Ohio fall away. This was what she cared about; this was where her heart lay . . . with Regina.

And having a happy daughter made everything worth it. It gave her hope, too. Hope for a future that was going to be better than she'd imagined. "I'm so glad," she murmured.

Roman glanced her way, making her realize that her voice was hoarser than she'd intended; thick with emotion. She shook her head slightly. "What I meant was, that if today was one of your best days ever, then I am mighty happy," she said lightly, moving closer to pat her daughter gently on the back.

Mrs. Keim didn't look fooled for a moment. She was gazing at Regina steadfastly. As if she knew exactly what it was like to feel pain. "Amanda, won't you join us for some hot chocolate?"

She wasn't really thirsty; she'd just had that cup of tea with Marie. But the offer was kind, and she couldn't pass up an opportunity to sit with Regina and share the treat.

"*Danke,*" she said. When Roman sat down, too, and started

chatting with Regina, Amanda realized that it wasn't just her daughter who'd had a wonderful day. Something special was happening with her, as well.

At the moment, she was happy. Happy almost like she used to be.

chapter twenty-one

Opening the door of the outhouse and stepping into the sun was one of the hardest things Viola had ever done.

Actually, as Ed stared at her in concern, his handsome face expressing no disdain, only worry, Viola realized that she'd never been more miserable in her life.

Well, perhaps she'd been more miserable when she'd been twelve and had been besieged by chicken pox and strep throat at the same time.

But this certainly came in at a close second.

"Edward, I'm so sorry," she murmured yet again as they started walking back into the main building of the mission house. "I don't know what happened to me."

"There's no need to apologize, Viola," he said as he waved to a few of the local children sitting under the shade of a tree. When they waved back, he smiled, then continued to lead the way across the compound.

As she followed, Viola knew it wasn't okay. Everything in Roman's body language told her that he was upset with her. With the children, his smile was easy, genuine.

But now, every time he looked at her, he looked upset.

She didn't blame him. Of course he had to be upset about the first impression she'd made with all his coworkers. Embarrassed about the way she'd gotten sick, practically in front of everyone.

No, she didn't resent his disappointment. She felt the same way. She'd reacted in the worst possible way and now it was going to take everything she had to start over on the right foot.

If that was even possible.

So, though she still felt queasy and lightheaded, she grabbed his hand and tried her best to infuse some life into her voice. "Edward, we could continue our tour now, if you'd like."

He stopped and looked down at his feet. The brim of his straw hat shielded his face from the sun . . . and effectively blocked her from seeing the expression in his eyes. "I think it would be best if we stopped the tour. At least until tomorrow."

"I don't want to stop."

"Viola—"

"Ed, I promise, I do feel better." Distressed, she pointed to one of the crudely built buildings. "Would you like to show me what those buildings are?" she asked quickly, her words practically tripping over themselves. "They look like barns to me."

"They are barns." Finally, he lifted his chin. "Viola, I think it might be a good idea if I took you to your room and let you lie down for a while."

"But—"

He interrupted her and started moving back toward the main building. "It's getting late, anyway. I bet you are anxious to get some sleep."

"I'm not that tired." But even to her ears, her voice sounded shrill. Like an exhausted child's.

"I've got a lot of work to do anyway, since I've been away all day. It would be best for both of us if you got some rest."

Though she knew all of this was her fault, she felt rejected.

Quietly, she nodded, then let him lead the way into the main building, down a narrow hall, and back into the central gathering room.

Unlike before, when it had been teeming with energy and excitement, it was now empty. Only the faint scents of the meal they'd prepared in her honor remained. "Um, where is everyone?"

Ed looked around the room, then shrugged. "Oh, they, ah, decided to give us some privacy."

She knew she'd made a fool of herself, but for them to put away the celebration? They must have felt that she hadn't liked them. "I really do feel horrible about this, Ed. I want to make amends."

"You shouldn't feel bad, and you certainly don't need to make amends. No one can help getting sick."

She hadn't been able to help herself, that was true. But she also realized that her illness had been triggered not only by the heat, but also by her nerves. She was scared to live somewhere so different from Berlin.

But she was also just as afraid to lose Edward.

But if she corrected him, it would only make things worse.

After they crossed the large, empty room, he led her down another narrow hallway. Only a bare lightbulb illuminated their way. Finally, they stopped at a door. To her surprise, he pulled a key out of his pocket and unlocked the door. "Here we are," he said.

She stepped inside and almost gasped. Inside was a double bed, neatly made with a pair of quilts and what looked like ironed, white sheets. Pegs lined the wall, and hanging on them were Edward's clothes. "This is your room, isn't it?"

"*Jah*. I thought you might like to use it while you're here. It's clean, and will give you some privacy and quiet."

It was obvious that he'd very carefully cleaned what was clearly the nicest room in the mission complex.

Seeing how much trouble he'd gone to, how much preparation he'd made for her arrival, she felt even worse.

Oh, he must be so disappointed in her.

"Where are you going to sleep?"

"I'll bunk with some of the other men in one of the dormitory rooms."

"I can't take your room, Edward." As she glanced around, at his shirt hanging, at the pile of notes and loose change on his chest of drawers, she was certain that every little thing was going to remind her of him. Even his scent filled the room. But then again that helped her finally feel a little more relaxed, as if she really wasn't so far from home.

And that new glimmer of well-being was so wonderful, she wanted to hug him close and promise that she'd never embarrass him ever again.

But she wasn't sure that she could promise him that.

"Viola, this is really the only appropriate place for you to sleep." He stepped away. "Plus, I, ah, I had imagined you'd want to see where you'd be sleeping when we married."

"Had imagined?"

"Yes." He shrugged. "But perhaps this isn't the best place for you."

"What do you mean? Where else would I go?" All the hotels that they passed coming in from the airport looked too far away and too expensive.

"Perhaps you'll want to stay home."

She heard what he was saying, but it didn't want to register. "You mean Berlin?"

"*Jah.*" His face looked expressionless. Stoic.

"Where would you be? You wouldn't quit, would you?"

"No, I told you, I have a commitment to the mission. My chance to withdraw was back in February, when I came out here the first time. I can't leave now, it's my job." He cleared his throat. "But, like I told you, some wives stayed behind."

"I thought perhaps that was out of necessity. That they were raising *kinner* and wanted them to be at their schools and such."

"It's also by choice." He shrugged. "There's no need to make any sudden decisions, but I want to assure you that if staying in America is something you need to do, I'll understand."

"But you said—"

He cut her off. "I said a lot of things, Viola. We both know that just because I want something to happen, doesn't mean it will. I think it was wrong of me to push you so. I didn't want to be away from you. I wanted to marry you quickly. I wanted you here, by my side. But I should have asked what you wanted to do."

It almost sounded as if he were trying to find a way to break things off. "Edward, I love you."

"And I love you, too, Viola. Of course I do."

"Then give things some time. Give me some time. I mean, I only got here a few hours ago, Edward. Surely you don't expect us to make decisions about the rest of our lives in just a few hours? Do you?"

"You're right, of course." Gently, he reached out and caressed the side of her cheek. She looked into his eyes and realized that he looked sad. "Get some rest. We'll talk more in the morning."

"All right," she murmured, waiting for him to caress her cheek again, and then hold her close.

Instead, he turned and closed the door tightly behind him.

Dismayed and yet again on the verge of tears, she took off her shoes and sat on his bed. She lay down and curled on her side, inhaling the comforting scent of him on the sheets.

He was right. They could talk more later. Who knew what that conversation would be like, anyway?

She could only hope it went better than the one they'd just had.

"I don't know the last time I laughed so much," Lovina said with a smile as she sat with Aaron at the kitchen table the morning after Amanda and Regina's arrival. "That little Regina has already drawn a ring around my heart."

Aaron smiled at her over the rim of his coffee cup. "I have to agree that the child is a delight. I hope her mother and Roman can come to some kind of agreement and soon."

"They must be feeling something if she's bringing her daughter up here to see Roman."

"And us," Aaron corrected. "I recall Roman saying that he wanted her to meet his whole family."

"Sam and Lorene are coming over tonight. We'll either scare her off, or scare Roman," Lovina joked. "The Keims all together can be overwhelming."

"I suppose so." Her husband looked to add something more, then kept his tongue.

"What is it?"

"Oh, I was just wondering how you first felt when you met my family."

"I was overwhelmed, too," she said with a burst of laughter. "I wanted to please you." Almost shyly, she gazed at him through lowered lashes. "Of course, I was afraid your family would shun you for even thinking about dating an *Englischer*."

He scratched his beard, as if he was trying to remember. "They were surprised I fancied you, for sure. But they were happy I was smiling again."

Leaning back, he rested one foot over the opposite knee—the way he used to sit all the time. "After Laura Beth, I didn't smile so much. You changed that."

She was touched. So rarely did they speak to each other like this. To cover up her deep feelings, she said, "I was always doing something wrong. I'm sure everyone had a lot to laugh about."

She looked at her husband fondly, not seeing his unruly, thinning gray head of hair. Instead, she recalled how his hair had once been thick and the color of dark caramel. His eyes had held a tired expression . . . like they'd seen too much.

Except when he gazed at her.

Years ago, it had felt as if she were the only person in the world.

"To be honest, I'm not really sure what I thought about when I met your relatives. All I remember was that I wanted to change," she murmured. "And that I wanted you." To her surprise, she felt her cheeks heat. Even after forty years, he could make her blush.

"We were two souls in need of fresh starts. I had lost Laura Beth and Ben. You had lost your boyfriend."

"We were both in need, for sure," she agreed.

"Well, the chores aren't going to do themselves. Best go see if Roman needs a hand." Aaron was always the practical one. Meanwhile, her head was still in the clouds, remembering Jack, when Aaron closed the back door with a thud.

Thinking about how she'd sneaked out of her house the day after the accident and took the bus to the hospital to see Jack.

When she'd gotten there, his parents had barely acknowledged her existence.

Even worse was when one of the nurses had told her that Jack didn't want to see her. Right in front of a bunch of his friends.

She'd realized that she had never really meant all that much to him. Not even after all the things they'd done. Especially not after Billy's death.

But after he'd left for basic training, Jack had written her a carefully penned note that had revealed more than he'd ever told her in person.

In it, he'd told her that after he'd left for boot camp, he'd thought about her more and more. She'd made an impression on him, for the better. And because of that, he wanted to change. He wanted to be a better person, and he hoped she'd give him another chance. He'd asked her to write him back.

And so she had. They'd exchanged a few brief, hesitant letters. Each filled with grief and regrets about Billy.

Then, of course, things had changed again.

And Lovina had realized that the pain she had been feeling, while bad, had only been a taste of what was about to come.

chapter twenty-two

The day had been wonderful. Now, as he and Amanda sat on the couch in the front parlor, Roman finally understood what Viola had felt with Edward.

Now he understood why his sister was willing to pledge herself to a man who was determined to live all over the world. Feeling the way he did about Amanda, Roman knew he was willing to change his idea of his life, of who he was, of who he wanted to be.

That's what happened when a person was in love, he realized. Love made everything in life worthwhile . . . and much in life seem hardly significant at all.

As he turned to the beautiful woman he was falling in love with, he noticed that she'd become increasingly withdrawn over the last few minutes.

"You're pretty quiet," Roman said after he brought them fresh cups of coffee. "Is something wrong?"

She shrugged in that winsome way he noticed she did when she was at a loss for words. "Not a thing. I'm simply content." After taking a sip of her coffee, she added, "I guess I've been quiet because I'm so used to Regina constantly chattering in my ear. Perhaps I've forgotten how to have a real conversation."

"My grandparents have become smitten with her and her chatter."

"I think she feels the same way. She is enjoying being around a big, gregarious family."

Her comment surprised him. "I would have thought she would be used to being around so many people, living close to Wesley's family the way you do."

"We live close to them, but it isn't the same as what you have here."

Her words seemed a bit evasive. "Why not? Did Wesley not have a lot of siblings?"

"No, he only had one sister and they were never terribly close. But the main reason is that the Yoder family isn't loud by nature. They're fairly quiet people, I guess," she said after some reflection. "Then, of course, Wesley's sickness and death cast quite a dark cloud over us all. It was hard to concentrate on anything but the cancer, and that he was fading from us in spite of our prayers and the doctors' drugs and treatments. We all became quieter after his death."

Roman was again reminded of their different life experiences. His naiveté embarrassed him. Until he'd met Amanda, he'd thought of himself as someone who was strong because he'd shouldered many of the farm's responsibilities. Now, he realized that his strength couldn't hold a candle to hers. "Sorry, I didn't mean to be so thoughtless."

Resting a slim hand on his arm, she shook her head. "Oh, Roman, don't think that. You're not being thoughtless. Truthfully, I never thought about why we are the way we are. I just always accepted it . . . for better or worse."

She smiled at him, her smile turning the dark night a little brighter. "Though Marlene and Micah have been good grandparents to Regina, I think their grief for Wesley dominated their actions. They've been kind, but a little standoffish." She wrinkled her nose. "*Nee*, that's not quite right. Anyway, they haven't spoiled her near as much as she would like them to. Not like your family is doing, anyway."

"I never would have imagined anyone saying that my grandparents were the spoiling kind."

"They pay attention to her. That's what counts. Roman, haven't you seen how she practically glows around your mother and grandparents? She eats up their attention like a hungry caterpillar! In a lot of ways, Regina is just a little girl aching to fill the gap of all that she's lost."

Something about the way she said that made Roman realize that Regina wasn't the only one who was trying to fill the gaps in her life. Amanda had been so focused on taking care of her husband and now her daughter that she'd put her own needs aside. Now, she seemed just as eager as Regina to try new things, to have some fresh experiences.

Now, that was something he could help with.

"Hey, I thought I could take you for a ride in our sleigh. What do you think about that?"

"I think it's freezing out!"

"I know, but we could bundle up under some wool blankets." He waggled his eyebrows. "We could sit really close to keep warm that way." Just to tease her, he added a little bit of a challenge. "Unless you think your Florida blood can't take the Ohio cold?"

"I was born in Pennsylvania. I can handle the cold and snow."

He raised his brows. "Are you sure about that?"

"Perfectly sure," she countered, then chuckled. "Boy, you got my gander up, didn't you? You are incorrigible, Roman."

"Sometimes being incorrigible has its advantages."

"And what are those?"

"It lets me get my way." Taking a chance, he slid closer to

her on the couch, wrapped his arm around her shoulders. "Take a chance, Amanda. Come for a sleigh ride with me."

"Just the two of us?"

"Of course." He would be happy to take Regina for a sleigh ride one day. But at the moment, all he wanted to do was tease and cajole Regina's mother. And maybe, kiss her in the moonlight.

He was, after all, incorrigible.

"Come on, Amanda," he whispered. "What can it hurt?"

Amanda felt a burst of alarm flash through her. His words were igniting all sorts of feelings she'd long ago resigned herself to that she'd never experience again. But here they were, alive and well inside her.

Realizing how eager she was for Roman's attention was more disconcerting than the feel of his arm around her shoulders. Was she even ready for this?

Wesley hadn't been demonstrative with his love for her. Even when they were alone, he hadn't been one to touch or hug her. He was far too reserved for that. But she was finding herself to be much like her precious daughter. She, too, was enjoying the sensation of being around someone who was so open and affectionate.

In her own way, she was soaking up the warmth as much as her daughter was.

But of course, she knew what getting so close to Roman could do. It could hurt her very much. She could get her heart broken.

His arm fell away, making her skin feel chilled.

"Amanda?" he murmured, his gaze searching. "Have I upset you? Did I push too hard? Talk to me."

She was still focused on her arm. The way it felt so cold with his hand gone. Who knew an arm could be so sensitive, anyway?

But that feeling cemented her decision. If she stayed away from him, if she stayed safe and wary, then chances were very good that she wouldn't be hurt. She could get used to being a little bit cold. Soon, she would forget what it felt like to be warm. She would forget how much she'd ever craved another person's touch.

She could go back to her life, and go back to work. She could find comfort in stranger's smiles.

But she was so tired of being cold.

"That sleigh ride sounds like a good idea," she finally replied, making her decision. "It sounds *wunderbaar.*"

Roman gazed at her like she'd made his day. "That's great. I promise, I'll bring extra blankets. And I'll heat some bricks for our feet. I won't let you get cold, Amanda."

She was staring at him, her lips slightly parted, thinking about everything he wasn't saying, when they heard footsteps approaching.

"Mamm?" Regina called out.

Pushing all those thoughts of romance to one side, she turned to find Regina and Elsie. "Hi, you two. Were you looking for me?"

"Regina here was wondering where you two were," Elsie said. With a meaningful look directed at Roman, she added, "I thought it might be a good idea to find you."

Regina scampered forward. "Mamm, Mrs. Keim said we could start making cupcakes for the wedding."

"Truly?"

"My aunt Lorene and aunt Mary Beth are coming over tomorrow," Elsie explained. "Lorene thought pretty cupcakes iced in different pastel colors would a nice change from the traditional wedding cake. We need to bake over two hundred. Three hundred if possible. We're going to refrigerate them until Monday or Tuesday when it's time to add icing. We'd love your help."

"And I would love to help you. Regina, you will like making the cupcakes very much."

"Are you going to make them, too, Roman?"

"Definitely not. Baking and icing cupcakes is a woman's project."

"What will you do?"

Looking terribly put upon, he sighed. "I suppose I'll have to work."

"Where?" She wrinkled her nose. "In the smelly barn?"

"That very place. But wait a minute, weren't you just telling me a few hours ago about how much you liked the barn and all the animals?"

"Oh, I like them."

"Even smelly Sam?"

Her lips curved up. "Especially smelly Sam."

He chuckled, then to Amanda's surprise, he scooped Regina up and twirled her around.

Regina grabbed hold of his arms, squealed in delight, then said, "Again!"

Amanda felt her insides turn to mush as she realized what was happening. She was falling in love.

Just as she was pretty sure Regina was, too.

With every tug and hug of her daughter, Amanda felt the last of her resistance slip away.

Later that night, Roman ignored the knowing glances of his mother and sister as he prepared the sleigh for their ride. While Amanda and Regina were helping with the dishes, he'd gathered a pile of fluffy quilts and a sheepskin cover for the cold leather seat.

Then he'd buckled up the horse to the sleigh. As Roman expected, Chester was excited about being out in the snow. He was shaking his head impatiently as Roman fastened his reins. "Settle, boy," he said soothingly. "I know you're excited. I am, too, but we need to bide our time. Amanda will be out when she's ready. That's a woman's prerogative, I guess." And something, he realized, that he might have to get used to.

And though his sisters' dawdling had always annoyed him, now he was finding that he wouldn't mind waiting for Amanda whenever she needed him to.

Chester, obviously not in the same frame of mind, snorted and pawed the ground with a hoof.

"Sorry, horse, she'll be coming along soon. She said she was only five minutes behind."

In the distance, he heard a familiar laugh. "Are you speaking to the horse about me?"

"Guilty," he replied with a laugh. "Talking to the animals is a longtime habit of mine, I fear." As he watched Amanda approach, he added, "I see I'm going to have to watch my mouth in the future. You have ears like a hawk."

"I believe it's ears like an elephant, and eyes like a hawk."

"Whatever the case, your hearing is good enough for me to learn to be a bit more circumspect in the future." Simply thinking about a future of watching for her made him happy. "I'd sure hate for you to hear something best kept secret."

"Animals do keep the best secrets."

He held out a hand to help her into the sleigh. "I'm glad you're dressed warmly. You look pretty. I like your violet sweater."

"Elsie let me borrow it, and the scarf, too." She tilted her head up at him as he climbed in the sleigh beside her. "I'm surprised you didn't recognize it."

He wanted to tell her that he rarely noticed much about what his sisters were wearing, but thought that might sound mean. So he concentrated on rearranging the quilts around her more carefully. "Are you warm enough?"

She snuggled a bit closer. "I think so. Where are we going?"

He slipped on his gloves. "Nowhere special. Only down a few roads."

"Do you use your sleigh much?"

"Hardly ever, if you want to know the truth. I think my father or grandfather bought it in a romantic moment. Or a moment of weakness," he added after some thought. Actually, he only remembered his parents taking him, Viola, and Elsie out on Christmas mornings. "Right now I can only remember them using it once a year."

"Whatever the reason, I'm glad you are taking me out."

"Me, too." He jiggled the reins and Chester trotted forward, pulling the old sleigh with an eager jerk.

Amanda laughed as they got on their way, then laughed some more as they increased their pace. "I didn't think we could go so fast!"

"Chester is feeling frisky. I hope you're not frightened."

"Not at all, Roman. I think this is *wunderbaar*!"

Feeling like he was the king of the world—or at least someone terribly special—he clicked the reins, giving Chester permission to continue his brisk pace.

In answer, the horse almost pranced down the road, kicking up bits of snow in his path. The breeze kissed their cheeks and made his eyes water.

But all he seemed to be able to concentrate on was the feeling of her beside him. She felt warm and comfortable. Perfect.

He curved an arm around her shoulders, and after only the slightest hesitation, she snuggled closer. Close enough for him to drop his hand to her waist and give in to temptation by pressing his lips to her cold cheek.

She smiled in return.

He felt euphoric. Lifted. So blessed. He'd found his soul mate, and she felt the same way about him. Before long, they could start discussing weddings and house sites.

After another twenty minutes, Chester finally grew weary and slowed. Roman let the horse set the pace, only gently guiding him to follow the well-worn path back to their home.

As Chester quietly clip-clopped along the gravel path, and the white fields and bare trees glimmered in the snow's reflection, Roman felt as if the whole world was at peace. "I love this," he whispered. "I love right now. I love this very moment."

"I love it, too," Amanda said after a moment. "I don't know how to tell you this, but this, this right now? It's one of the best moments of my life."

"It's one of my best moments, too, Amanda. Being with you like this—it almost surpasses my dreams."

Her eyes widened at his flowery words.

Then, to his astonishment, she started crying.

Roman froze, not knowing what to do, not understanding why she was crying.

Not understanding anything except that for some reason all this happiness made her sad.

And he had no idea about what he was supposed to do next.

chapter twenty-three

After a good night's sleep, Viola felt better. Oh, she still felt awkward and out of sorts, but the haziness of travel and the uneasiness she'd felt being in a foreign country had lifted. She was starting to feel more like her usual self.

Thank the Lord, her mood had improved as well. Even though she was still unsure about Belize and still unsure about her ability to do God's work as a missionary's wife, she couldn't have felt more sure about her relationship with Edward. From the moment she spied him waiting for her at the airport, she'd felt the same strong feelings of happiness and love that she'd experienced when they'd been courting in Berlin. They were meant to be together. She was sure of it.

Now, all she had to do was find a way to make it work.

Late last night, one of the women handed her a thin cotton dress, telling Viola that she might find it more comfortable in the heat and humidity.

Viola had accepted it gratefully.

Now, as soon as she put on her borrowed light blue dress with its short sleeves, white apron, and *kapp*, she felt a thousand times cooler than when she'd arrived.

With a feeling of hope, she gathered up the pot holders her grandmother had made, left Roman's room, and ventured out to the kitchen area. The kitchen was a unique combination of her mother's kitchen at home and the commercial kitchen at Daybreak. Though it had an oversized oven, outdated refrigerator, and large range, somewhere along the way, people had added some lovely hand-stitched hand towels, and a collection of brightly painted ceramic jars.

And though the spices that permeated the room smelled unfamiliar, she also saw two loaves of bread, glass jars of homemade jams and preserves, and a stoneware pitcher.

Two women about her mother's age looked up when she tiptoed through the doorway. "*Gut matin,*" one said, her smile as bright as her blue dress and matching apron.

"*Gut matin.*" Feeling awkward, Viola smiled slightly.

"Would you care for *kaffi*?"

That definitely sounded like heaven. "*Jah. Danke.*" When one of the women went to reach into one of the top cupboards to grab her a cup, Viola waved her away. "Please, I can help myself. Just show me where everything is."

"I can do that," the slim brunette offered. "The cups are here, and you'll find milk and sugar on the table."

Viola opened the designated door, found a large collection of white and blue mugs, and gratefully poured herself a cup of the fragrant brew. "This smells heavenly."

"The *kaffi* is wonderful here, for sure," the brunette said as she lifted her own mug. "Especially after a day of travel. I'm Amy, by the way."

"I'm Viola. Did we meet last night?" she asked hesitantly. "I'm afraid my mind is a blur."

"Only for a moment." With a look of concern she asked, "Are you feeling better?"

"Much." She bit her lip, then decided to plunge forward. "I know I got off on the wrong foot with all of you. I promise, I don't intend to act like that in the future." Presenting the pot holders, she added, "My grandmother made these. I thought you all might be able to put them to good use."

The other woman came forward and patted Viola on the back. She took the quilted pot holders with a pleased smile. "These are lovely. We will, indeed, put them to good use."

She then leaned over and looked Viola straight in the eye. "Don't fret, dear. There's nothing to say, or to apologize for. We felt bad for ya."

The lady's words were kind, but how could they be true? Viola had a feeling no one had ever made as poor of a first impression as she had.

"And I'm Rachel." After playfully winking at Amy, Rachel added, "If you want to know the truth, we all enjoyed our director fussing over you a bit."

"You did?"

"Ah, yes. Your man? He is a bit of a whirlwind, Viola. Our young director always seems to be working on two projects at a time."

"At least," Amy added.

With a chuckle, Rachel continued. "Edward has a real gift for connecting with people. Truly, I've never seen him flustered. So, it was kind of nice to see him at such a loss."

"It was obvious Ed was worried about you something awful," Amy added.

"I feel bad about that."

"Ach. Like I said, not a one of us thought you were being difficult or unseemly."

Viola took another bracing sip of coffee. "Truly?"

"Definitely. See, all of us have been through the same thing a time or two."

"Or five," Rachel added with a grin. "We've got a few years on you, Viola. I promise, I've had my share of embarrassing moments."

The women's frank talk did more to ease her nerves than Ed's gentle reassurances ever had. "I can't tell you how relieved I am to hear you say that. I was thinking that I was the worst sort of woman."

"I promise, you're in good company," Amy said after pulling a tray of biscuits from the oven. "A woman's first taste of this life can be overwhelming, and that's a fact. Our families enjoy sheltering us, and we enjoy being sheltered. That's *wonderful-gut* when we don't have to do anything out of the ordinary. But going to work as a missionary in a foreign country is anything but that."

"How do you like mission work now?"

"I enjoy it."

Amy looked at the clock, then motioned to Viola. "I'll tell you more, if you come with me," she said, then walked straight toward the food pantry. She looked over her shoulder. "Care to help me get the rest of our breakfast together?"

"I'd be happy to." Reaching out her hands, she grabbed the basket Amy held out to her while Amy began putting little boxes of cereal, jars of canned fruit, crackers, and nuts into the basket.

She said, "I've been with CAMA seven years. I have three months to go before I return to Missouri."

Viola put the filled basket down, picked up the next one, and followed Amy toward where the shelves were filled with paper goods. "Do you ever miss home?"

"Before I started, I thought I would. I was sure I would. But it hasn't been bad."

"Why is that?"

"Viola, have you ever been away from home before?"

For the first time in her life, she was embarrassed to have been so content to stay in Berlin. "*Nee*."

"Ah. You're much like I was. Being away from home can be hard. Well, you might think differently, but I've noticed that when I first leave, I always think of home. I find myself comparing where I am to where I've been. But then, as the days pass and I begin to feel more comfortable, I begin to see my new place more clearly."

She still wasn't sure she understood. "More clearly?"

Amy shrugged. "I guess I stop seeing only generalities. Little by little, I don't just notice that people or places are different. I start to think of them by name."

Finally, she understood what Amy was talking about. It comforted her to think that her perception about the mission might change with time, too.

But then she remembered the look of dismay on her fiancé's face. "I hope Ed will try to understand and give me time to get settled."

"He will. If he seemed disappointed to you, it may be because he's forgotten that sometimes a person's first impression isn't always the clearest. Especially for a man like him, who seems more suited to this life than most."

"I hope you're right. I want to be able to fit in here. I think I was so nervous and warm that I made myself sick."

Amy chuckled. "Like I said, I understood your reaction." Taking the basket from Viola's hands, she said, "I think we have enough paper cups, napkins, and plates. Let's go put them on the tables."

As they headed toward the main room, Viola followed

Amy's sure strides, carrying the basket filled with cereal. They set the table and arranged the food.

She was just picking up the empty baskets to return them to the pantry when Edward walked in.

"Viola? What are you doing in here?"

"I'm helping. I mean, I'm trying to help," she corrected sheepishly.

A line formed between his brows. "Are you sure you're up to that? You were so sick last night. Viola, you should have asked someone to find me when you woke up."

"I didn't want to bother you and I wanted to be of use."

"You are doing okay?"

Remembering the other women's reassuring words, she nodded, "I think that maybe last night I was a little overwhelmed. I feel better now." Fingering her dress, she said, "I'm much cooler, too. That helps, I think."

He fell into step beside her. "How did you sleep?"

Feeling more like herself, she risked teasing him. "I slept very well in your bed, Edward."

To her great amusement, his cheeks heated. "You shouldn't say such things," he said under his breath. Just as if a dozen people were actively listening to their every word.

Finally, she felt as if they were on more even ground. She didn't know how to live as a missionary. She found Belize scary and the idea of living here as his wife more than a bit overwhelming.

But his embarrassment and sudden awkwardness merely made her feel a little bolder. Here, at least, she felt comfortable. She was used to teasing Roman . . . and after bantering back and forth with his father for months, she felt she was pretty capable of holding her own with Ed.

"If you don't want to know how I slept in your bed, then you mustn't ask such things," she teased. "Now, I must put these baskets away. Would you like to help me carry them?"

"Of course." As he took both from her, he cast her a sideways glance. "Viola, this is what life is going to be like with you, isn't it?"

"Like what?"

"You're going to flirt and tease and laugh and cry." He looked her over like she was the most unique of persons. "You are going to be such a girl."

"I am a girl, and a far from perfect one at that, Ed," she said, all traces of humor gone from her voice. "I'll try my best for you, but I fear there are sometimes going to be moments like last evening, when we both are at a loss for what to do or say."

Still staring at her intently, he exhaled a heavy breath. "That's *gut*. Because I, too, am far from perfect."

Unable to help herself, she rubbed the smooth skin of his cheek. The smooth skin that would one day soon be covered with a beard, signifying their marriage. "I don't want perfect, either."

"If we're in agreement on that, then I suppose we will be all right," he said before leading the way to the pantry.

With a lighter heart, Viola followed.

Maybe, just maybe, everything was going to be fine after all.

It was beautiful out. The air was brisk and still. Tiny snowflakes dotted their skin and clothes, feeling like cold kisses on her face.

Roman beside her was everything she could have hoped for—a man who understood that she'd loved before but was willing to love her all the same. A man who understood how much Regina needed someone in her life who could bring light and happiness into her dark days.

He was offering her a future again. It was *wonderful-gut*. It felt almost perfect.

So why couldn't she seem to stop crying?

Amanda covered her face and inhaled deeply, hoping the cold shot of frigid air would clear her head and calm her nerves.

Or at least temper her tears.

But it was useless. The tears just kept coming of their own accord.

"Amanda?"

She waved off his concern. "It's nothing. Don't mind me."

"Don't mind you?" With a light chuckle, Roman pulled back on Chester's reins, then guided the horse to the side of the road. When they were stopped and not another noise could be heard—beyond her sniffling tears—he turned to her. "Amanda, right at this very moment, I can think of nothing but you."

Ah, the romance of it. His words were the stuff of a girl's dreams. The kind of dreamy words that Wesley had never even said.

Which, of course, made the tears fall harder. She swiped at them in frustration, then stilled as she felt his thumbs gently catch the tears on her cheeks and brush them away. "Amanda, cry if you want to, but I'd rather you tell me what you're feeling. If something is wrong, I could maybe try to help."

"Ah, Roman." She took a deep breath, then turned to him. When she looked into his brown eyes, she noticed they were gazing at her steadily. There was compassion there. And affection. And complete confusion, too.

She didn't blame him; she was feeling pretty confused herself. "I'm sorry," she said. "When we were riding down the road, I suddenly felt so happy, it caught me off guard. Before I knew it, everything kind of came tumbling down around me." Hopefully, she glanced at him. Perhaps he knew what she meant?

He didn't. Instead of nodding in agreement, he continued to stare at her in confusion. "You don't seem happy, Amanda. In fact, you sound pretty sad."

"Oh, I am sad, too. I'm happy and confused, sad and hopeful. I'm everything."

"What are you talking about? Did I do something wrong? What did I say?" His hand clenched the edge of the leather seat, like he was striving for control. "Did I push you too much? I know when we talked about you coming out here, we promised not to have too many expectations."

"But did you mean that?"

"Yes," he said quickly, then, slowly, he shook his head. "*Nee,* that's not the full truth. I had hopes that you would see that there was something special between us. I wanted that to happen."

This was why she was falling in love with him. He was so kind to her, so eager to be the man she needed him to be. "You didn't do anything wrong, Roman."

"Then why the tears?"

Even though she didn't think she had the words to try to explain herself, she knew she had to give it a try. "For so long I've been missing Wesley that I didn't think I could feel anything but dead inside. At first, I was sad. Then, I felt empty. Then, little by little, I began to look around at other men in my life. But not a one interested me. I started to think that I was destined to spend the rest of my life alone."

"But now?"

"Now I feel hope." She smiled. "For the first time in a long time, I feel like I have something to look forward to. It's, ah, overwhelming. That's why I was crying. I can hardly believe that I really am going to be able to say goodbye to my past."

He took off his stocking cap and tossed it on the bench beside them and ran his hand through his hair. "So, even though you're crying, it's for a good reason."

"I think so."

He brushed a finger under her eye, catching her tears as delicately as if he were trying to catch a butterfly. "I wish you weren't crying."

"I do, too. But all in all? These tears aren't a bad thing. I'm starting to realize that my future can be special because of you."

"I like the sound of that . . . we need to string special and future and you all together more often."

She chuckled, as she knew he'd hoped she would.

Yes, she still felt guilty about Wesley, but she was also starting to realize that he'd been right when she'd sat by his bedside and he made her talk about a future without him in it.

"If that's the reason for your tears, then you can cry all you want," he said with a smile as he leaned forward and lightly brushed his lips against her cheek. "You make me happy. Both you and Regina make me happy. I can hardly wait for us all to be together one day."

It was almost a proposal, Amanda realized. He wasn't going to push her, but his intent was clear. Wiping away the last of her tears with a swipe of her mitten, she said, "Roman, I can hardly wait for you to return to Pinecraft. I'll take you all around, and we'll start to make plans."

"That sounds great. You know, Sam and Lorene have been

talking to my uncle Aden. I think my family might even buy a cottage there. That way we'll have a house to go to when we visit."

"Visit?"

"Yes," he said with a smile. "I know we're jumping ahead of ourselves, but I didn't want you to ever think that I mean to take you away from everything in Florida."

"Roman, I've never considered living anywhere else."

"Not even here?"

"No. I need to stay in Florida." That was where Regina's grandparents were. That was where Wesley was buried. Where all their memories were. Even though she might be ready to move forward, she certainly wasn't ready to forget about everything she'd had with him.

He pulled away from her. The two-inch gap that now lay between them chilled her skin. Just as his words froze her heart.

"Amanda, I can't move to Florida." He ran a hand through his hair again. "I thought you understood that."

"*Nee.*" With a sense of dismay, she felt their future slipping away as fast as Roman said the snow melted in spring. As fast as she knew the water receded from the shoreline during low tide.

"Amanda, my life is here."

"In Florida, you told me you weren't happy here."

"My family is going through a rough patch, for sure. That was what I needed to get away from."

"But you said you loved Pinecraft."

"That was true. Of course I love Pinecraft. What's not to like? It's warm and sunny. Everyone there is more relaxed. People are smiling. The beach is there."

"Then what has changed? Why do you sound like you now could never make a home there?"

"Now that I've been home, and things have settled down, I realize that I had only needed a vacation. And though I do like Florida, I realized I loved Pinecraft because you were there. I realized I was unhappy because I didn't have you in my life. That's changed."

He scooted closer again, obviously eager to press his point. "If you move here, we can still have each other. I know right now all this cold and snow feels strange, but in time you'll get used to it. And summer does come." He smiled slightly. "It always does."

He was missing the point. She wasn't worried about the weather. She was thinking about her life! She couldn't just up and leave it. She couldn't plan for a future where she had to give up practically everything she had.

After all, she'd already given up so much already. She'd already lost Wesley. Did she need to lose everything else, too? "Roman, I don't think you're seeing things from my side."

Though he looked in her eyes, he wasn't seeing her. "We can figure this out, Amanda. Don't worry. You'll like it here, and I feel certain everyone's going to love you."

"But—"

He spoke again, effectively stopping anything she had to say. "Amanda, I'm a farmer, and this is where the farm is. And I just accepted the preaching position in our church district. I'm a leader in our church community now. That's a serious commitment."

"But wouldn't a marriage to me be a serious commitment, too? I mean, that is what we are discussing, right? Marriage."

"Of course."

But he hadn't actually asked, had he?

And he hadn't actually mentioned love, had he?

The shine of happiness faded as the realities of what they

were discussing came to light. "I think it would be best if we went back."

"I'd rather we stayed here and talked things out."

"Please, it's time to go back."

"Amanda, we don't have much time."

"Of course we do," she said impatiently. "You've waited your whole life for some woman to be just 'right' for you."

"And you are." He reached for her hand. "You're perfect for me."

She snatched her hand right back. "There's more to a relationship than that. I can't only be the woman who fits in with your plan. I need to be the woman in your life who you want to move heaven and earth to have."

Even in the evening night, she could see his bemused expression. "Move heaven and earth? I would have thought you would have been long past spouting such fanciful phrases, Amanda."

"And I would have thought you'd be more than ready to spout them," she replied sharply, trying to cover up her embarrassment. "Please take me back. Now."

He clicked the reins and motioned Chester forward. The bells on the side of the sleigh jangled as they glided forward. They sounded merry and bright.

Snow was still gently falling, but whereas before it had felt magical and special . . . now it only felt cold and wet.

Amanda scooted farther away from Roman. Needing space as her future evaporated and became what it had been all along . . . just spun dreams that dissolved with the night.

So quickly grasped . . . too easily gone.

chapter twenty-four

"You, brother, are a fool," Elsie declared when she entered the barn just as the sun began to rise the following morning.

Glancing over his shoulder, seeing her bundled up in her thick black cape and bright pink mittens, he almost smiled. But nothing, not even Elsie's pink mittens, could lighten his mood. "*Gut matin*, to you, sister," he said sarcastically. "What brings you here on a Sunday morning?"

"Oh for heaven's sake, Roman. Is that really all you have to say? I heard Amanda crying last night."

"I feel bad for her but I don't see how her tears are any concern of yours."

"I know why she was crying."

"And you know this because . . . "

"Because I went and knocked on her door, of course."

"Last night?"

"Yes, Roman. Last night," she replied matching his sarcastic tone. "She told me about not wanting to leave Pinecraft and you not wanting to leave here."

"I'm glad you're caught up to speed. Do you have anything else to report? Maybe you went and listened outside Mamm's door, too?"

She stopped him with a hand. "Don't be like that."

"Elsie, I don't want to talk to you about my personal life right now. No, make that ever."

"Well, I'm not going to let you settle back into your old ways. I'm not going to let you hold everything inside. Not this time."

"There's nothing to talk about, sister. Amanda and I are at an impasse."

"Not necessarily. People can change their minds. Maybe she'll come around. Or, maybe you will."

He was so frustrated with the situation, with his life, he jerked his arm away from her touch. "Elsie, there is no coming around for me. I have responsibilities here." Bitterly, he said, "Haven't you heard that Daed is gone and Viola is too?"

"Daed will be back soon. And the rest of the family can help you farm. Lorene's John said he'd help in a heartbeat. You only have to ask."

"It's not just the farm that I'm concerned with. There's my new position with the church. I'm taking my responsibilities as preacher seriously, Elsie."

"I'm sure people will understand if you say you have to move. People do move, Roman."

He was annoyed that she seemed to have all the answers. Life couldn't be manipulated as easily as she seemed to think. Sometimes certain things were more important than a single person's selfish wants. He truly believed that.

He wasn't happy about it, but he believed it.

"Roman, you're making things too difficult. You need to put yourself first sometimes. I promise, there are many able men who will make a good preacher. And we will find a way to work the farm."

Oh, her confidence grated on him. "It's not just the land or the church I'm worried about, Elsie." He didn't want to say it. Didn't want her to know how much they worried. But how else would she understand? "To be honest, I'm thinking about you. I promised Viola I'd look after you if she left."

She stepped backward. "Me? Wh-what do you mean, you promised Viola?"

"Since Viola is going to be living far away, it's up to me to stay here. We talked about it, and it's fair."

"I don't need you to stay with me. Why on earth would you think that?"

Her expression was incredulous, and he knew she was completely baffled. So, even though he didn't want to hurt her feelings, he realized he had little choice. He had to be honest, there was no other way. "Because you're going to need help," he said quietly. "One day, a lot of help."

"Because of my eyesight, you mean?" She adjusted her eyeglasses over her eyes, maybe in another attempt to see better. But Roman knew those thick lenses could never fix her eyesight. Elsie was going blind . . . and she seemed to be the only person who was in denial about that.

"Of course, because of your eyesight, Els. Even though it's hard, you've got to realize that you have special needs. You're going blind, and you're going to need help. It's inevitable." Lowering his voice, he said, "And I don't mind, Elsie."

"But I'm not blind. I can see."

"Not well. And it's going to get worse. And Mamm and Daed won't be able to take care of you forever." He looked down at his boots, hating the way she was staring at him, full of hurt.

But just like their father had to own up to his problems, and their grandparents had to admit their pasts, Elsie needed to finally face her future.

"I know you hate to talk about this, but it will be easier if we both face the facts."

"Which is that you're planning to give up everything in order to take care of me, your poor, blind sister."

"I don't mind," he repeated. "I really don't."

She flinched. "Roman, do you really think I'm going to be sitting around the house, expecting to be waited on hand and foot?"

"You are twisting my words, Elsie." He shook his head in frustration. This conversation was hard for him, she had to see that. "You know what, never mind. We'll talk about this another day. When there isn't so much going on."

"Oh, really? You're going to make that decision, too?"

"Elsie—"

"Roman, you might be shocked to hear this, but listen to me well. I *am* going to be married one day. I'm sure of it! I'll be taking care of my own *kinner* and husband and *haus*. I won't be needing you to be hovering around me. I can promise you that."

"I hope that's what happens. I really do." But of course, what he wasn't saying was what they both heard, clear as day: That he didn't really believe it would ever happen.

"Until that day comes, I advise you to make some plans of your own. Hasn't everything that's happened in our family given you a wake-up call? Bad things happen. But the Lord never promised us an easy life, only that he would be there for us. Let Him shoulder some of your burdens, Roman. And take a chance with your heart while you're at it."

Too tired to argue with her anymore, he didn't reply, only stood stoically until she turned with a grunt of contempt.

Wearily, he followed her back to the house, hoping to make things better between them. But by the time he'd removed his muddy boots and hung his coat on a peg, she was nowhere to be found.

Needing something to warm his insides, he poured a cup of coffee and sat down.

He was still staring at his filled coffee cup when Regina came in.

"Hi, Roman!" she said, pattering over to him still in her nightgown.

"And hello to you. How are you this morning?"

"I'm *gut*." She smiled. "We're gonna make some cupcakes today, 'cause there's gonna be a wedding soon and Elsie says we need tons of 'em."

He'd been so focused on Amanda's visit, and his new duty at the church, he'd completely forgotten. "That is true," he said gently. "Aunt Lorene's wedding day is coming up on Wednesday. That's sure to be a special day. Have you been to a wedding before?"

"Uh-huh."

"Then you know it's going to be busy around here for the next few days. I bet all the women are going to be cooking."

She nodded. "Mamm said a wedding takes a lot of hands. Marie said lots of ladies were coming over to set things up."

"I think tonight when everyone's cooking, we'll have to go out for pie and then go for a walk in the snow."

Her eyes lit up. "We can do that?"

"We can if you want to."

She clapped her hands. "Can I go see Sam now?"

"Sam only likes to have visitors who are dressed in warm clothes. I'll take you to the barn when you're bundled up."

With a little cheer, she scampered off.

He smiled at the sight . . . and wished all his problems could be solved by a visit to a cold barn and an irritable pig.

Moments later, he was brushing down Chester, when the barn door opened. He turned, prepared to greet Regina.

But was faced with Amanda instead.

"Did you come out here to see Sam, too?"

"*Nee*. I came to tell you that I got a reservation on the Pioneer Trails bus today. Regina and I are going to leave."

"Today?"

"I think it's best."

He was so stunned, so hurt, he blurted the first thing that came to his mind. "But what about the cupcake making? Regina just told me that you two planned to help all the ladies bake today. She's excited about it."

"I'm sorry, but I can't do that. I can't bear to think about another wedding right now."

"Because it will only remind you of Wesley?"

She blinked, as if he'd surprised her, then nodded. "Yes. Because of that."

Well, that was that, then. No matter what he did, he was never going to measure up to Wesley Yoder. He turned away to hide his hurt. "I guess you better pack then."

He felt her presence, then breathed a sigh of relief when she turned and walked back out of the barn.

She was only a few steps away, but it felt as if she'd already walked out of his life.

chapter twenty-five

Marie gripped the phone a little harder as she finally heard her husband say the words she'd been praying for.

". . . so I should be home before you know it. As long as the weather stays clear and we don't get any snow."

Doing her best to stifle the annoying cough that she couldn't seem to wish away, she said, "Peter, I'm so happy about this."

"I am, too, Marie." His voice sounded hoarse, a little choked. "It's been a difficult couple of weeks, but good ones, too. I'm a better, stronger person now. And I'm done trying to hide behind a bottle of alcohol."

"I'm so proud of you. Going to the clinic was the right decision."

"I think so. I'm only sorry that this right decision has made your life so difficult."

Now that she knew he was coming back, her whole world felt brighter. Even all the things she'd been so worried about didn't seem that overwhelming. She had a feeling his return would even make her body feel better, too. Of late, she'd been so tired it hurt to move. "I'm okay," she said lightly.

"Are you sure? You sound a little off."

"Oh, I've still got this little cold I told you about. It's nothing to worry about." Brightening her voice, she said, "Peter, we're all going to be just fine now."

"All right, if you're sure." He paused. "So, tell me what's been going on. How is Roman's young lady?"

Thinking of what had been happening with their son, Marie frowned. "She is a lovely woman, but they're having some trouble, I fear."

"I'll look forward to meeting her."

"I don't think that's going to happen," Marie murmured as she glanced at Amanda's suitcase standing by the door. "She's leaving today."

"What?"

Rubbing the lines that had formed between her brows, she said, "That is a story better told in person. I'll let you know everything when we see each other again."

"All right. I suppose I should get off the phone anyway. Goodbye, Marie. I'll see you soon."

After speaking to him for a few more precious seconds, she hung up the phone and stared hard at that suitcase.

So many people had been coming and going lately. She didn't know why they all had to travel so much to find their way, but she certainly hoped that everyone would elect to stay in one place very soon.

Otherwise, she was going to be the one who needed a vacation from the drama in their lives.

Roman was as stubborn as a mule. From the moment he'd come into the kitchen, he'd glared at her with his hands stiffly folded across his chest.

But instead of changing her mind, it only made her more eager to get out of his house.

"This isn't easy for me, Roman. I wish you wouldn't make it more difficult," Amanda said as she prepared another peanut butter and jelly sandwich for the long bus trip home.

"I haven't tried to stop you. I'm merely offering my opinion. I think you're running away."

"I guess it's good that I've discovered your true colors," she retorted. "You're not nearly as easygoing as you were in Florida."

"I was on vacation then. And that has nothing to do with you refusing to see my side of things."

"That is not what is happening," she said sharply. Wearily, she neatly sliced through the center of the sandwich and wrapped waxed paper around it.

"Well, something is. Amanda, I think there's more going on here than just my desire not to move. What is it? Is it that you've changed your mind about me?" He paused, then raised an eyebrow. "Or is it more likely that you changed your mind about yourself?"

She flinched, hating his words. Hating that he was right. She wanted to hold her irritation with him close to her heart. It was so much easier to blame someone else than to face her demons all over again.

At the very least, she owed him her honesty. "I don't know."

"Why not?"

"You came into my life unexpectedly, Roman. I didn't plan to meet you on vacation. I didn't plan to start waiting for your phone calls. I didn't plan on Regina liking you so much." Though all that was the truth, it wasn't the full truth. What she wasn't brave enough to say was that she didn't plan on liking him so much.

He gazed at her, his expression a combination of dismay and anger. That made her realize that he, too, knew she still wasn't telling him the whole truth. She still wasn't sharing everything in her heart.

Which was a problem.

"All right," he finally said. "I'll go take your suitcase out to the front porch. The driver should be here soon."

"A driver is picking us up?" She'd thought he'd take her to the German Village in his buggy.

"Yes. I think that's for the best."

"Yes. Yes, I imagine it is." Carefully, she screwed on the peanut butter cap and set the last sandwich on the top of her lunch sack. "I'll go get Regina and meet you on the front porch."

When he walked away, she washed her hands, pressed a damp paper towel to her cheeks and forehead, hoping to cool her flushed face, then strode to the *dawdi haus,* where Regina had been from the moment Amanda had told her that they wouldn't be making cupcakes today. Instead, they would be going home.

Her knock was quickly answered by Lovina. "Is it time already?" she asked as she led Amanda to her tidy kitchen. There, Regina was sitting at the table with Aaron. A small puzzle with large pieces was spread out in front of them.

The older lady looked as distressed as Amanda felt. But it would do no one any good to see how she really was feeling. "It is. Uh, Roman was able to hire a driver to take Regina and me to the shopping center to wait for the bus."

"But Momma, we're not done with the puzzle."

Amanda was familiar with what Regina was doing. She was concentrating on things she could control instead of what she couldn't.

She'd done that often while Wesley was sick, arguing over what dress to wear, or what food she would eat.

To see that the painful habit had returned broke Amanda's heart but it didn't change the way things were. "I'm sorry about the puzzle, but we're on the bus's schedule, dear. We must go now."

"But I don't want to." This was a comment Regina had made often before. Usually it came out as a babyish whine. This time, though, was different. Regina looked genuinely distressed. She spoke in a soft whisper. Yet again, Amanda felt that rush of guilt.

But she had to be strong enough for the both of them. Already they were too involved with the Keims. Already she could imagine living in their midst, attending church in their district. Watching Roman preach, encouraging him, being by his side.

But if she did all these things, she'd be saying goodbye to her life in Pinecraft, and that would be wrong. She might be thinking about moving on without Wesley, but she had never intended to leave her life with him completely behind.

"It is time, Regina," she said with iron in her voice. "Maybe we'll meet some nice people on the bus," she added brightly. Just as if they were on the way to the county fair.

But no one was fooled for a minute. Both Mr. and Mrs. Keim looked glum, and Regina was on the verge of tears.

She had to get out of there. Had to move on. Stepping forward, she reached for her daughter's hand. "Let's go, now."

Regina jerked back her hand. "*Nee*."

"You have no choice." Through clenched teeth, she turned to Lovina and Aaron. "Thank you for being so nice to Regina."

"It was no trouble. We enjoyed being with her," Aaron said.

"She's a *wonderful-gut* girl, Amanda," Lovina added. "*Wonderful-gut*."

"*Danke*." Amanda didn't know what to do with her hands. She ached to hug Lovina and Aaron goodbye, but it didn't seem right. "Well, goodbye."

The couple exchanged looks. Then Lovina nodded. "Goodbye, Amanda. Safe travels."

Just as she started to turn away, Regina rushed over to Aaron and hugged him tight.

While Amanda simply stood and watched, Lovina went to her husband's side and hugged Regina, too. Then, when Regina started crying, the woman bent down and whispered to her, carefully calming her.

As seconds passed, Amanda felt like the worst mother ever. Especially when Regina turned from the security of the couple's embrace and calmly announced she was ready.

"Let's go then," Amanda answered. Surprised she could even speak around the lump in her throat.

The next five minutes were excruciating. They said goodbye to Marie and Elsie. To Lorene, who was over making cupcakes for the upcoming wedding.

The wedding that Amanda had promised Regina that they'd get to attend. Through it all, Roman remained to one side while Regina stayed silent.

Only the beep from the van's horn offered any relief.

"We must go," she said, after double- and triple-checking that she had her purse and their lunches and Regina's stuffed dog. After getting Regina settled in the van, Amanda looked at Roman. "Thank you for inviting us to Berlin. I'll never forget it."

"You're welcome. Goodbye, Amanda."

She halfheartedly waited for him to ask her to call him when they got home. Waited for him to say that he understood, that he would change his mind about where he wanted to live.

But he did none of that. Instead, he stood stoically while she turned away and got into the van. While she fastened her seatbelt, he closed the van's door. Then he turned away as they drove off.

Beside her, Regina was hugging her stuffed dog tightly, looking for comfort there instead of from her mother.

And that was when Amanda realized that she'd been terribly wrong. It certainly was possible to feel that all-encompassing pain again.

But unlike Wesley's cancer, she'd been the one in charge of this loss.

Yes, it turned out that she was perfectly capable of causing pain and heartache and loss, all by herself.

Walking back to their house, Lovina blinked back the tears that she hadn't been able to will away but luckily had held back until no one else saw them. "I'm going to miss that little girl," she said.

"Me, too," Aaron said. "I don't think I'm going to be able to finish that puzzle without her. Half the fun was cheering with her whenever she got a piece in the right spot."

"We'll put it away so you won't have to be reminded of it." Uncertainly, she glanced at Aaron's stoic profile. "Do you think, perhaps, we'll need it for another day? For when she comes back?"

"Hope so." He stuffed his hands in his coat pockets. "It's a real shame Amanda and Regina had to leave. That grandson of ours shouldn't have let that happen. He won't do better than that pair."

"Sometimes our grandchildren can be so stubborn and silly."

"That is a fact." Slowly, the sides of his mouth turned up. "I wish I could say I've never been that way, but I can't."

"Truly?"

"Oh, *jah*. Lovina, I've certainly done my fair share of stubborn things. For sure, I have."

Rarely had Aaron ever admitted a mistake. Never could she remember him pointing out his own faults. "Like what?"

"Like . . . making you keep your past a secret. I know now that was a foolish idea."

"Not so much. I kept it secret for twenty years," she reminded him.

"But at what cost?"

Just a few weeks ago, when the secret had first come out, she'd been sure that their relationships with their children and grandchildren were lost. But as each day passed, things had seemed to ease. Time really did heal all wounds. "Maybe that secret didn't cost as much as we feared," she said. "We still have our family."

"Things are strained."

She stopped at their front door. "That's because everyone is now focused on your first family."

"My first family?" he echoed sarcastically.

She ignored his tone, choosing instead to focus on what was important. "You need to talk about Laura Beth and Ben, Aaron."

"I can't." He opened the door and stepped inside.

She followed on his heels all the way to their sitting room. "Why are their deaths so difficult for you to talk about? It's not like you caused the accident."

Gripping the back of his chair, he looked at her directly. "Some thought I did."

"Who did?"

"Laura Beth's brother." After a pause, he added, "Every year on the anniversary of Laura Beth's death, he sends me a letter. Inside are always the same two things—a photocopy of the news article, and a letter from him. In it, he says he still hasn't forgotten his sister's death or forgiven me for my part in it."

Lovina was stunned. "I never knew about the letters."

"That's because I didn't want you to know about them."

"But you don't take the notes seriously, do you? I mean, for someone to continually send you the same thing, year after year? That's ridiculous!"

Aaron shrugged.

Feeling assured that her husband clearly needed some sense talked into him, Lovina continued, her tone stronger. "Laura Beth died forty years ago. Her *bruder* must be mentally imbalanced or something." She walked toward him, ready to grasp his hand. To show him that even though she didn't understand all the secrets, she believed in him.

Believed the best of him.

But instead of curving his palm around hers, he stiffened. "Lovina, there's something else I never told you."

"And what is that?"

"I was driving that buggy. Her death really was my fault."

Once again, Lovina felt her world tilt. "I don't understand. You said she was driving."

"I never wanted to tell you the truth."

She was beyond dismayed. "Aaron?"

He rushed on with his explanation. "The police deemed it an accident, but we all knew better. She and I were fighting, arguing. I was yelling at her while I was driving the buggy in the rain."

"But—"

"After it was all over, I couldn't take the guilt," he whispered. "I knew I needed to get away, to start over again. . . ."

His voice drifted off, but now Lovina realized she could fill in the gaps.

Now she understood why he'd courted her, even though she wasn't Amish. Now she understood why they'd moved to Ohio and never went back to Pennsylvania.

All this time, she'd imagined it was because of her painful memories, but it had been for his.

"I killed my wife and son, Lovina," Aaron said, his voice flat. "Then I married you on top of a pile of lies and moved you far away so I could pretend it never happened."

She felt like all the air had been forced out of her. "For forty years, you did a good job of it."

"Possibly." He shrugged. After a few seconds, he added, "Lovina, I don't know what else to say."

"I think I do." Abruptly, she made a decision. "We need to go back. Aaron, we need to go back to Pennsylvania and face our pasts."

Even from her position across the room, she could see every muscle in his body tense. Then, with a sigh, the fight left him. "Lord help me, but I think you are right."

Meeting his gaze, she saw everything she was feeling reflected in his eyes. He looked terrified, and pained. Weary.

But a new resolve was present, too.

"Please, Lord, help us both," she murmured.

With her words still echoing in the air, she walked to the kitchen and filled up her kettle with water.

At long last, there was nothing more to be said.

chapter twenty-six

"I can't believe it's already time to leave," Viola said on Monday afternoon as she stood outside the airport's entrance. "I'm not ready."

Under his straw brim, she saw Ed's blue eyes twinkle. "That's quite a change of heart from when you first got here."

Even under the hot sun, her cheeks were able to hold a fierce blush. "Are you going to remind me of my behavior for the rest of our lives?"

"I hope not . . . but maybe." His tender gaze, mixed with the way he held her hand between his two lessened the sting of his words. "Everything's fine now, though. Ain't so?"

"Everything is more than fine," she agreed. It was amazing the way the Lord had worked through her during the last few days. She'd gone from being nervous and insecure to feeling braver than she thought possible.

And the best thing of all . . . she'd come to look at the mission as her home, and the people there as potential friends. Not just her future husband's coworkers or people who were in need of help. She'd been transformed and made stronger . . . and none of it would have been possible without Edward in her life.

Now she couldn't imagine merely living her life in Berlin. Now she couldn't imagine getting as much satisfaction at her job at Daybreak. Here in Belize, by Edward's side, she felt needed and valued and worthwhile.

A car horn blared behind Edward, making them both jump.

He let go of her hand. "Don't forget to call me when you get back. I know phone calls here are expensive, but I'll worry otherwise."

"I'll call."

He gently touched the end of her nose. "Promise?"

"I promise."

"*Gut*. And I promise that I'll be back soon, and we'll get married."

"That's another three months." Right now it felt like a lifetime. A very long, very lonely lifetime.

"But then we'll always be together." Wrapping his arms around her, he hugged her close. "I miss you already. And I love you, Viola. Don't forget," he whispered before stepping away.

"I won't forget." She swiped away a tear.

"Please don't cry. Now, off you go." He raised a hand. "Bye."

Slowly, she raised her hand, too. "Goodbye, Edward. I love you, too."

And with that, she turned and walked inside, right to the ticket counter.

"Going home, miss?" the lady said as she examined Viola's plane ticket and passport.

"Yes. I'm going home for now," she replied.

And found herself already counting down the days until she was coming back to Belize. As Mrs. Edward Swartz.

"Do you think your wedding will be like this?" Elsie whispered to Viola ninety minutes into Aunt Lorene's wedding service on Wednesday morning.

They were sitting about four rows from the center on the women's side in the barn. The barn was packed with at least two hundred people, and overly warm, because the cold weather prevented too many doors from being opened. Because of that, the three-hour wedding ceremony felt longer than usual, especially for the Keim women, who'd had next to no sleep for the past twenty-four hours.

They'd been cooking and cooking and cooking. Even at that moment, a group of women were in the portable kitchen they'd rented, putting the finishing touches on all the dishes. Four women who worked with Lorene at the cheese shop were setting out paper napkins, placemats, and plastic silverware on the long tables under the white tent Roman and their uncle Sam had put up the day before.

"I imagine my wedding will be much like this," Viola answered. "But hopefully it will be a little cooler in this barn. I'd be *verra* grateful to have fresh air to breathe."

Elsie shifted yet again and pulled the collar of her dress out from her neck. "Fresh air would be a blessing," she murmured.

"I'm *verra* glad that Edward and I are getting married in May."

"It will be here before we know it."

Viola glanced at her with worry. This wasn't the first time Elsie had made a comment like that. Viola feared Elsie was dreading their separation as much as she was. Of course, their circumstances were different. Viola would miss Elsie terribly, but she had a new life with Ed in Belize to look forward to.

And Elsie? All she could look forward to was a series of adjustments at home. She was going to have to pick up some of Viola's chores . . . and also learn to do without Viola's help.

As Viola thought about Elsie being home without her, a fresh new wave of guilt slammed into her.

It was likely Roman was going to move out soon, too. Either he and Amanda would have their own home in Berlin, or he would move to Florida. That is, if they ever decided to stop being so stubborn and learned to compromise.

But Elsie? Elsie was destined to live with their parents. Poor Elsie.

"Viola, you all right?" Elsie whispered.

Viola realized she'd been clenching her hands together. "I'm fine."

One of the elderly ladies turned to them and frowned. "Shh."

"Sorry," Viola mouthed, then returned to the service again.

At the center of the barn, in between where the rows of men and women on benches faced each other, Viola watched Lorene sit primly in her lovely navy blue dress and black *kapp*.

Directly across from her, John Miller sat primly as well. His matching blue shirt drew all their eyes, though he probably had no idea. It looked as if he was hardly aware of what the ministers were saying.

No, it looked like he only had eyes and ears for Lorene.

Viola shifted as two girls scooted past their row, purses in hand. Two rows back, a young boy left his mother's arms and walked directly across to the other side of the barn, quickly locating his *daed*.

And still the minister talked.

"I wish Daed could've been here," Elsie whispered after another ten minutes. "It don't seem right that he'd miss his sister's wedding."

"Mamm said she expects him home any day."

Elsie grunted, a terribly untypical response. "She told me that, too. It was kind of her to be so nice and vague."

Viola treaded carefully. After all, usually she was the one who was impatient while Elsie was the one who kept things positive. "I'm sure he wishes he were here, twin."

Elsie opened her mouth, then shook her head in a gesture filled with regret. "I'm sorry. I sound awful, don't I?"

"Is something wrong with you?"

"Other than I seem to be the only one out of the three of us who hasn't fallen in love?"

Viola pursed her lips. There was nothing that she could say to make things better. Poor Elsie was not likely to ever fall in love.

But Elsie took her silence as another offense. "You don't think I ever will have a husband, do you?"

"I didn't say that."

"Viola, how do you think I feel, knowing that no one in the family believes that I have a future?"

"You're putting words into our mouths. We all think you have a future," she said.

Another lady turned around and shushed them again.

Thankfully, further conversation was prevented by the minister raising his hands and calling them all to stand.

A thick silence settled over the congregation as the bishop gestured for Lorene and John to stand up. And then, after reading several verses from First Corinthians, Lorene and John began to recite the vows that everyone had heard a dozen times, and that many of the assembled girls had even practiced saying late at night, in the privacy of their rooms.

Viola felt a thrill go through her as she realized that her wedding might very well be the next one the community attended. Most likely she, too, would only have thoughts and eyes for her beloved.

Across the room, she met Roman's eyes and wondered what was going to happen with him and Amanda. She felt certain that he, too, had found his perfect match. All he and Amanda needed to do now was figure out a way to live together.

Obviously, she knew that wasn't always an easy task, but it could be done . . . if they wanted a life together.

Moments later, the vows were completed, and only the ending prayers needed to be said. It was the family's cue to leave and prepare for the arrival of the wedding guests and the bride and groom in the celebration tent.

Picking up her own purse, Viola led the way for her and Elsie to exit the barn. Behind her, Elsie stumbled but quickly righted herself. It took everything Viola had not to reach for her, to hold her hand.

But she couldn't refrain from looking her way.

"I am fine," Elsie said irritably. "I am fine."

Viola nodded. Even though they both knew Elsie wasn't fine. Not at all.

Late that night, after Lorene and John Miller had driven away, after the party had continued into the night, and most of the chairs and tables and trash had been put away, Roman came to a decision.

He wanted what Lorene had. He wanted what his parents and grandparents had. What Viola was looking forward to.

He wanted marriage. He wanted vows. He wanted his family and friends around him, encouraging him, teasing him.

Being there.

He wanted it all. Most important, he wanted it all with Amanda and Regina. Only that lady and that little girl would make him feel happy, and would give him the life he'd been dreaming of. A fulfilled life, one with laughter and tears. With excitement and contentment.

He realized that he'd been letting everything else get in the way of his happiness. Yes, he had responsibilities to his family and their farm, but he instinctively knew that he would only grow to resent those responsibilities if he gave up his happiness for them. And that wasn't how he wanted to be. He wanted to joyfully give of himself, not do things begrudgingly.

And though he hated the thought of going to Bishop Coblentz and telling him that he couldn't be a preacher, Roman had to think that the Lord wouldn't be too disappointed in him. After all, He had been the one who had put Roman and Amanda next to each other in Pinecraft. Surely He hadn't intended for them to meet and fall in love . . . only to be apart because of a church job?

And so he was going to have to reach out to Amanda. To call her and make some changes.

Suddenly, he realized that he didn't want to simply call her on the phone. He needed to see her face when he told her that he wanted to move to Florida, if that was the only place she could live and be happy.

But as he thought of the countless hours he'd have to wait on the bus down to Florida, with its many stops along the way, he made a decision. Yes, if Viola could go gallivanting about on planes for love, he could, too.

After a lifetime of being restrained and dutiful, he was ready to throw all those traits out the window.

Being in love really did make a man different, he decided. It made him impulsive and excited.

Actually, it made him better.

chapter twenty-seven

Just when she thought it would never come, Marie got the phone call she'd been waiting for. "Peter, where are you?" she asked the moment she heard his voice.

"I'm at the bus station in Berlin."

"Where have you been? I thought you were going to be here two days ago?"

"I tried to get there, dear, but my counselor's child got sick, so we couldn't meet on time, then I missed my first bus, then the second one broke down. It's been quite the adventure."

"I guess it has." She felt bad for him, but she wished she could turn back time, too. He'd missed Lorene's wedding, Amanda's visit, and now Roman was back in Florida.

"But I'm here now. Do you think you can come pick me up?"

Her smile was so wide, she could hardly speak. "Of course. I'll be there as soon as Chester and I can make it."

"There's no reason to rush, Marie." He paused. "Marie, you sound much worse. How sick are you now?"

She did feel dizzy and short of breath. But that was nothing compared to the happiness she was feeling. "It's nothing. I'm still just a little under the weather."

"Why don't I call for a driver?"

"Don't be silly. It's only a cough. I'll be better when you're home, I'm sure of it."

"All right, then. Well, I'll be here waiting, so take your

time. I don't care how long it takes you and Chester to get here."

His romantic words melted her heart, and renewed her spirit. Maybe things would be better between them. Maybe their troubles were over. They'd been through their difficult patch but things were better already. "I can't wait to see you."

When she hung up, she turned to her mother-in-law, who was cutting up vegetables for the evening's planned supper of chicken and dumplings. "Peter's come back."

Lovina paused in her cutting. "I figured as much. That is *gut* news."

"I'm so glad he's home."

"Me, too." She smiled.

Marie's mind was spinning as she looked from her dirty apron to the dust rag that she was somehow still holding. "I feel light-headed, I'm so excited."

Her mother-in-law laughed. "Reunions have a way of turning us all into young girls. My advice is to wait until you get your bearings, then hitch up the buggy and go find your husband."

"Yes. Yes, that's what I'll do." After switching her apron, she ran outside toward the barn, fastening her cloak and tying the strings on her bonnet as she did so. When her cough forced her to stop to catch her breath, she told herself that she'd sit down to rest later.

In no time, she'd hitched up Chester and guided him out toward the main road. As she drove the horse, her mind was filled with dreams and questions. She wondered what it would be like, to see her husband again after his month's absence.

Wondered if things really would be the same like she

hoped . . . or if they would be different like Peter said they would.

And then there were all the other things to consider. Like how his relationship with his parents would be now. Better, hopefully?

And how would Roman treat him after his absence? Though her son had never confided in her about this, she feared that Roman resented his father for forcing him to accept so much responsibility around the house.

By the time she pulled the buggy up to the front of the German Village Market, she felt dizzy and feverish.

"Marie!" Peter called out. But then his happy smile turned to worry. "Marie? Marie, you're sick."

Vaguely, she was aware of him holding her, then calling out to a pair of men walking by.

"Marie, we're calling a driver. I'm taking you to the hospital."

"There's no need. And Chester—"

"They're going to help me with Chester. I'm back now. Trust me, Marie. I'll take care of you now."

As his words sank in, she let herself lose control. Gave in to the fever and the cough. Gave in to the headache and the ache in her chest.

And was hardly aware when her husband and another woman helped her into a van.

The beach had never looked so empty. Or so depressing. Devoid of people, only the rhythmic churning of waves broke the silence of the evening.

Over and over again they crashed to the shore, spitting water and debris onto the packed sand, reminding Amanda that much of her life had been spent like that. She'd been stuck in a rut, doing the same things, even when it only dredged up more hurt and painful memories.

Beside her, Regina walked stalwartly like a small soldier, silently staying by her side, though whether it was by choice or habit, Amanda didn't know.

Ever since they'd left Roman's grandparents' house, Regina had been depressed. She'd laughed rarely, smiled even less.

Feeling desperate, Amanda went to the shelter and signed the papers to make Goldie theirs. Now, only the silly dog's antics made Regina smile.

And only Regina's smiles were able to lift Amanda's broken heart.

It had been a difficult two days, trying to be strong, attempting to resign herself to being without Roman. Doing her best to pretend that she'd made the right decision, and that sometimes, it was a mother's lot to give up her wants. To put her daughter's needs first.

But this time, a small, needly voice whispered, *Wasn't it your wants that took precedence?*

"Momma, watch this!" Regina exclaimed as she threw a stick and Goldie ran to the edge of the water to retrieve it. "Look at her go."

"She does love those sticks, that is true," Amanda said, glad to concentrate on anything else besides her drab thoughts.

When the current lapped against her paws, the dog scampered away, then trotted out into the water a little farther. Then, tongue hanging out of her mouth, she began dog-paddling in the shallow current. Standing back on the beach, Amanda crossed her arms over her chest and chuckled. "She is getting mighty wet."

"Goldie loves swimming!"

"She does."

Goldie leapt out of the water, gave a good shake, then trotted back to Regina, the stick in her mouth. Tail wagging, she stopped right in front of her and dropped the stick on the ground. Regina dutifully picked it up and tossed it again.

With a happy bark, Goldie ran off to retrieve it . . . and then went for another swim.

"I'm glad we got Goldie."

"I am, too," Amanda said. Now this, at least, was something she could be completely truthful about. This dog was sure to be a perfect pet. Already housebroken and, at four years old, already out of the precocious puppy stage, Goldie wanted to play with Regina, but so far seemed just as content to spend much of her days on her soft dog bed while Amanda went to work and Regina went to her grandparents' house.

Last night, Goldie had seemed to know exactly what each of them needed the most. She sat between them on the couch and snuggled, seeming to enjoy their petting as much as they enjoyed the dog's unspoken love and comfort.

"Goldie needed a home, Momma."

"Yes, she did."

"Being at the dog shelter was no fun," Regina added seriously. "Remember how noisy it was there? Poor Goldie!"

Amanda struggled to hold off her smile. They'd had this conversation several times already. Her daughter was intrigued by the idea of animals needing homes.

"It was no fun for Goldie, for sure. Now she's happy, though, wouldn't you say?" she asked as they watched the half golden retriever, half who-knew-what dog come trotting back to them with that same stick secured in her mouth. "Now she lives in a nice, cozy home. And has a fluffy dog bed, too." Tickling Regina's back, she added, "Plus, now that she's in an Amish home, it's mighty quiet."

But instead of nodding in agreement, Regina shook her head. "*Nee*, Mamm. That's not it."

"No?"

"Mamm, Goldie is happy because she's around people who love her," Regina said. "That's why."

"Ah, yes. I suppose that is what matters the most," Amanda murmured, then felt a lump form in her throat as the meaning shone through.

It was being loved that mattered, Amanda realized. That had been what everyone, from Roman to Regina to Wesley had been trying to tell her all along.

A person couldn't live a life on memories. Not a good life, anyway.

No, the past was in the past, and the future was in God's hands. All she had was the present. What she did now was what counted . . . not what she'd done years ago . . . or what she hoped to do one day.

And what really mattered, when all was said and done, was love.

And she'd had that. She'd been loved. Deeply. She'd been blessed to be loved not once but twice. Both by good, upstanding men.

But what had she done?

She'd clung to her grief and ignored the precious gift she'd been given. She'd pushed Roman away, pushed the future she could have with him away. For some reason, she'd decided that it would be easier to live in the past. Had it been fear that had driven her? Perhaps.

But even knowing it was fear that had driven her, it didn't make her consequences any easier to bear. She'd hugged her misplaced sense of loyalty to Wesley like a badge of honor. But now she realized that she hadn't done it for him.

When he'd known his time was coming, he'd told her time and again not to mourn for him. He'd told her over and over that life was for living, not simply for wishing.

And definitely not for grieving.

She'd promised him she wouldn't do that. But she hadn't even tried to keep that promise.

She'd fallen into an uneasy habit of living alone, and never imagining that her life could be better or different.

And worse, she'd made her dear daughter live that way, too.

It was time, Amanda decided. It was finally time to live, to grasp happiness, even if it was as shimmery as a hazy ray of light.

Even if it meant moving and changing and giving up some of her security.

Just like that silly dog, who had a past no one knew about but had happily found love again, she could, too.

It was time, time to go home and make that call. Call Roman and tell him she'd been wrong. That she'd been afraid to want more, to ask for happiness, but she wasn't any longer.

"Momma, look!" Regina called out, pointing just behind her.

"I will. In one second. But first I want to talk to you about something."

"But—"

Amanda knelt down. "Regina, just for a second, listen."

"But, Mamm—"

"Please, Regina."

Blue eyes widened. "Yes?"

"Regina, what would you say if I thought we should move to Berlin, Ohio, after all? To live with Roman and his family? What would you say if I told you that I know I was wrong? That I now know I was wrong to leave?"

Regina's eyes widened, but then they crinkled at the edges as she beamed at her. "I'd like that."

"Sure?"

"I'm sure." Her smile widened. Almost as if she had a secret.

Amanda hugged her tight. "*Gut*. Then that's what we'll do. We'll gather up Goldie and walk to the condo and—"

"Mommy!"

"What?"

"This time, you need to listen."

"All right. What is it that you need to tell me?" Panic coursed through her. Maybe Regina was changing her mind? Maybe she was upset? Maybe . . .

Regina pointed behind Amanda again. "Mommy, just look over there, will ya?"

"All right." Amanda turned around and gaped.

There was Roman, standing tall and handsome, his gaze warm and loving. Just as if she'd conjured him from a daydream. "Roman, look at you," she whispered.

After giving Regina a little wink, Roman walked forward. He was carrying a pair of brown work boots, thick socks tucked into the tops of them. "You look surprised," he said after hugging Regina.

"I am."

"Are you upset?" His gaze studied her face, obviously looking for clues about what she was thinking.

"I was just telling Regina that we needed to call you."

He got to his feet. "Were you, now?"

"Yes. I . . . I wanted to tell you that I'm sorry, Roman. You were right about everything. We can be happy everywhere. Anywhere."

"Listen, I wasn't right about everything. I was too impatient. But," he added boyishly, "I am younger than you, remember. We young men sometimes need a little bit of guidance."

"I'm only two years older."

He laughed. "Two years still counts."

Regina beamed up at him. "Momma said we're going to call you about Berlin."

"Really? Are you going to come for another visit?"

"No. We're going to live there," Amanda said softly.

He stared in shock, then closed his mouth. "Amanda, I appreciate that, but, ah, you don't have to. I mean, I know you want to be here, where your life with Wesley was. It was wrong of me to expect you to leave everything. If this is where you need to be, then I can be here, too."

Amanda felt so loved. Roman said so much with those words. "I loved Wesley, but he's gone. I'll always love his memory. And I'll always be grateful that he gave me Regina. And I'll treasure the memories of our brief time together. But you're my future, Roman. I know you are."

"If you want to stay here . . . I decided that you were more important to me than even my church obligations."

"That much?"

"Amanda, I don't want to lose you."

"You haven't lost me. I'm ready. I'm ready to start over. Both Regina and I are. Right, Gina?"

"Yes. But Goldie needs to come to Ohio, too."

Roman grinned at the dog, who was currently digging in the sand. "Do you think Goldie will mind the cold weather?"

"I think she's a pretty resilient dog," Amanda said as she rubbed the dog's shaggy head. "I think she'll be happy as long as we're there."

"Then that's settled," Roman said with a grin. "As soon as possible, we're all going to go to Ohio."

"We're getting married, Roman?" Regina asked hopefully.

"Yep. We're all getting married as soon as possible."

There were so many more things to say. And so many things that would probably forevermore be left unsaid. But all that mattered was that moment.

Where they were all together. The three of them plus one shaggy dog.

And this moment would one day rest in her memories, tangled in a hundred, a thousand moments of her life. She'd remember the time Roman had appeared on the beach, loving her enough to give up everything.

At almost the same moment that she'd decided the same thing.

She'd remember the way the sand had felt under her feet, the way she spied the sun sinking low over the horizon. She'd remember the sharp smell of the ocean and the faint scent of Regina's faded sunscreen.

She'd remember feeling exhilarated and awake and so, so very alive. She'd remember feeling in love and happy.

She'd remember it all for the rest of her life.

Forever.

Roman had just leaned close to kiss her when the condominium manager called her name.

Surprised, Amanda turned to him. "Yes, Mr. Conway?"

"Amanda, we just got an urgent message for your beau," he said as he came rushing out to greet them, seemingly oblivious to the way the sand he was kicking up was sticking to his dark slacks. "Son, are you Roman Keim?"

Roman strode forward. "I am. Is something wrong?"

"I'm afraid so. We just got a call from your grandmother. Your mother has just been admitted to the hospital."

"What?"

"That's all I know." He thrust a piece of paper into his hands. "But here's the phone number of the hospital. Your grandmother asked you to call as soon as you can."

Turning to her, Roman's face was a study of disbelief and grief. "Amanda, Regina, I don't know what to say."

"I do," she said simply. "We had better see if Pioneer Trails has room for us on the next run to Ohio."

"You're sure you want to go back right away?"

"I'm positive. I want to be there for you. I want us to be together."

"What about Goldie?" Regina asked.

"We can put her in an animal carrier and she can ride the bus, too," Roman said. "She won't like it, but she'll do all right."

"I don't deserve you," Amanda whispered.

"Of course you do. We all deserve each other," Roman said with a smile. "We're a team now, you, Regina and I. Together, we'll be able to get through anything."

Roman reached out for both of their hands. Then, the three of them started the long walk back, Goldie for once walking sedately at their heels.

Though so much in life could hurt and go so wrong . . . at the moment nothing felt more right.

epilogue

This is how life goes, Lovina decided as she took a turn by Marie's bedside in the intensive care unit at the hospital. Some days it was wonderful. And other times? Not so much. Life was truly a series of hills and valleys.

Sometimes it was also downright scary.

The doctors said that Marie was going to be better soon, and Lovina hoped and prayed that was true. Currently, Marie had a number of tubes and cords attached to her, as well as a noisy machine that helped her breathe.

She'd woken in fits and spurts, but had been so drowsy and feverish Lovina didn't think she understood where she was.

The rest of the family was coping with her sickness the best they could. Aden and his family had come in from Indiana. Lorene and John had cut short their wedding trip and were back in Berlin, too. The house was as full as it had ever been, and the noise and commotion brought back memories of when their five children were still small.

As the machines beeped and blipped and Marie's slumber continued, Lovina stretched out her legs and let her mind drift.

First, she thought of happier times, such as when Roman and Amanda had returned to Berlin together and announced their engagement. Or how radiant Lorene had looked on her wedding day.

Oh, indeed, her daughter had looked so happy. So, so different from the last few years, when Lorene's demeanor had seemed so bleak.

Remembering that, of course, took Lovina to another time, back when she was simply Lolly.

When everything about her life had felt bleak and dark, too.

She remembered going to the market, her arms full of miscellaneous items for her mother. Near the checkout counter she'd seen Jack's parents, their steps faltering when they caught sight of her.

She'd ached to dart back down an aisle, but experience had shown her that hiding solved nothing.

Lifting her chin, she strode forward to meet them. "Hi, Mr. and Mrs. Kilgore."

Almost reluctantly, they stopped. "Hello, Lolly," Mrs. Kilgore said.

With a start, she noticed that Mrs. Kilgore's eyes were red-rimmed, and the lines around Mr. Kilgore's eyes looked deeper than she remembered. They both looked haggard. Exhausted, really. They also were staring at her. Glaring, really. Almost as if they were daring for her to challenge them.

Or maybe they were daring her to speak?

She felt thoroughly confused. "How are you both?" she asked reluctantly, feeling as inane as her words sounded.

Mr. Kilgore blinked, just like she'd managed to surprise him. "Lolly, have you not heard?"

"I don't know what you're talking about. Have I not heard what?" But of course, the moment she said the words, a curious buzzing started to ring in her ears.

And she knew.

"Jack is gone," Mrs. Kilgore said through clenched teeth. "His helicopter went down over Saigon."

Lovina blinked, hearing the words, but not fully comprehending them. "Went down, you say?"

"The helicopter crashed," Mr. Kilgore said flatly. "Our boy died in Vietnam."

Jack was gone. Gone, just like Billy. Just like their innocence. Just like all her dreams, and all the silly, too sweet dreams she'd had about her future.

Gone.

Her world began to spin.

"Lolly? Lolly!" Mrs. Kilgore exclaimed. "Jim, I think she's about to faint."

Vaguely, she was aware of being helped to the ground. Next thing she knew, she was sitting on the cold linoleum of the grocery store floor, leaning up against a shelf full of canned tomatoes.

When her vision cleared, she looked up at Jack's parents. The couple she'd imagined would one day be her in-laws. "I'm so sorry," she murmured, just as tears started falling down her cheeks.

The couple, now looking like all the fight had filtered out of them, hovered ineffectually over her. Mrs. Kilgore was wringing her hands. "Lolly, dear. I am sorry we told you like this. I guess we should have thought to have given you a call. Or called your mother. . . ." She continued to talk, with Mr. Kilgore adding something every now and then.

But it all sounded garbled to Lovina. She hardly understood what they were saying.

Well, perhaps she didn't remember it now, Lovina reflected as she returned back to the present.

Somehow she'd made it home. A couple of weeks later, she'd moved on and got a job working as a clerk at the local bank.

And then, one day, in had come Aaron. Looking so healthy and proud and Amish.

Looking so different from any man she'd ever known.

Then, of course, everything had changed. They'd started talking, one thing led to another . . . and she'd left all the pain behind.

Well, she'd thought she had.

"Lovina, I hope you're not worrying too much," Aaron stated from the doorway. "Peter just spoke with the *doktah*. He said Marie's health is improving."

"That's *gut* news."

"It is *gut*, indeed. Marie will get better. She has to. Why, all of us are praying for her recovery."

Once again, she looked at her husband. Thought about the trip they were planning to take to Pennsylvania in an attempt to finally put their pasts behind them. If they could find the strength to do that, why, she was sure that Marie could find the strength to regain her health.

Slowly, she got to her feet and met him at the door. "I was just sitting here, thinking about how time marches on."

To her surprise, he took her hand and gave it a little squeeze. "One day this, too, shall pass. Just like everything else." In an obvious effort to cheer her, he said, "Why, it seems like not so long ago that we were corralling our *kinner* at the grocery store."

The memory made her smile. It had been exhausting, trying to get five children anywhere on time. It had been fun though, too. "It was more like they corralled us," she said. "Some days, I fell into bed feeling like I was the tiredest woman on earth."

"They did have a way about them," Aaron agreed, his eyes bright. "They were busy and rambunctious and loud."

"So loud!" she agreed, remembering all the arguments and joking and giggles.

"But they turned out okay."

"Better than okay," Lovina said fondly. "I'm proud of them. They're *gut* people."

"Soon, we'll be marrying off more grandchildren. Viola next."

"And maybe Roman . . . "

"Yes, and maybe Roman sooner than we realize." He yawned. "Peter is outside, waiting for his turn with Marie. I think we should let him come in. Are you ready to leave?"

"Almost. I'll be there in a moment."

He paused, almost looking as if he was going to say something else. But then simply nodded. "All right."

Quietly, Lovina walked back to Marie's bedside and opened the blinds a bit. Let the sun shine into the darkened room, brightening things up.

And though Aaron was waiting for her and Peter was anxious to sit with Marie, Lovina sat down and watched the rays of sunlight stream across the sheets and blankets that covered Marie.

Little by little, the constant noise from the squeaks and pings of the machines drifted over her and faded into the background. Until she hardly heard them anymore.

When she was sitting in silence again, she felt peace settle over her. One that was as calming and sustaining as it was unexpected.

Here in the hospital room, when everything seemed so dark, she recognized the feeling for what it was . . . a glimmer of hope.

A chance for happiness that she'd almost forgotten existed.

Until recently, hope was something that she'd long ago given up on. Something that, over time, she'd twisted and turned and damaged . . . so much so that she'd even started to imagine that the emotion had never existed.

Or at least had passed her by.

But now she saw what it was. Hope was a ray of light in a life filled with regret and disappointment. It had always been there, lurking in the background. As perfect and as endearing as God's love.

"Light shines on the godly, and joy on those whose hearts are right," she whispered.

Yes, all she'd had to do was open the blinds covering her heart a bit. Let in the light.

"I believe," she whispered to the Lord. "I believe," she repeated to Marie.

And then, carefully, she reached out and grasped Marie's hand and gently moved it to rest in one of the rays of light shining on the bed.

And felt the warmth of the sun cover both of their hands.

She closed her eyes and gave thanks.

And basked in its glow.

About the author

About the book

Read on

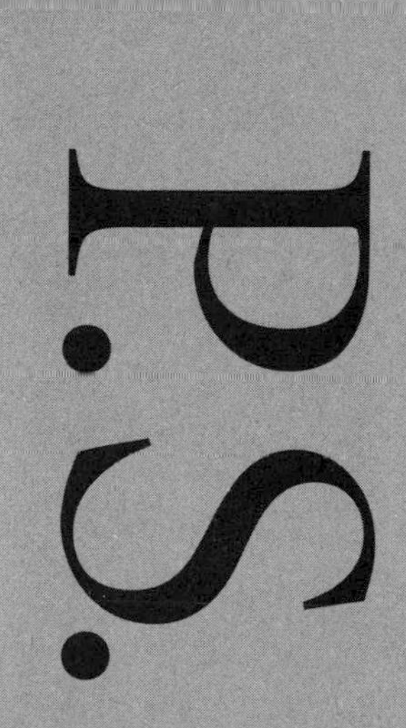

Insights,
Interviews
& More . . .

Meet Shelley Shepard Gray

The New Studio

I GREW UP IN HOUSTON, TEXAS, went to Colorado for college, and after living in Arizona, Dallas, and Denver, we moved to southern Ohio about ten years ago.

I've always thought of myself as a very hard worker, but not "great" at anything. I've obtained a bachelor's and master's degree . . . but I never was a gifted student. I took years of ballet and dance, but I never was anywhere near the star of any recital. I love to cook, but I'm certainly not close to being gourmet. And finally, I love to write books, but I've certainly read far better authors.

Maybe you are a little bit like me. I've

been married for almost twenty years and have raised two kids. I try to exercise but really should put on my tennis shoes a whole lot more. I'm not a great housekeeper, I hate to drive in the snow, and I don't think I've ever won a Monopoly game. However, I am the best wife and mother I know how to be.

Isn't it wonderful to know that in God's eyes that is okay? That from His point of view, we are all exceptional? I treasure that knowledge and am always so thankful for my faith. His faith in me makes me stand a little straighter, smile a little bit more, and be so very grateful for every gift He's given me.

I started writing about the Amish because their way of life appealed to me. I wanted to write stories about regular, likeable people in extraordinary situations—and who just happened to be Amish.

Getting the opportunity to write inspirational novels is truly gratifying. With every book, I feel my faith grows stronger. And that makes me feel very special indeed.

Letter from the Author

Dear Reader,

Every few weeks, I host a group of women in my living room. We started out studying a workbook provided by our church, but over time, our little group began our own routine. I started making a cake or cookies to eat while we studied. Eventually, we started sharing things that were going on in our lives and praying for each other. Now, we mainly talk and laugh and pray.

Not too long ago, one of the women said she felt God's presence with us. I agreed. And since I was working on this book, I mentioned that they were my rays of light. Their honesty and friendship have meant the world to me.

Other rays of light are the many people in my "writing world." I doubt I could ever fully describe how much I've grown to depend on my agent for her guidance and support, or for my editors for their ability to make my novels so much better than I ever imagine they can be. It's amazing how one encouraging word from them makes forty hours of writing a week so much easier.

There are so many other folks at HarperCollins who shine on me, too. I'm blessed to work with Joanne, who painstakingly does a thousand things to set up book signings, interviews, and other appearances. Jen and Mary and Shawn and everyone in the marketing department have placed ads in magazines, given away Nooks, and promoted my books in ways that I could only dream about.

But perhaps my favorite rays of light are my readers. I can't tell you how grateful I am that you have taken the time to reach out to me. Whenever I read a kind note, or when I hear that someone loaned one of my books to a friend or family member, my day is brighter.

I hope you are enjoying the Keim family, and will join them in *Eventide* as Lovina and Aaron journey to Pennsylvania to finally confront all the secrets of their pasts, as Peter works to heal both his family and Marie, and as sweet Elsie finally has her chance at romance and love.

With blessings and my sincere thanks,
Shelley Shepard Gray

Shelley Shepard Gray
10663 Loveland, Madeira Rd. #167,
Loveland, OH 45140

Questions for Discussion

1. Roman Keim has spent much of his life trying to stand apart from his family—even going on vacation while his father is away. Ironically, going away enabled him to become closer to them all. Have you ever felt the need to "step away"?
2. Amanda struggles to move on after her husband's death. Do you think there's an appropriate timeline for grief? What has helped you during the grieving process? How does one know when it's time to move on?
3. New Order Amish are allowed to have a phone line in their home. Do you think this makes their lives much different from the Old Order Amish?
4. Little by little, Aaron reveals more about how his first marriage ended. What do you think was harder for Lovina to hear—that he never told her about his brother-in-law's letters, or that he was, in fact, driving Laura Beth and Ben in their buggy?
5. Viola's first impression of Belize is different from what she expected. She's deeply embarrassed about her behavior and worries about disappointing Ed. Have you ever gotten off on the wrong foot in a new town or with a new group of people? How did you make amends?

6. How does Regina grow and change during the novel? Is it surprising that she has an easier time adjusting to life with the Keim family than Amanda does?
7. Amanda is Roman's Ray of Light. Who is yours? Why?
8. What do you think will happen when Lovina and Aaron go back to Pennsylvania to visit?
9. I used the following Scripture verse to guide me while I wrote this book. What does this verse mean to you?
   Light shines on the godly, and joy on those whose hearts are right.
   —Psalm 97:11

A Sneak Peek of Shelley Shepard Gray's Next Book, *Eventide*

An exciting preview of Eventide, *the final book in Shelley Shepard Gray's The Days of Redemption Series*

THERE WERE NOW three machines attached to her mother. Each one made a different noise, and in the silence of the intensive care room, they clattered and wheezed and rang in a type of discordant melody.

Elsie was almost used to it now.

Six days earlier, her mother had collapsed when she'd gone to pick up her father from the bus station. When her father had seen how ill she was, he quickly hired an *Englischer* to take them to the hospital. The doctors at the hospital discovered she had a severe case of pneumonia, a terribly high fever, and several other complications.

Well, that was what Elsie had heard.

Now, her mother seemed to be drifting in and out of consciousness with sluggish ease, much to the physician's dismay. It seemed most people responded to the medication and were much better after a day or so. That wasn't the case for Marie Keim, however. No matter how much any of them begged or prayed, she didn't seem in any hurry to return to them. So they'd all had to make do with holding her hand and hoping for a miracle.

Elsie was okay with doing that,

though she'd privately given up on waiting for miracles years ago. Now that she was twenty-two, she had quite a bit of experience with the Lord's will. If He wanted something to happen, no amount of prayer or wishing could change His plans.

"Ahh, Mamm," she said. "When are you going to get better? We need your help at home. Things are a real mess, and they don't look like they are going to get calmer anytime soon."

Though she didn't really expect an answer, Elsie stared at her mother, hoping against hope that she would suddenly open her eyes and tell her what to do.

But of course, the only sound she heard was the steady beeping of the machines.

"How's she doing today, Elsie?" Dr. Fisher said from the doorway. He was a pulmonary specialist, and he headed up the team of doctors who checked on her mother. Dr. Fisher's hospital rounds always seemed to coincide with Elsie's visits.

She was glad of that. She liked the man from Alabama. He had a chatty, kind way about him, and she trusted him. Far more than the rest of the family did.

Perhaps it was because she was used to doctors poking at her head and staring into her eyes, or asking her to lie down in fancy MRI machines.

Looking back at her mother, Elsie said, "I'm afraid things seem about the same, Dr. Fisher. Every once in a while, she opens her eyes, but closes them fast ▸

A Sneak Peek of Shelley Shepard Gray's Next Book, *Eventide* *(continued)*

again." She pointed to the little computer that all the doctors and nurses used now. "What do you think?"

"About the same thing." Pulling up a metal chair, he sat down next to her. "I'm sorry, Elsie. I thought she would have recovered by now."

"Me, too," she said softly. "Mamm is always okay. It feels strange to go home and not have her bustling around the kitchen."

"I bet." He stared solemnly at the machines, paying close attention to one of the screens that showed little lines rising and falling. "How are you doing?"

"Me? I'm fine."

"Your sister told me that you've been in the hospital before for tests."

"Only for my eyes." Lifting her chin, she peered at him through thick lenses. "I'm slowly going blind, you see. I have keratoconus." As she heard her voice, sounding so prickly and combative, she inwardly winced. She had quite a chip on her shoulder about her disease, and it didn't seem to be going anywhere, either.

But instead of being taken aback, she saw his lips curve upward. "Your sister also told me that you had more spunk than your demure nature suggested."

"That might be true."

He chuckled. "Well, if you need something, be sure and let me know, Elsie. Either for your mother, or for your eyes. I happen to know a couple of good specialists."

"*Danke*, but I have Dr. Palmer. He's at the Cleveland Clinic." Inwardly, she winced. There was that spunk she couldn't quite seem to turn off.

"You are in good hands. Even I have heard of Dr. Palmer. He is a good doc." Standing up, he said, "I'll be back this evening, Elsie." Playfully, he wagged a finger at her. "But you had better not be here."

She smiled. "I won't. My visiting time is almost up. There's so many of us, we have to take turns."

When he left, Elsie leaned back again and watched her mother sleep, hoping that before long, Mamm would soon be wide awake and bossing them all around.

Closing her eyes, Elsie prayed that would be the case. And as the machines beeped and rang around her, she gave herself over to the rhythm and prayed some more.

"Hey, Elsie?" her father said from the doorway, "the driver has arrived. Viola's going to take her turn now, so we need to head on home."

"All right." After kissing her mother's paperlike cheek, she followed her *daed* out to the waiting room, pausing only briefly to glance her twin's way.

Then they walked outside into the bright sunlight, where the van was waiting.

The sudden change in light stung her eyes something awful. If she'd been alone, she would have stopped and ▸

A Sneak Peek of Shelley Shepard Gray's Next Book, *Eventide* *(continued)*

pressed her palms to her eyes in a puny effort to shield her vision.

But her father was there, and he already had so many worries, she was afraid if she added one more burden, he might not be able to handle it. So she squinted and walked across the small, covered portico.

Pretended she felt no pain.

And tried not to show how upset she was that the light of day was making her ache for the dark of night. It didn't seem fair that she was longing for the darkness when soon that would be all she had.

It was going to be time to call Dr. Palmer again, and soon. He'd warned of this.

But she wasn't going to call, not quite yet.